PRAISE FOR BURLESQUE RIVER

Burlesque River

"This was one of the most beautiful love stories. Mike and Amanda have been friends and together since she was 11 years old. After high school they were set to marry, but Amanda's rough childhood compared to Mike's normal family life weighed to heavily on her and she never felt good enough for Mike. For 12 years the both floated along, never finding love or anything close to what they had. When Amanda's Burlesque troupe performs at Mike's bar completely by chance, the two are reunited and feelings come flooding back. Emotional struggles are hard enough, but Amanda has a secret that can tear them apart. Four steamy days together bring these two on quite the roller coaster and we get to go along for the ride. Beautiful, emotional, perfect." ~MidnightMaiden

"I haven't read many romance novels, but the few I have read lack the depth of emotion on display in Kitty Bardot's Burlesque River. *Bardot tells the story of young lovers, Amanda and Mike, separated by life's unique cruelty, thrown back together 12 years later. Mistakes are made, arguments are had, and the lovers are forced to deal with the ramifications of their actions, some of which have left terrible scars. Also...in true romance novel style there is a lot of sex and a lot of different kinds of sex, always a good thing in a book like this. Most significantly though, there is a literary thrust (no pun intended) to it that elevates* Burlesque River *above similar novels. I, for one, can't wait for the sequel."* ~Kimberly

"Even though it was an easy read, there was a great depth to the characters and story line. Not to mention this book is hot, hot, hot. I really enjoyed it, and can't wait for book number 2." ~MrsBates2U

"Romance is not my usual thing but I picked this up and ended up devouring it in two days. The love story is heartfelt, the sex is passionate, and the characters are all lovable and real. Definite recommend and I'm looking forward to the next book in the series!" ~Joshua Kahn

Burlesque on Bourbon

"I devoured this book in one night as soon as the pre-order purchase went live. I am a fan of Kitty Bardot's real life connection in her books, its so easy to put yourself in the world and lives she creates. I connected so much with the character Bridgette, and I fell completely in love with Henri and his slow dripping southern drawl. I was completely hooked just a few pages in at "you have to be careful when dealing with papa legba cher"... 10/10 would recommend this book, I was sad when I flipped the last page. This Author is a rising star, and I am excited to read everything that will be coming next!" ~NO.5

"Burlesque on Bourbon *is a sensually enticing tale that you will want to read nonstop from start to finish. The excitement, chemistry, and intensity explode off the pages and keep you enrapt in Brigette's adventure with Henri. The characters are authentic, realistic and perfectly matched. I highly recommend this tale."* ~Chef Rose

"This is a sizzling romantic story between two people who have undeniable chemistry. They both also have a past that has left them with damages that are difficult to overcome. I really liked the book, I couldn't figure out how it would end. Kept me on the edge guessing." ~Sandy L

"From the beginning, the reader has the impression that Henri is very shallow. He is a known playboy picking up women and discarding them just as quick. He comes from a different world than Bridgette tossing money around without a thought to how others see him. Even so, Bridgette sees there is more depth to Henri than a pretty face so she throws caution to the wind and takes a chance to

get to know him better. The more Bridgette and Henri are together, readers can see Henri's mask slipping. It is difficult for Henri because he has never known a woman such as Bridgette. The more time they spend together and the more comfortable they are, secrets are bound to unravel in the most spectacular fashion. With Bardot at the wheel, her descriptions heighten the senses while the characters leap off the page wanting to tell their full, complete story." ~Brenda

BURLESQUE BABY

Burlesque River – Book Three

Kitty Bardot

Boroughs
Publishing Group

www.BOROUGHSPUBLISHINGGROUP.com

ISBN: 978-1-953810-51-9

For the love of my life who inspires me every day. And for my burlesque family, growing and changing as the years go by, but always there when I need them.

ACKNOWLEDGMENTS

Special thanks to my family and friends for their continued support and encouragement. Also, to Michelle for her hours of editing, the emails, phone calls, and most importantly – guidance.

BURLESQUE BABY

Chapter 1

"Oh shit." Olive scrambles out of bed, her alarm clock blinking twelve pm on the bedside table. "God damn it." Her small, shabby bedroom rocks and creaks as she hurries to the pile of clothes lying on the only chair in the room. She grabs her uniform from the top, where she'd left it earlier that morning when she got home. It smells like cigarettes and despair. Like the Lady Luck Casino. *They can't expect me to wash it with only six hours between shifts,* she thinks as she squeezes into the tight bodice. She has thirty minutes to get ready and bike across town before she's late again. "No contacts today," she says to her reflection in the tiny mirror above her equally small sink. Her normally bright eyes look back at her dull and tired through her plastic black-rimmed glasses. She brushes her teeth, combs her hair into a high ponytail, and slaps on some lipstick. *That'll have to do for today.*

Cringing as she sees the sink full of dirty dishes, she grabs her backpack from the counter and hurries through the kitchen door and out onto the deck, locking up behind her. The houseboat rocks beneath her as she rushes. With one awkward step over the water, she runs down the dock as it bounces under her quick steps.

Her bike is waiting at the end, chained safely to a post. Still rushing, she rolls the combination into place and releases it, tucking the chain into her bag. She checks the road ahead and takes off, standing on the pedals like a little kid, her tiny black skirt fluttering in the wind.

The weather is beautiful. It's the kind of day she would love to spend floating down the river, sprawled on her hammock, listening to some Waylon Jennings or Otis Redding while watching the clouds float by. It's not an option, though. Not today. Nope, today and every day for the foreseeable future she'll be going to work at the goddamned Lady Luck Casino.

She rides quickly down the road, lost in her thoughts, focused on the pink elephant a few hundred feet ahead of her. Old Pinky is there every day to greet Olive with bleary eyes and a crooked top hat. As much as she enjoys the elephant's quirky existence, the sight of Pinky makes her heart sink. The elephant is a symbol of every distasteful thing existing within the Lady Luck's walls: drunks and gamblers wasting their lives away in dingy, smoke-filled rooms. She hates all of it. Mostly she hates serving them their drinks with a smile, pretending they're funny or charming in any way. She shudders to think of how often their hands wander to the small of her back, or to her hip.

"Fuck," she screams as she skids her brakes to a halt, before careening into the rusted door of an old pickup truck.

"Jesus. Are you okay?" Olive looks up into a shadow of a face surrounded by a glowing crown of golden curls. "Miss?" he asks, kneeling beside her. Another man is standing above him in a baseball cap, his big red beard catching the sunlight like amber glass.

"She came out of nowhere," red beard says. "Is she all right?"

"Fuck," Olive grumbles, as she struggles to untangle herself from her broken bike. Her pantyhose are snagged and running in a half a dozen places. She pushes her glasses back up on her nose and swats the golden-haired man's hand away as he tries to help her up. "I'm fine. I should've been watching where I was going," she says, standing up on shaking legs. Her elbow aches and she can feel a bruise already growing on her hip. Red beard bends down to pick up her bike while golden hair watches her with a curious gaze.

"You don't look okay," golden boy says quickly with a smooth voice. Olive looks from him to his large friend, who seems like he's going to rebuild her bike right there on the side of the road.

"I'm fine, okay. I'm running late already, so if you don't mind," she says to red beard, nodding at her bike with its bent front tire. "I'll take my bike and be on my way. I can fix it later. It's not a big deal." She reaches for the handlebars.

"Let me get you my insurance information at least, and my phone number," red beard says, reluctantly handing the bike over to her and crossing to the passenger-side door. He starts rooting around in his glove box while golden boy watches her. Olive stands waiting, holding her handlebars, not okay at all. Her whole body aches. She's fighting to keep herself from trembling and falling into pieces where she stands. Golden boy's stare is unnerving and she's going to be late again. Her boss had been clear the last time that it was the *last* time.

"Here it is." Red beard appears from behind her. He wears a big friendly grin and holds out an unmarked envelope. "Here's all my information. Are you sure you're all right? You don't want us to call anyone?"

"No. I'm fine, really." She shifts from one foot to the other, ready to get on her way. "I'm running late and I need to get to work." She snatches the envelope from his hand and hurries across the road, doing her best to hide the limp. Her heart is racing. She can feel them watching as she does her best to walk proudly away, pushing her bike with its wobbly tire. Most days she would chain it out front and head through the main doors. Today, however, with the admittedly handsome truck brothers watching her every move, she feels it would be wise to stash her bike out of sight and enter through the backdoor. Added bonus, if she sneaks in through the kitchen, she can get cleaned up in their employee bathroom and punch in before her douchebag boss catches her coming in late.

The rich, heavy smell of grease and the clanging cacophony of the kitchen greets her as she pushes through the sticky, heavy doors. Pedro and Eddy are leaning against stainless worktables chatting comfortably. "Hey, hey, *chica,*" Pedro calls over the loud music. "Kyle is on the warpath today. He's looking for you. You better get moving."

"Ah shit," Olive groans, dropping her head back, her gaze settling on the grease-stained ceiling tiles. "Are you for real?" she asks, slipping her backpack off her shoulders.

"Yeah, for real. What happened to you?" Pedro asks, stepping toward her, his usually smiling eyes looking concerned. They fall on her torn stockings and scraped knees. "You look like shit."

Olive looks down at her rumpled and dirty uniform. Her ponytail hangs loosely on the side of her head. She takes a deep breath and looks at the two cooks in their hairnets and stained aprons. Men who have become her friends over the years. "I hit a truck."

"You what?" Eddy asks, stepping closer alongside Pedro. "You got hit you mean?"

"No," she says, looking from one to the other. "I hit the truck. I was coming down the road on my bike and I wasn't watching where

I was going. They were stopped and I hit them," she rambles. "My bike is pretty busted up."

"You're pretty busted up," Eddy says, pulling a bucket down from a nearby rack with one of his large hands and turning it over. "Sit down." He leaves no room for argument. Olive sits and looks at them. Her hands start to shake, then her whole body. Her heart is thumping so hard, she's sure her chest will crack open.

"I'm okay, really I am. I have to go get cleaned up is all." She stands, and the room spins around her. Pedro reaches out to steady her.

"You are not okay, Olive. Come on. Let's get you out of here." He leads her out of the kitchen with his hand on her elbow. They make their way to the women's locker room.

"Stop, Pedro. I'm all right. Really." She pulls her arm away from him and rubbing her elbow. "Once I get cleaned up, I'll be fine."

"Why didn't they call an ambulance?" he asks, looking her over. "Why didn't you file an accident report?"

"I wouldn't let them. I told you, I'm fine. I'm a bit shaken up, but fine." He looks at her with his dark shining eyes and offers a reluctant smile.

"All right. I don't believe you, but I get it. Come find me if you need anything though," he says, looking her over again. "I know you're tough, *chica*, we all do. Even tough guys can't compete with trucks."

***

"Where'd she even come from?" Mike asks, glancing Vic's way as they start back on the road heading out to Mike's bachelor party, which is really a camping weekend. Not Vic's idea of a rockin' good time. He'd rather be in Vegas. At least Mike brought whiskey.

"I don't know, man. She came flying down the road. Good thing we were stopped. Shit could've been a lot worse," Vic says, watching the woman push her bike away from them. She's walking with quick short steps, her shoulders straight, head held high. He can't imagine how badly it must have hurt to fly into the side of the pickup the way she did. He had to admire her pluck. She picked herself up, dusted herself off, and tried not to make a fuss. "You think we should let her walk away like that? Think she's really okay?"

"She seemed all right," Mike says, watching the road. "I slipped some cash in the envelope for a new bike and my phone number if she needs anything. I'm sure she'll be fine."

Vic turns around to watch out the back window of the truck. The ridiculous pink elephant seems to be waving at them as the dark-haired bicyclist disappears around the corner. "I bet she works in that casino," he says, thinking out loud.

"Think we should go back and check on her?" Mike asks.

"I mean, don't you?" The truck slows down, and Mike lets out a long slow breath.

"We're losing daylight." Mike flips on the turn signal. "You're right though. We should at least make sure she made it to work all right." He turns around in a small, tight parking lot and heads back to the pink elephant.

"It won't take long. We gotta make sure she's not in worse shape than she let on. Not banged up and out of it. She hit us pretty hard."

"I'm not arguing." They pull into the lot beside the elephant and climb down from the truck. Vic looks down at his camp clothes, concerned he's underdressed. Then he watches an elderly couple walking ahead of them to the door. They look about ancient, and dressed for a Saturday at the farmers' market to sell produce. *We'll fit in fine.*

Inside is the same sad scene of every casino in the Midwest. The large room is poorly lit, colored lights flicker and flash all around. The air is thick with smoke and an odd sort of music blends with the beeping and ringing slot machines. Vic narrows his eyes and searches the room for the girl from the accident. He sees a few cocktail waitresses, all wearing the same uniform as the mystery girl. "Looks like we're in the right place," he says with a nod toward them.

"Yep. Now let's go find her and make sure she's all right so we can get back on the road."

"I know. We're losing daylight," Vic teases as he scans the room. Mike heads to the bar, talking over his shoulder.

"It's not like I don't care if the girl's all right," he says loudly over the noise. "I bet you anything she is. She didn't seem like she wanted us here."

"Maybe not," Vic says, catching up with Mike, "but I'll sleep better knowing she got here safely." They stand at the bar, waiting for the bartender to come their way.

"Yeah, me too," Mike agrees, nodding to the bartender, who rushes over with a bright smile.

"Hey, fellas," she says with a hint of seduction. "What can I get for you?" she asks looking from Vic to Mike, then back at Vic.

"Hi there," Vic says, turning up the charm. Though from the look in the bartender's eye, he doesn't need it. "We're looking for someone. I think she might work here. There was an accident out front, we wanted to make sure she's okay. It wasn't too long ago, looked like she was heading in here." The bartender looks disappointed to learn they hadn't come in to spend the night drinking and flirting with her.

"Well, we did have a shift change not long ago. And it looks like we're still one short." She scans the room. "Can I get you a drink while I go check on her?"

Vic looks at Mike. "What do ya say, Mikey? A beer while we wait?" he asks, realizing this is as close to Vegas as he is coming this weekend. Mike looks at him, his mouth set and serious. Then he looks at the bartender and smiles.

"Sure, what the hell."

"Two Mexican beers please, whatever you've got," Vic orders for them both. The bartender smiles and presents them with two icy cold bottles of Corona with limes stuck in the heads, then goes off in search of the missing cocktail waitress. "Well, it's not Vegas, but here's to you, friend. I'm happy for you." They raise their beers and drink. Before the bartender comes back, Vic spots her. She's near the wall, with a lump of a man in a polo pointing in her face. Vic pats Mike's shoulder and points. "Look, there she is." His feet are moving before the words are out of his mouth. Mike's following close behind.

"Hey, there you are," Vic says as he approaches. He already hates the man who's snarling at the cyclist. His nametag says *Kyle, General Manager*. Kyle looks up, annoyed and ready to snap, and changes his demeanor quickly after he sizes up Vic and Mike.

"How can I help you gentlemen?" he asks with a sickeningly fake smile, which makes Vic want to punch it right off the asshole's face. That he's clearly bullying this woman makes him want to do it even more.

"Well, you can show a little respect for the lady, for one," Vic says smoothly, clenching his right hand into a fist. It's been years since he had to punch the pompous out of someone. This guy looks like he could benefit. He shifts his attention from Kyle to the dark-haired waitress. She's wearing a name tag that says Olive. Olive's gaze flashes from his to Kyle's, then to Mike, who's standing behind Vic. Her eyes are deep mossy green and are glistening with unshed tears.

Mike speaks up, his voice full of authority, "She *was* in an accident. Surely you can see that." Kyle looks from Vic to Mike and back to Olive.

"It's true then?"

"Yes, it's true," Vic growls through his teeth, still clenching his fist.

Mike says, "She hit my truck with her bike. Can't you see the scrapes and bruises?" he asks, stepping between Vic and Kyle. Vic can't blame him. Mike knows him well enough to intervene. If he doesn't step in, they'll never make it to camp 'cause Vic is likely to create *a situation.* Kyle steps back, away from Mike, looking small and weak. Vic looks at Olive and catches a tiny smile on her deep red lips. There's something about her that's intriguing. She doesn't look like she belongs in a place like this. She's too... He's not sure what it is about her, but she has all of his attention. Her thick cat-eye glasses suit her large eyes, slender face, and slightly pointed nose. The delicate rise of her sun-bronzed cleavage peeks out from her tight bodice. She covers her mouth as the tiny smile grows, and then she clears her throat.

"Listen, Kyle. These guys are vouching for me. I'm sorry I was late. I'm here now and I'll stay late to make up the time." Kyle looks from Mike to Olive, and then Vic. Vic stares him down, a rage in his chest he hasn't felt in a long time.

"All right, Olive. One more chance," he says, before turning on his heel and bustling away.

"Thanks for coming in." She looks at them, then down at the ground. Vic takes a survey of her injuries. There's a bruise on her elbow the size of a softball, and bandages on both of her knees. Her legs are bare, though she'd been wearing pantyhose on the street. He wants to take her home, clean her up, then take her to dinner. "He's such a prick," she says, shifting her weight from one foot to the other.

"Are you sure you're okay?" Vic asks, trying his best to look at her face and not at her breasts.

"Yeah. I'm good. It's only some scrapes and bruises. I'll be in rough shape tomorrow, but I'm a fast healer."

"That's good to hear," Vic says. Her mossy green eyes sparkle, she smiles and snorts out a small laugh, which is cute. Endearing.

"I've gotta get to work. Thanks again for coming in…" She looks at him and raises one brow.

"Vic. I'm Vic. This is Mike."

"Yeah, I got his name. Thanks for the cash by the way," she says turning her attention to Mike. "It's way more than my bike is worth. But, with pain and suffering, we'll call it even."

"If you need anything, though," Mike responds with a nod. "Don't hesitate to call. I feel terrible about the accident."

"It was one hundred percent my fault," she says, waving both hands in front of her and shaking her head. "Besides, it saved my job. I was going to be late either way. Because of you, I get one more chance." She snorts again, and then turns to walk away. "Thanks again, guys," she calls back. Vic notes what small steps she takes on such long legs and the gentle sway of her hips. He remembers the beer in his hand and wets his dry mouth.

"Shall we?" he asks Mike. "We are losing daylight after all."

"Fuck you," Mike says quickly before finishing his beer. "And we are." They leave the casino through the front doors, Vic eyeing Kyle until he scurries out of sight like a cockroach in the light.

"Should've let me punch him a few times," he says to Mike as they climb into the truck.

Chapter 2

Olive sits down in the staff lounge, taking her lunch break. At least that's what they call it. Though thoughts of lunch are far from her mind at ten o clock at night. It's the halfway point of her shift and she's not hungry. Her body hurts, she needs rest, and possibly a doctor. Who could afford to see a doctor? Only squares have real jobs and insurance. If her folks had given her anything in life, it was the deep-seated education on how to not be a square. She laughs softly to herself, rubbing her swollen elbow and looking around the room. It's dim, and grimy with a patina of desperation. From the stained plastic tabletops to the overflowing ashtrays and the flickering light of the snack machine.

Janice sits across the table, her thick legs outstretched, tiny feet resting on another chair. A burning cigarette hangs from her fingers as she holds the newspaper in front of her face. Olive takes a sip of the terrible coffee brewed in the ancient pot on the counter. She winces at the taste, remembering what coffee on the farm tasted like. It was one of her parents' biggest splurges. They bought the beans and roasted them at home, then ground them fresh every morning. There was nothing like a hot cup of fresh ground French press coffee mixed with heavy cream and brown sugar. She sighs then swallows the memory down with another drink of the tasteless brew.

"You know what you should do?" Janice asks, dropping the paper and looking across the table. Her heavy makeup is caked on her face and neck and does more to reveal her age than hide it. Her ample cleavage has a watery nature, shimmering and waving as she ashes her cigarette somewhere near the ashtray.

"What's that?" Olive asks. Though there is at least twenty years between them, Janice has become her best friend at the Lady Luck.

"You should tell Kyle to go fuck himself, get in that little houseboat of yours, and cruise down the river to Rock Island."

Olive cocks her chin. "That's oddly specific, Janice," she says, stretching her back gingerly through the aches and pains from the accident.

"There's more." She flips the paper around and lays it flat on the table before her. "Check this out." She points her brightly polished fingernail at a small ad on the bottom of the page.

Wanted:
Dancers, musicians, comedians, magicians, jugglers, performers of all kinds. All shapes and sizes. Contact the Speakeasy in Rock Island, IL for details on how to join the wild and wonderful world of burlesque entertainment.

"Oh, come on. I'm not a dancer," Olive says, leaning back against the hard plastic chair.

"You're pretty," Janice says with a large, bright grin.

"Thanks for the compliment. I think it's more than being pretty. I don't see how I could possibly be entertaining to watch."

"Oh please." Janice takes a drag from her cigarette. "If I was as young as you and had that body, I'd already be there."

"Shit, Janice, do it." Olive sits up. "It says all shapes and sizes. You're beautiful and vibrant. I bet the stage would love you."

Janice bats her lashes and tries to hide her blushing cheeks behind her cigarette hand. Her bracelets jingle on her wrist. "Don't be ridiculous," she says with a sigh, staring into space. "Once upon a time, girl." Her voice is wistful. "Carl would have fucking kittens." She laughs her deep, hearty laugh that turns into a coughing fit, then she snubs out her cigarette.

"I bet he'd think it was hot," Olive offers. Janice is an absolute gem, and though Olive's met Carl only once before, she could see Janice was his everything.

"You think?" Janice stands, smoothing her uniform. She pops her hip a couple times and shakes her shoulders, sending her fluid breasts into a fit of shimmers.

"Get it, girl," Olive cheers from her seat.

"Yeah right." Janice composes herself. "*You* should." She slides the paper closer to Olive. "At least go check it out. You never know what you might find."

***

Vic watches Mike pull another trout out of the river. Though Mike will deny it, Vic's pretty sure he hears him giggling. Mike's dad tends to their breakfast at his handmade camp kitchen, a clever contraption he built, which holds all the essentials and folds out into a table, stove, and sink. They're having a wholesome moment. The entire weekend has been wholesome. Even when the whiskey came out, things didn't get rowdy. They passed the bottle and shared stories and laughter. Vic feels out of place. He's always known they'd come from different worlds. Spending two days with Mike, his family, and childhood friends makes Vic question how they ever became close in the first place. As sleepy men crawl from their tents to retrieve coffee, he wonders what his life would've been like had he been raised like this.

Family camping trips weren't a part of his history. His dad had been too busy drinking. From when he was a small boy, he remembers the way his dad looked at him with disdain. How he seemed to get angrier whenever he would enter the room. How his dad's shoulders would go rigid every time he spoke. He did his best to be small and invisible, especially after the booze took hold. Instead of tents and laughter there were closets and holding tight to his mother while she shushed and rocked him, quiet sobs heaving in her chest. He believed, even in those early days, his tiny arms could keep her safe.

When the day came he was strong enough to stand up to his dad, his life changed forever. Dad's rage grew. They fought often. Eyes were blackened and lips were bloodied more often than not. His soft and pudgy frame became a well-hewn machine, wound tightly and ready to snap. His rage spilled over into everyday life. Schoolyard fights were nothing compared to the knock-down drag-out brawls he had with his old man. Guys learned to fear him. Girls started noticing. It wasn't until his freshman year in college when he met Mike, he learned there was more to life than proving his worth with his ability to land a hit and take one.

Mike approaches with a grin, his fly rod over his shoulder. "Caught my limit already." He chuckles and fills an enamel mug with coffee.

“Of course, you did.” Vic shakes his head and stands to fill his own mug. He recalls the first party they went to on campus at a frat house, filled with newfound freedom, hormones, and too much alcohol. “You remember the first party we went to back in school?”

“There were so many.” Mike shakes his head and sips at his steaming cup.

Vic remembers dragging his new roommate out for the night. How Mike had stood on the wall stubbornly nursing a beer. “You didn’t want to be there.” He laughs.

“Oh, come on. You make me sound lame,” Mike defends.

“You kind of were. At first, anyway.”

“What?” He looks away, shaking his head.

“You were. It wasn’t until we came back from Christmas break you finally started enjoying yourself.”

“I suppose I was waiting at first,” he says with a sigh and a far-off look.

“Waiting?”

“For her to come back.” He gives a little half grin. They share a brief silence before Vic clears his throat.

“Well, it took her long enough, but she finally did.” He pats Mike’s shoulder.

“She finally did,” he agrees with a broad smile, nodding.

“Remember that girl you rescued though? From those jocks?”

“Hmm.” He looks up, thinking.

“Dark hair, pretty?”

“That narrows it down.”

“I think her name was Sally,” Vic says, wondering how Mike could forget. She’d followed him like a puppy, fawning over him for weeks. Vic found her in the kitchen with several frat boys encouraging her to drink her fill of their sugary sweet booze. He remembers hanging back, watching. Then her catching his eye over the shoulder of a particularly burly football player. She was scared. The familiar rush of adrenaline surged as he clenched his fists and prepared to intervene. As he stepped toward the group, ready to attack, Mike entered the kitchen. He assessed the situation, including Vic’s rage, and stepped in.

Vic doesn’t know what Mike said, only that the frat boys disbanded with little more than a few words and a look from Mike. He did it without swinging, and Sally was his for the taking.

"You might not remember, but you saved me a lot of trouble that night."

"What?" Mike asks, clearly not remembering.

"For real. I was about to start swinging on all of them. Can you imagine what would've happened if I'd started a brawl? You saved my ass that night and you didn't even know it."

"Come on," Mike says, looking away humbly. "I was looking for the keg."

"Sure thing." Vic shakes his head, his chest full of gratitude for the best friend he never knew he needed. "I'm happy for you, brother," he says with a nod and a tight-lipped smile, hiding the admiration welling in his heart. "If anyone deserves to be happy in this world, it's you."

***

The weather is perfect. Olive lounges in her hammock on the deck, reading. A warm breeze blows over her face. Birds sing in the trees along the beach of the small river island nearby where she's anchored her houseboat. It's her first day off since the accident and her body aches in places she never knew she had. Her knee is swollen, her hip throbs, and she's blooming with black and blue marks. If only she had a tub. She remembers falling out of a tree when she was a kid, and how her mom, after making sure nothing was broken, had drawn her a warm bath with Epsom salt and essential oils to soak away the pain. That was back when she believed her mom was magic. When a kiss on a bruise could make it vanish. Before she learned the truth about her parents. Then she'd had an actual house with a tub. Not a rickety houseboat with a closet for a shower. Before everything she'd ever known had been taken away from her.

Her breath catches in her throat and tears well as she recalls childhood memories of running wild and barefoot through acres of woodlands, her little brother following her on all her adventures. "Oh Eli," she whimpers, letting her paperback fall to the wooden planks beneath her.

She sobs quietly into her hands as the images of government agents pulling her brother from her mother's arms surface. Most days, it's easy. She works and sleeps and doesn't think. She pushes the memories from her mind and keeps moving. Today, however, under the perfect sky with bright green new leaves all around, and the pain from her accident, her defenses against the past are weak. Every happy thing she ever knew is tarnished by that last day on the farm. Eli had been twelve at the time. She was seventeen and had been completely oblivious.

"Run, baby," she remembers her mom saying, standing in the open doorway, her silver-streaked hair gleaming in the sunlight. Olive stood behind her, confused. Her mom turned her head slightly so Olive could see her profile. Her normally smiling lips had fallen into a deep frown and her hand shook on the doorframe. "Olive, baby, run. Run out the back door. Find your brother and run out the back door. Run to the woods and stay there."

She'd never known a day of fear in her life. The look on her mother's face was enough to change that in an instant. Her heart raced, and her skin buzzed. The tiny hairs on her neck and scalp went stiff. She ran. She didn't find Eli. She ran until she reached the tree line and hid. Then the commotion began. She watched from her hiding place as her father was gunned down by men in black suits. They said he was armed.

She stood among the trees and saw her beautiful, gentle, gray-haired father be shot and killed with a fiddle under his chin. He'd been playing while her little brother danced. It was Lammas. One of the lesser holidays. One where they celebrated as a family, unlike the solstice and equinox celebrations, when people would come from all over to celebrate. Lammas was late summer, the first celebration of the harvest. They would play and dance all day and night. Almost eighteen, she'd grown weary of many of the games and dances. Eli still loved them. More than anything, he'd loved to dance while their father played.

Olive watched, hidden as her mother ran to her father's side and gathered him in her arms. The sound of her mother's wails and her brother screaming haunted her days and her dreams. That she hid in the trees and did nothing while they dragged Eli kicking and screaming from their grieving mother's side kept her awake most nights. "You're a child, Olive. What could you have done?" her mother asked from behind the prison glass.

"I could've gone with him. I could've kept him calm," she said through her tears. "I should have been there with him."

"You can be there for him now." Her mom seemed to have aged a decade in a month.

"How, Mama? I don't know what to do." Her mom pressed her lips tight and blinked her tears away.

"We'll figure it out, baby. We'll figure it out," she said, nodding vigorously. They didn't figure it out. Her mother was convicted of a special class B felony, manufacturing and distributing illegal substance. She was sentenced to forty years in prison. Eli was forced into one foster home, Olive another. She lived with strangers for five months. Christian strangers who shook their heads and gave her sad smiles whenever she mentioned her home and family.

Eventually, she learned the many people she called friends and family were employees, running drugs tucked neatly inside straw bales all over the country for her parents. Her folks had called their grow farm the medicine tents, and they were off limits to children. She'd snuck in once when she was young and found large stinking plants and eerie pink lights. They brought to mind the terrible concoction her mom drank for her nerves. Olive never liked the smell and never gave the medicine tents another thought. That was until she learned her parents' secrets.

At eighteen she left the strangers' foster home; she did what she could with what she had. Which was next to nothing. The only home she'd ever known was seized. The money she never knew existed was gone. All she had was the houseboat her dad built out of scrap materials. He left it docked on the Mississippi, licensed under another name. He called it his contingency plan.

Olive never considered the meaning of why he'd need one. She enjoyed watching him build the boat. When the time came for its maiden voyage, she laughed happily with her parents and baby brother as her dad broke a bottle of champagne on the side.

They floated down the river that day and many after it. As she sits in the same hammock she and Eli had swayed in together for years, she cries for the child she was, and for the years lost to her parents' mistakes. Her broken heart and aching bones are heavy.

***

Vic sits at the head table, tears misting the golden light of the crystal chandeliers. Amanda's maid of honor, Bridgette, is giving her speech through tears of her own. The ceremony had been beautiful. Mike and Amanda spoke their heartfelt vows surrounded by spring blooms in the gardens of the botanical center, the bright and lovely flowers overshadowed by the colorful cast of characters who stood on the bride's side. Vic had stifled his laughter, standing beside Mike, witnessing for the first time their worlds colliding. On one side was Mike's good-natured, small-town family with great-aunts and uncles, children, and cousins all dressed in their Sunday best. On the other, Amanda's menagerie of friends and fellow performers with hair in all the colors of the rainbow, and clothes to rival the best- and worst-dressed list on any red carpet.

It had been nearly three years since Burlesque A la Mode had come into their lives, a whirlwind of sequins and feathers via the only woman Mike ever loved who brought with her the wonderfully entertaining world of burlesque. Their club, the Speakeasy, had never done better. With regular visits from A la Mode selling out every other month, Vic, Mike, and Amanda had decided to start a troupe locally. Vic was overjoyed at the prospect. Not only for the money it was sure to bring in, but also for the much-needed excitement in his life.

"Vic?" Bridgette sniffles, clutching her rose-pink gown in one hand. She's standing behind Mike and Amanda, holding the microphone out to him. Lost in thought, he missed the end of her speech. He was up next and terribly unprepared. Clearing his throat, he stands and takes the microphone. Mike's sitting, his tuxedo jacket hanging over the back of his chair. Amanda looks radiant in her pearl-studded gown. Mike's arm is draped casually over her shoulder, and they are beaming like the summer sun.

"Mike, buddy, I never thought I would see the day," he says, looking down at them. A chuckle rolls through the hall. "Until I met this one." Amanda smiles bashfully and flutters her lashes at Mike, dabbing at the corner of her eye. "In all the years I've known him, I've never seen him happier." His words catch in his throat as he watches them, lost in each other's gaze. "I can see why. Amanda, since I've met you, you've become like a sister to me. I couldn't imagine a better mate for my best friend." He clears his throat again, emotions welling, and lifts his glass. "Here's to all the happiness that the world has to offer, and a lifetime of adventure." He tips back his glass of bubbling pink champagne, and then sits down to the sound of cheers and whistles. The music starts and people begin to mingle.

Vic watches with delight as the boldest of Mike's nieces approaches a table of Amanda's friends. He can't hear what she's asking, though he's sure it has to do with the man in makeup and high heels. When the rest of the children see she's well received, they follow suit. It's not long before the table is swarmed by a dozen curious little ones. Smiling, he scans the room for single ladies. A date for the wedding would've been easy enough to get. He chose to come alone though. There was no telling what a night with Amanda's crew would bring.

Over the rainbow sea should be the title of her guest list. Vic spies several lovely women, none of whom are her regular crew, leaving him free to do as he pleases and still uphold his rule of never mixing business with pleasure.

As it had after the camping weekend, his mind turns back to Olive, and he wonders how she's doing. On more than one occasion, he thought to go over to the casino to check on her. Yeah, okay, to ask her out, but then he thought maybe she'd find that creepy. Him hitting on her after she slammed into his side of Mike's truck. He didn't want her to think she was a charity case. He'd turned it over so many times in his head, he waited too long. She probably wouldn't even remember him.

Tonight though, he's the best man, single and ready for anything. Anything turns out to be small and curvy with shining black hair and bright blue eyes. Her leopard print dress hugs her curves. Her shapely legs are pegged into impossibly high heels. She's been watching him all night, boldly. Her plump red lips smile as she twirls a section of her long hair with both hands. He's several drinks in. The traditional wedding games and dances are done. The old folks and children have retired. All that's left of the party is the revelry.

Vic crosses the room to the dainty brunette, standing at the bar. "Hello, beautiful." He slides up beside her. "Can I get you a drink?" he asks.

She smiles again, looking up, still twirling her hair. "I'm not thirsty," she challenges.

"No?"

"Bored actually," she says, flipping her hair over her shoulder, revealing her smooth creamy cleavage. Vic steps closer, she smells sweet like candy.

"I could help you with that," he says smoothly, raising an eyebrow.

"Yeah?" She gets even closer, her small frame emitting more heat than he expected.

"Wanna get out of here?" he asks.

"Yes," she breathes.

His room is a blur. Her thick lips around his cock, hands everywhere, skin so soft. Her hair all around him, a curtain of vanilla and smoke. He lifts her easily. They tumble over his bed. Flashes of body parts coming together. Hands and hips, ass and thighs. Mostly lips, lips and hair. Words were surely spoken, and evaporated with the dawn. It could have been hours or moments for all he knew.

He wakes in the morning sprawled, naked on his bed alone. Several condom wrappers, empty beer cans, and cigarette butts with dark red lipstick floating in a water glass tells him the night was longer than he thought. *That's gonna cost me,* he thinks as he remembers the hotel smoking policy. Standing with a heavy head, he wonders if his new friend is coming back and heads to the shower to wash his hangover down the drain.

Chapter 3

"You're looking a lot better." Janice gives Olive the once-over in the locker room, assessing her fading bumps and bruises.

"I'm feeling a lot better. Thanks for letting me use your tub. I knew all I needed was a nice long soak," Olive says over her shoulder while adjusting her tights.

"I wish the hot tub had been up and running. You could have soaked for hours."

"Hey, anything is better than what I have at home." The word hurts her to speak. The houseboat isn't home. It's a contingency plan, as her dad had called it. A contingency plan she'd been living in for ten years.

"Well, I'm glad to see you with some spunk in your step again. This place isn't the same with you shuffling around like a geriatric."

"Thanks, I think." Olive looks at Janice, sitting on a bench, holding a pen in her fingers where a cigarette should be. She's trying to quit.

"Oh, you know what I mean." She waves the air between them.

"Yeah, I do. I'm glad to be moving easily again. I almost buckled and went to the doctor. Glad I stuck it out."

Janice looks at her seriously. "You've got to get over yourself someday. Sure, you're young now, and you bounced right back. Someday, you'll be old and frail like me."

"You're anything but frail, Janice." She laughs.

"You know what I'm saying."

"I do," she agrees. They sit in silence.

"Well, we should probably get to it." Janice stands, twirling her pen before sliding it in her apron.

"Yep." Olive follows Janice from the locker room to the dingy casino lounge for another night of serving watered-down cocktails to people who barely look up from their slot machines.

***

"Olive." Kyle approaches her from behind. She turns from the bar with her tray of drinks. "I need to see you in my office."

"Um, okay," she says, gesturing to her tray.

"Deliver those and come back. Janice can cover for you," he clips before walking away quickly. She catches a glance from Janice and shrugs. Janice hurries over.

"What's that all about?" she asks.

"Not sure. Can you watch my section for me?"

"Sure." Janice takes her loaded tray. Olive heads to Kyle's office.

He's sitting behind his desk looking smug. She imagines his legs dangling from the chair like a child's and stifles a laugh. "What's up?" She leans on the doorway.

"Come in and shut the door please."

"Okay," she says slowly, doing as he asks.

"Have a seat." He motions to the chair across from him with one pudgy hand. "How long have you been with us, Olive?" he asks, sitting up straight and leveling his gaze on her.

"I don't know. Three years maybe?" she answers, counting the months in her mind.

"That's about right." He lifts and taps a stack of papers on his desk. "You passed a background check when you were hired, correct?"

"I would think so. I didn't hire me," she responds with a shrug, her heart racing at the thought. She knows she didn't. The old manager before Kyle hired her because he liked the look of her tits. His words exactly. She took the job because she needed it. Shortly after that he was let go and Kyle was brought on. She'd thought after three years she was in the clear.

"Well, it looks to me like you didn't. It's required all employees pass a background check before they can be employed here. Not sure how you got around it. You're the only one on our payroll who hasn't had one." He looks at her across his desk, tapping the papers again.

"Okay. What does that mean?"

"It means you have to pass your check before you can continue your employment with us." Olive looks down at her hands in her lap.

She's not sure how she got around it for so long. She's not even sure what her background check will look like. Her chest feels heavy with dread as she counts the many reasons why she might not pass one.

"That is," Kyle says, lowering his voice and standing from his seat. He walks around the desk and stands behind her, placing his hands, soft and clammy, on her shoulders. "If you had an arrangement with Jo before me, we could possibly work something out between the two of us." He squeezes her shoulders gently. She can feel the heat radiating from his soft belly, hear a tremor of excitement in his words. Her cheeks blaze with rage at the thought of what he's proposing. Olive stands quickly, turning to face him. He steps back, the blush of arousal draining from his face. Her stomach twists and her pulse races. Anger rises from her gut. With a deep breath she moves around her chair, backing him against the door.

"You're a disgusting little man." She spits the words with all the rage she's bottled up over the years. "The fact you even think you can touch me makes my skin crawl. There was never any arrangement with Jo. If there had been, it most certainly doesn't clear the path for you to place your gross, sticky little hands on me. You can take your background check and your fucking offer and shove them both up your ass." She stares him down and watches as he turns to a puddle between her and the door. He steps aside quickly. She pushes through the door and stalks down the hall, her stomach rolling with rage.

She storms through the lounge. Janice follows her quickly to the locker room. "What happened?" she asks.

"Kyle is a fucking pig," Olive says, shaking out her hands and arms as if she could shake away the memory of his unwelcome touch.

"What did he do?" she asks with a look of shock.

"He fucking thought he could touch me. Called me out on not having a background check. He's lucky I can't throw a punch," she says, pacing.

"He can't do that," Janice says.

"He can't, but he did. I quit." They stand, looking at each other.

"Oh honey, what are you going to do?" Janice opens her arms, Olive hurries into them.

"I don't know."

"You can stay with me if you need to."

"No. I'll be okay. I've got to keep moving. You know?" Olive sniffs.

"Oh, I know. You'll keep moving. Know that you'll always have a place at my house."

"I know." They squeeze each other tightly. Janice rubs Olive's back vigorously.

"We're going to miss you here."

"I'm going to miss you too." Olive pulls out of the hug and turns to the mirror to check her reflection. Janice hands her backpack over. "Thank you for everything."

"Good luck." Janice wipes at her tears. "Wish I could leave with you. I've got to get back out there though."

***

Vic sits in his office in the back of the Speakeasy, scrolling mindlessly through social media. Pictures from the wedding flood his page. So many smiling faces. Mike and Amanda grinning endlessly. A glimpse of the small fiery woman in the leopard print dress. She never came back to his room. They spent the night together, sharing their teeth and tongues. What he remembers from the haze of sex and booze is hot. She'd been passionate, insatiable even, coming back for more again and again. The breaks in sex were sprinkled with words forgotten as they fell from their lips. The words didn't matter. It was all about the skin, the touch, the nearness of another body. He'd only wished he had a name. He could send flowers.

Maybe she never gave one. He searches Amanda's friends list for her. *Maybe she wanted it to be anonymous.* He can't seem to find her. He's learned over the years burlesque girls have at least two personalities. Like superheroes, they have their mild-mannered day persona. Then, behind the glittering armor of sequins and lace, they become something undeniably different. Amanda is a perfect example. She can make herself damn near invisible if she chooses to, and when she's on stage, no one can help to stare. Vic leans back in his chair, admiring the photo on his screen. Amanda somewhere between her two personas, looking ethereal and full of joy staring at Mike, who's never been happier. His heart swells with appreciation for how she's changed his friend for the better.

He's always known Mike was eventually going to fall for someone, get married, and start a family. He was raised for that shit. Generations of happy families making babies and memories. Not him, though. Vic isn't the marrying type. Marriage turns men like him into monsters. His dad was proof. The best thing he can do is keep it casual. Like Amanda's mysterious friend from the wedding.

Was she on the list in front of him somewhere, invisible behind a clean face and sweatshirt? No, he would know those lips in an instant. It seems they are the only thing he remembers clearly. Beautiful lips smiling, biting, smoking… His cock stirs. "Fuck." He breathes. "I'll have to ask Amanda about her when they get back," he says to the empty room, closing out the open tabs on his computer. He's gotten used to Amanda's presence at the Speakeasy since she came to live with Mike.

Mike prefers to be there only for the big decisions and lifting of heavy things. Amanda has taken to her role of bar manager beautifully. She and Vic spent hours together working out the details for drink specials, schedules, and new acts to book. He laughs to himself. She's the partner Mike had been years before, even better in some ways. He understands fully why she was so hard for Mike to forget.

Vic turns his mind to the future, looking over the schedule for the upcoming auditions. They're fast approaching with a promising list of potential performers signed up. Some of Amanda's people from A la Mode are coming in to help with auditions. He's excited for what's to come. Maybe his little leopard vixen will make an appearance.

***

Olive sits on her bed, scrolling through help wanted ads. Prospects in the small town of Marquette, Iowa are few and far between. The room creaks as she shifts in her bed. Her backpack falls from its place, spilling its contents on the floor. She slides off the bed to gather her things and sees a folded piece of newspaper. The ad Janice had shown her before is circled in bold permanent marker. The words DO IT, followed by several exclamation points.

Even though Olive knows nothing about burlesque, it tempts her. Something about running away from her life to pursue one filled with dancers, musicians, comedians, magicians, and jugglers sounds wonderful. She remembers the celebrations her parents would host with food piled high and drinks flowing like water. People would eat, drink, laugh, and eventually pull their various instruments from their tents to play together. All the people would dance. On occasion there would be fire dancers, twirling blazing batons and blowing enormous fireballs.

She dabs at tears, overwhelmed by nostalgia. The only life she ever knew was a mystery to others. It hadn't taken too many mentions of solstice celebrations and fire eaters followed by uncomfortable looks from her foster parents for her to realize her new world was nothing like the one she grew up in. She'd been sheltered from the real world, never knowing what life was like off the farm. No television, no internet, no formal education. Art had been a huge part of her childhood. She spent hours in a room filled with windows, plants, and as many paints and canvases as she could want. Music was always playing. Bluegrass, country, soul, funk, blues, classical, even opera. Her parents would sip coffee together listening to Sunday Morning Baroque on public radio. Mom said it was her favorite hour of the week. Olive and Eli would skip and twirl to the sound of a harpsichord.

She pushes away the memories of happier days and looks to the future. Diving into the world of burlesque, she reads all she can about it on the internet. Then after watching hours of videos of different performers, she convinces herself she can do it. After, calculating how long she can live on what she has saved, she calls the number from the ad.

A pleasant voice answers after two rings. "Thanks for calling the Speakeasy. This is Bunny."

"Um, hi. I'm calling about the dancers wanted ad?"

"Perfect. Do you have any stage experience?"

"Not really."

"That's okay. Are you familiar with burlesque?"

"Somewhat," Olive answers, unsure of her ability to actually go through with an audition.

"That's better than some," Bunny says with a chuckle, which puts Olive at ease. "We'll be holding open auditions Thursday and Friday next week. We'll start at seven with some stretches and a warm-up. Then we'll teach you all a simple routine as a group. Don't worry, it's remedial. Mostly to see how you carry yourself on stage. After that, if you make the cut, you'll have an opportunity to show an individual routine. It doesn't have to be anything extravagant. Don't concern yourself too much about costuming. We want to see your personality, get a feel of your stage presence. After that, we'll hold interviews off stage. It seems like a lot. It's not. I promise. It'll be fun."

"Sounds like it," Olive says, swallowing her trepidation. "I'll be there Thursday, if that works."

"Yep. We'll see you at seven."

"Great. See you then." Olive disconnects and racks her mind for a routine idea. *What song? What song?* She runs through the soundtrack of her life through the many records her mom and dad had played. She remembers the subtle shift in the music once she and her brother were sent off to bed. The songs that would lull her to sleep were soft and bluesy. She recognized the sensuality without understanding it. As she runs through many of them in her mind, she keeps coming back to one. Taj Mahal, "Here in the Dark." It's smooth and sexy. She sways as it plays on her phone, the boat rocking with her movements.

What to wear? She considers the many glittering costumes from her research. The layers of sequins and sparkle. Confident women peeling them off with crowds cheering them along. Her uniform lies on top of her clothes pile. It's a somewhat shimmering bodice reminiscent of a corset. With her matching black bra panties and some heels, she's one trip to the drugstore for stockings away from a complete costume.

***

Standing on a new dock miles away from the farm and the dock she'd spent the last decade, Olive is filled with a sense of adventure. Her steps feel lighter. She climbs on her newly purchased bicycle and rides along the river. As she rides, she's listening to her song, and goes through her choreography in her mind.

The riverfront is full of people enjoying the early summer evening. A modern playground bustles with children and parents. Teenagers zoom past her on skateboards. A tall red and white antenna stretches above the buildings a few blocks away. It's the landmark she identified from pictures online, across the street from her destination. She heads toward it, excitement bubbling in her chest. Interesting metal art pieces hang along alley walls. Bright murals cover many of the buildings.

On the corner stands an old theater with beautiful architecture and enormous windows that seem to be staring down at her. She spies the Speakeasy's sign on the much smaller building next door. Out front a group of people are laughing and talking. She pedals slowly across the road, trying not to be seen watching them. They're colorful, to say the least. She's immediately intimidated. Though they seem to be friendly, she can't imagine she'd shine brightly enough to compare with any of them.

Riding past the theater on the corner, she turns down the alley and comes around the side of the building through a small parking lot. In her t-shirt, shorts, and sneakers, and with her backpack on her back, she feels like a child compared to the women in their dresses and dancewear. Their faces are painted brightly, their hair as well. She parks her bike quietly and chains it to a light post. As she approaches the group, a tall and lean black man spots her. "Are you here for auditions?" he asks, his voice smooth as velvet. His eyes are like liquid amber. She tries to focus on them, but everything about him demands to be seen. His full lips and facial piercings, his springy golden dreadlocks, his beautifully sculpted and tattooed chest and shoulders are on display behind a neon pink muscle shirt with the word "Freak" in bright letters across the chest.

"Um. Yeah. I think so." She looks from him to the other people behind him. Several of them lean against large windows, looking as awkward as she feels with their bags and their nerves.

"I'm Calvin. Nice to meet you," he says, offering her his slender hand. She takes it, surprised by the softness. He smells like heaven.

"Um, Olive." She nods slightly, continuing to survey the other folks. Two blonde women who look like sisters are having their own conversation a few paces away. A shorter woman with a wild rainbow afro-hawk peeks from behind Calvin's shoulder. She's dressed to kill in a lace shirt, skintight vest, and painted-on jeans. Her earlobes have more earrings than Olive can count, sparkling necklaces hang from her slender neck, most nestled in her cleavage.

"Look at you," she says, stepping between Olive and Calvin. "You look like a dancer." She looks Olive up and down with large dark eyes like a cat.

"Uh. Not really." Olive chuckles nervously and steps back. "I mean, maybe. I guess."

"I bet you can move, though."

"I hope so. That's what I'm here for." She shrugs.

"Hmm." The small woman squints at Olive then smiles.

"Nice to meet you, I'm Cin D'Lish. I'll be teaching the choreography for the group routine."

"Okay. Cool. Nice to meet you too." Olive adjusts her backpack on her shoulders and nods to them both. "I'm a little nervous," she says quickly.

"Don't be," Calvin soothes. "We're all a bunch of awkward outcasts here. Nothing to be nervous about." For the moment she believes him. Then, the look on Cin's face says otherwise.

"Is this everyone, Bunny?" Cin asks over her shoulder. The blonde holding a clipboard looks up from her conversation then glances down at her list and then over to the crowd and begins counting.

"We're still missing Em," she says. Cin rolls her eyes.

"Of course we are."

"How about you three go talk with John? He's in the sound booth. I'll give these guys a quick rundown about tonight. If Emily isn't here by the time we're done, we'll start without her."

"It's your show," Cin says with a shrug and heads inside, her tiny backside switching with sass.

"We'll be ready when you are, Bunny." Calvin follows Cin.

"Good luck, you guys," the unnamed blonde says before heading in with the others.

"Hi, Olive." Bunny approaches with her arms open for a hug.

"Hi." Olive hugs her back awkwardly.

"I'm a hugger. You were the last one on my list, other than Emily, and you aren't her." She laughs and motions for Olive to join the others along the window. "All right, guys, I'm really happy you all made it out," she says, looking at the slight man with dust-colored hair and shining gray eyes behind thick plastic glasses. He nods back with a smile. "Everyone is here for dance auditions, short of you, Marty. Right?" The group of four others nod their agreement.

"Perfect. Then we have five, six when Em gets here," Bunny says to herself, looking at her clipboard.

"What we'll do is head inside for stretching. Then Cin, Calvin, and Bridgette will teach you the steps of our "Bourbon Street" routine. Don't worry. If I can do it anyone can." She laughs again. "After that, we'll get you on stage and see how you do. Again, it's okay if you don't get it spot on. We're looking for confidence, mostly, and control of movement. After that, you'll get a chance to show a routine you've put together yourself. Then I'll do quick one-on-one interviews with each of you." She looks over the group with a broad smile that continues to put Olive at ease. "And you, Marty." She points at him with her clipboard. "I'd like you to sit with me while they learn the steps. If you're going to be my emcee, we've got a lot to talk about."

"Sure thing," Marty says with a nod. He has a soft unassuming voice that makes Olive think of a dozen different things. None of them emcee.

"Perfect." Bunny offers another dazzling grin. "Let's get started then."

***

"It's open," Vic calls to the knock at his office door. He's sitting at his desk not doing much of anything, tempted to see how auditions are starting, but won't since Amanda made it clear she wanted him to stay put.

"Did you miss me?" A low, sultry voice surprises him. He looks up from his computer with a start. Her luscious lips smile as she closes the door behind her. He'd learned from Amanda that her name is Emily, and she's expected at auditions some night this week. As much as he hates to admit it, she's the reason he found an excuse to be here.

"Hello, stranger." He smiles, taking in her skintight leggings and low-cut tank top. "You're looking lovely."

"Am I?" she asks, stepping closer to his desk, biting her lower lip.

"I'd imagine you always do."

"That's sweet," she says with a pout. "I hoped I would see you tonight." She sits her ample ass down on his desk, inches from his laptop.

"How'd you get past the crew?" he asks, snapping his computer shut and pushing it away, a familiar excitement rising.

"I snuck in the back door. Someone left a brick in it." She laughs and levels her cool blue gaze on him.

"You here for auditions?"

"Maybe," she answers, kicking off her shoes and resting her bare foot along the side of his thigh. "Maybe I came to see you."

"Can't say I'd be upset about that." He takes her foot in his hand, angling his chair to face her. She shifts to face him directly. "Thought you weren't too interested…"

"Yeah, sorry for bouncing on you that night. I had to work," she says with a shrug. "You seemed content to sleep."

"I missed you in the morning."

"I bet you did." She leans in, her pale breasts spilling out of the black tank top. "Wanna hit that casting couch of yours?" She pulls her foot from his hands and wiggles her toes against his growing cock. "What do ya say, Vicky boy?"

"I'd be a fool to resist," he says, watching as she slides off the desk, lowering herself onto her knees. Her manicured hand sliding into the place where her foot had been. She grins up at him, her lips glistening with gloss. Her black hair is pulled back in a high ponytail, revealing her pale shoulders and neck.

"You would be," she breathes, pulling at his belt buckle and settling herself between his legs. "Well, hello there," she says warmly as his cock springs from his zipper. "You *are* happy to see me."

Her breath is warm on the swollen tip of his dick. She licks her lips, then brushes them against it. A shiver of arousal runs through him. He sighs and lets his head fall back as she sucks him into her mouth. Alarms go off in his head. Though there's nothing inherently wrong with what she's doing, it's not right either. Then again, she came to him. She lowered herself onto her knees unprovoked. Not to mention it feels phenomenal. He relaxes more, sinking back into his seat.

"Full disclosure," he says on a ragged breath. "I have no influence on the auditions."

"I know," she responds, her lips moving against his tip, her hand clutching the base, firmly. "I've been daydreaming about this cock for weeks now." His face warms with pride. His body shivers with delight as she lowers her head again, sucking hungrily. With a quick knock at the door, Amanda's voice startles them. He sits up quickly, and Amanda pops her head in and smiles, oblivious to the woman on her knees under his desk.

"We're waiting on one more. Emily is perpetually late, so we'll start without her. If you have to leave, use the back door, please. They're nervous enough as it is without you prowling around."

He clears his throat and rests his elbows on the desk. "You got it. Let me know when it's safe for me to come out." She nods and disappears as suddenly as she appeared. Emily giggles between his legs as he pushes his chair back.

"That was close." She stands and straightens her ponytail. "Sorry to leave you hanging," she says with a glance at his cock. "I should probably get out there, though." She slips her heels on. Then, bending with her ass inches from his face, she writes her number on his calendar. "Buy me a drink later?"

"Sure thing," he responds, shifting in his seat as she flashes a bright smile and leaves the room, closing the door behind her. Vic sits awkwardly, his nerves frayed with unspent desire.

"Bourbon Street" by Jeff Tuohy plays loudly on the other side of the wall. The piano and brass remind him of the purpose of auditions. They aren't to bring beautiful sensual women to his office for midday trysts. If Amanda had known that Emily was there, she would've been none too happy with either of them. Not to mention his own rule of keeping business and pleasure separate.

If Emily's seduction skills translate to the stage, she is sure to get a place on the new troupe, leaving him to question and most likely break his own rules.

How can he resist someone like her?

How can anyone?

Chapter 4

Olive stands with the other applicants in the middle of the Speakeasy. Tables and chairs are stacked along the walls to clear a space for them to practice. She listens intently to the music, watching as the three professionals move through the steps along with the beat. They're on stage with the houselights up, laughing and joking through the movements they've clearly done countless times before.

A girl, significantly younger than her with pink hair and a nose ring, looks nervous enough for the entire room. She's watching anxiously. A silver-haired woman slightly older than Janice watches with reserved glee. She's dressed like a college professor with bright colors, scarfs, and dangling jewelry. She winks at Olive and grins, tapping her hand on her hip with the beat. A woman, six feet tall, stands beside her in sweatpants and an oversize t-shirt. Her complexion is perfect, her smile sweet. She has her hair in a messy bun on the top of her head. A step or two ahead of them is a young man with an attractive build. He's moving through the steps with the precision of a Broadway hopeful.

Olive calms herself as she assesses the people around her. Though she doesn't have the confidence of the man dancing his heart out, she and the women to her left and right seem to be in the same place mentally: nervous and unsure of what they are doing here.

"He's really setting the bar here, isn't he?" The silver-haired lady leans close to Olive and chuckles.

"He is," Olive half whispers her response, still watching the people on stage. She relaxes her shoulders and smiles, opening her mouth to introduce herself.

"I'm sorry I'm late, Bunny," comes a shout from the doorway. Everything stops except the music. All attention is on the woman entering with her arms full. She drops her things on the nearest table and sighs heavily. "What did I miss?" Olive notes a change of the energy in the room. A quick glance in the direction of the stage shows annoyed expressions from Cin, Calvin, and Bridgette. The woman who Olive assumes is Emily stands with her hands on her full hips, skintight athletic wear, and perfect cleavage. Her thick black ponytail swings from high on the back of her head. With Bettie Paige bangs and full makeup, she looks like the burlesque dancers Olive has been watching relentlessly since scheduling her audition. She's immediately intimidated. Bunny stands up and crosses the room, wrapping her arms around the latecomer. The music stops.

"Glad you made it, Em. We're only getting started," Bunny says, releasing her and walking back to her place beside Marty.

"We're gonna take it from the top now," Cin says from the stage, looking to the sound booth, ignoring Emily as she hurries to take her place beside the young man between Olive and the stage. The music starts up again. Watching her from behind, Olive notes how confidently she moves through the steps, as though she already knows them. It seems the dancers and Bunny all know her too. Olive wonders about her story, how she fits in with the group. She's mesmerized by the way Emily's body moves, all wiggles and grace. If she doesn't make the cut, no one in this room will.

After several run-throughs, the crew from the stage come down to walk among the burlesque hopefuls. They all but ignore Emily, while smiling and chatting with the rest of the group. Calvin and Cin stand beside the young man, commenting to each other about his skill. Olive notes the look of pride on his face as he tries to focus on the moves. Bridgette is beside Olive watching her feet.

"You're doing great, everyone," she says. "I can't believe how quickly you've picked this up." She smiles and walks around the group to join Cin and Calvin.

"All right, guys," Cin speaks up as the music fades out, "we're going to arrange you on stage, three in front, three in back. We'll go through once that way. Then we'll move the folks in back to the front and do it again. You all ready?" she asks with a smile and an excited twinkle in her eye.

Olive's heart is in her throat. She takes her place on the stage where she's told to, on the right in the back line with Emily beside her, and the tall sweet-faced lady on the left. Broadway is in the center of the front line with Pink hair to his right and Silver hair to his left. Olive feels about as graceful as a newborn deer when the music plays. Her feet move without hesitation, though her insides are shaking violently.

"Step. Step. Pivot. Turn. Step. Step. Pivot. Turn," Cin calls from off stage with the beat. "Tap. Tap. Bend. Bend. Now slap that ass. Now up. Up. Bump. Bump. Grind. Grind. Bump. Bump. Grind. Slap. Pivot. Turn. Hip. Hip. Hip. Hip. Pivot. Turn. Annnnnnd, Shim…my. Shim…my. And take a bow, bitches. You did it." The small audience cheers and whistles from the floor. Olive's heart is racing. "You want a break before we go again?" Cindy asks. The group answers together that they want to go again.

The success of her first run-through is not enough to prepare her for standing in the front line. With the houselights down, the stage lights seem brighter than the sun. They shine in her face, nearly blinding her. She moves through the movements on autopilot, barely hearing the music, following Cin's calls from off stage. Thirty seconds seems to stretch out over time and space until the small crowd begins cheering from the floor again. Olive pants as the houselights come up. She looks around at the group of strangers panting too. All except Emily. She stands, cool and collected, appearing bored by it all.

"Great job, everyone," Bridgette cheers from her seat beside Bunny.

"No kidding," Bunny agrees. "You're all fantastic. Beyond what I had hoped for." She claps and stands to address them all. "Let's take about twenty minutes to catch our breath and get ready for your individual auditions. Anyone want to go first?" She scans the group of six still standing on stage. They look from one another with awkward apprehension. Then Emily speaks up.

"I'll go," she says with a shrug.

"Perfect," Bunny says with a quick nod, making a note on her clipboard. "Anyone want to volunteer for second?"

Broadway speaks up. "Me," he says, waving his hand and jumping up and down.

"Thank you, Chris." She makes a note and looks to the remaining four.

"Put me down," Silver hair says with the confidence that comes from years of learning to not give a fuck.

"All right, Susan." Bunny makes another note and looks directly at Olive.

"Okay. Yeah." Olive nods and looks at the remaining two.

"Thank you, Olive. Who's next?" Bunny asks, looking at the women who could hardly be any different. One small and pierced with short pink hair. The other towering over the rest, looking like she got lost on her way to the grocery store.

"I'll go," the tall one says with a soft, delicate voice.

"Thank you, Julie. That leaves you, Sophia," Bunny says with a quick nod. "If you all don't mind stepping outside for a bit, we're going to discuss your performance on the group routine. Then we'll bring you back in to get ready for your individuals."

Olive steps down the stairs with mixed emotions. She's not sure if she's got what it takes. The others follow her off the stage and gather their things to head outside. She takes her phone and headphones and hurries out to find a quiet place to practice.

***

Amanda pushes through the door without knocking. Vic jumps with a start. She's beaming. "That was amazing," she sings with a giggle and dances in the open doorway.

"Are you finished already?" He closes his laptop, hiding that he's playing solitaire to while away the hours between now and seeing Emily again.

"Oh goodness no. But the group we have tonight did a great job on "Bourbon Street." I didn't expect them to pick it up so quickly."

"That's great." Vic leans forward, resting his elbows on the desk. "How many do we have tonight?"

"We have six dancers, counting Emily. She finally showed up. And Marty, who desperately wants to be emcee. He's super sweet. I don't know if he's got what it takes though. I can see already that he's no Johnathan."

"Is there anyone who is?" Vic asks, remembering the emcee for Amanda's first burlesque troupe and his almost magic ability to woo any crowd.

"Not to my knowledge. Too bad I can't put him in a clone machine and get an exact replica. It would make this a lot easier."

"What are you thinking though? Since clones aren't an option."

"Well, we've got another round of auditions tomorrow night with a couple more comedians and a magician. So, I'm going to have him come back to run through his stand-up set with hopes that we find his perfect complement. I do like his energy."

"Can I come out and meet him? Or am I still on lockdown until all your fair maidens are safely out of sight?" he teases.

"You and I both know these ladies are not maidens. Some less than others," she offers a wry smile. "They are on break now though, including Marty. All out front if you wanted to meet them."

"I might wander out that way in a bit."

"Don't take too long. We're starting individual auditions in about fifteen," she says as she backs out of his office.

Vic sits back with a smile. He had known when he booked Burlesque A la Mode for a show years ago it was a good idea. But he could never have foreseen how good it was going to be. Amanda changed Mike's life, and in doing so changed Vic's as well. Her energy and excitement are contagious, taking their already successful venue and making it better with her woman's touch. Vic wonders what a woman's touch might do for his life. What a woman like Amanda might change for him. Then he considers Emily with all her brash sexuality and her unapologetic seduction. "Ah hell." He breathes out and runs his fingers through his hair before standing to leave.

He approaches the table where Amanda is seated with her friends. They're quietly discussing the merits of each performer. "I'm taking off for a while," he says to the group.

"You going out front?" she asks.

"Nah. Gonna head home. No sense in hanging around where I'm not wanted," he teases.

"Stop," Amanda says with the voice of a mother reprimanding her toddler.

"Okay, fine, where I'm not needed. Is that better?" Vic winks.

"Sure. I'll let you know when we're all done."

He says his good-byes to everyone around the table and walks toward the back door, shutting and locking his office on the way out. Sunlight shines around the heavy door to the alley still propped open with a brick. He pulls it open and kicks the brick out of the way then heads to the fire escape—his personal stairway to his apartment, leaving the main entrance out front to his tenants.

As he approaches the top of the stairs, he hears a shuffle on the roof he uses as a porch. Bracing himself for an altercation, he moves slowly, thinking of when he found a vagrant making himself at home on his chair. Peeking over the railing slowly, he spies a lovely frame swaying and spinning, headphones firmly in place. She's lit by the slowly setting sun, casting shadows on the roof. A pleasant and welcome surprise.

Her thick dark hair flows freely over her shoulders. Her long lean legs end in dirty bare feet, stained from the roof. With her back to him, she has no idea she's being watched. She bends and moves in true burlesque fashion, appealing to an invisible audience. As she begins to remove her imaginary bodice from over her loose tank top, she turns to him. A surprised squeal pierces the hum of the city. She jumps and covers herself as though she had removed an actual garment and was standing bare before him.

"Oh my god. You scared the shit out of me," she pants, lowering one arm and holding her chest with the other.

"I could say the same of you." He laughs and ascends the remaining stairs.

"I'm sorry, I thought I was alone."

"Well, you were. Until I showed up. What are you doing on my porch?" he asks, leaning against the rail.

"I thought it was a roof." She wraps her arms around her stomach and looks away. "I'm sorry. I'll get out of here." She moves quickly and stops a few steps away with a glance in his direction. "It doesn't look like a porch."

Vic chuckles while admiring the surprisingly familiar contours of her face. "I assure you it is." He points to the sun-faded lawn chair sitting beside his door.

"That's a chair on a roof," she says with a tilt of her chin. "Look, I'm sorry for trespassing. I've got to get down there though. I'm expected inside."

Vic steps away from the rail, making room for her to pass. "I don't want to keep you."

"Sorry, again. I really did think this was the roof." She smiles a shy smile. Her gaze meets his briefly, a mossy green sparkle, before she moves to the fire escape.

"Wait." He steps between her and the rail. "Have we met?"

“Um, yeah. Actually…” She chuckles and nods. “Now that you mention it. I think we have.”

“Where?” When her green eyes dazzle in the sunlight, he remembers. Holy shit. It’s Olive. Before he can say anything, she’s talking.

“I suppose you have women crashing into your truck all the time. I imagine it would be hard to keep us all apart.” She blinks and pushes her hair behind her ears with both hands.

“Jesus. Wow.” Vic smiles, shaking his head. “Looks like you healed right up.”

“Told you I would.” She grins and gives the air between them a playful punch. “As nice, albeit odd as this reunion is, I really do have to get down there. Don’t want to miss my big break.”

Vic steps aside to let her pass, watching as she descends the rusted stairway. An undeniably warm feeling is growing in his stomach. She’s prettier than he remembers her, and he’d thought she was cute when she was all banged up.

“Small fucking world,” he says to the sky before dropping onto his chair to watch the sun set on the windows of the buildings around him. What are the odds Olive would be auditioning to perform in his club? He wonders if it means anything.

For a few brief moments, the whole area glows with golden light, shining in the windows, warming the pale, yellow walls of the theater beside him.

“Small fucking world.”

Chapter 5

How strange, Olive thinks as she enters the Speakeasy. Though she should be thinking about her audition, the chance meeting with Vic has thrown her off-kilter. Sure, she'd been foolish to climb the fire escape in search of privacy, but she wouldn't've thought in a million years anyone would be up there. Least of all the handsome, golden-haired stranger whose passenger side door she rammed into weeks ago.

She takes a seat next to Susan, who's traded the layers of scarfs and bangles for a traditional burlesque costume. A black and purple corset with a black skirt gathered and bustled shows off her sleek figure. Black fishnet stockings adorn her shapely legs. "I've wanted to do this for years." She laughs.

"You look amazing," Olive gushes, lifting her backpack off the ground. She looks around the room. Bunny is sitting with Marty and the rest of the dancers at a table. They're lined up in front of the stage like judges from *American Idol.*

Emily exits the sound booth with a floor-length sequin gown. She offers Olive a tight-lipped smile and walks to the stage. Chris is in a tuxedo dancing in a corner. *What the fuck am I doing here?* Olive's tempted to throw her bag on her shoulder and make a run for it. *There's no way I can compete with this.* Then, she spies Julie coming out of the bathroom in a dated prom dress. Sophia is right behind her in what's clearly a cheap polyester Halloween costume. *You can do this,* she tells herself, standing and heading to the bathroom to change.

"You've got this," Susan cheers as Olive walks away.

"Thanks, so do you," she says over her shoulder then offers a broad smile to Julie and Sophia.

In the bathroom, she undresses in one of the two stalls, awkwardly wiggling into her stale-smelling uniform and fresh stockings. With her bag on the counter, she quickly makes up her face, then dabs sweetly scented oil on her hands and rubs all over her bodice to counter the stale cigarette smell. Running her fingers through her hair to fluff it one last time, she looks in the mirror, pleased with her transformation. It's nothing showy, but it's better than the Halloween costume.

Music blasts through the door, heavy bass and a slow beat. Olive hurries to see Emily's audition. The houselights are down and Emily is sparkling on stage. She slinks and moves through her routine with controlled grace. Olive can't believe a person can dance in heels that high. Surely, Emily has done this before. She looks almost bored by it all.

Bunny gives a quick hoot in the darkness while the rest of her table remain silent. The group of potential dancers watch spellbound as Emily peels off her sparkling dress to reveal a somehow more sparkling corset. Positioned on a chair to her right is a pair of bright white feather fans propped upright. She lowers herself and plucks them up, hiding her torso. Like magic her corset falls to her feet. She spins and twirls across the length of the stage, expertly hiding her bare skin. As the song ends, she holds the fans up behind her head like a peacock tail and shimmies her full, beautifully shaped breasts. Her audience of novices cheer and hoot along with Bunny, while the other three clap politely.

Olive's cheeks burn with embarrassment over what she's about to present as her piece. She looks down at her ridiculous uniform and again feels the urge to run outside. She would feel less foolish riding her bike down the city street in her uniform than she would following Emily's performance.

"Awesome, Emily," Bunny calls to Emily, ascending the stairs. "I didn't think to bring in a stage kitten tonight. Guess that's my job then." She laughs and begins to collect Emily's discarded costume pieces. Emily leaves the stage with a smug grin, her feather fans bouncing as she passes.

"You ready, Chris?" Bunny calls, shading her eyes from the stage lights. He jumps up and takes the stage before Bunny leaves it. Once she's settled, Louis Prima's "Just a Gigolo" plays. Chris moves through his high-energy routine, the whole room cheering and laughing throughout. He ends in a sparkling red thong, a bow tie, and a smile. Cin leaps from her seat, giving him a standing ovation.

"Better be careful, Bunny. We're gonna take this one home with us," she says with a large smile before running up the stairs to collect his clothes for him.

"You stay away from him, Cin. He's ours," Amanda calls from her seat. "Up next is Susan." She turns in her seat. "You ready?"

"Not sure how I'm going to follow that. But I'll try," Susan answers, standing to take the stage. She walks with elegance in her stiletto heels, ascending the four stairs that lead to the stage. "I'm going to start backstage." She shields her eyes from the lights and calls to the sound booth before hurrying behind the curtains.

"Hey Big Spender" begins playing. Susan's leg appears first, then her hand with a snap on the beat. She pushes through the curtains completely as the lyrics begin. Olive can see Susan's knees shaking as she moves through her carefully choreographed steps, singing along with the words. Bunny's table offers some gentle encouragement. Nothing like what they gave Chris, but enough, it seems, to give Susan a boost of confidence. She smiles and bats her lashes at the front table, slipping one long glove off then the other. She twirls and drops her bustled skirt, wagging her hips. Olive gives a little woot of her own as the group cheers her on right down to her twirling, bouncing tassels.

"Great job, Susan." Bunny stands and hurries to the stage, plucking up her cast-off garments. Susan exits the stage and plops herself beside Olive.

"It's harder than it looks." She sighs, fanning her face, looking at the remaining three.

"Thanks for the pep talk," Olive says, shifting in her seat, her heart racing.

"Olive, you're next," Bunny says, handing Susan her costume pieces.

"All right then. Here goes nothing." Bunny takes her seat, and on shaking legs Olive walks to the stairs.

Her music starts when she hits the top step. She moves without hesitation, forgetting about the small crowd watching. Her feet take over and her mind wanders to the roof where she'd been caught by the Vic with his gorgeous smile. Except this time, she doesn't jump with fright. Instead, she laughs at his curious gaze and keeps dancing, peeling off her clothes as he watches with awe.

Cheers from the audience bring her back to the present as she drops her skirt and lowers herself onto the floor. Slipping off her worn old heels, she kicks her legs, pointing her toes. Then slides one stocking down slowly from her thigh to her toes. Bunny squeals with glee while the others hoot and holler along with her. Olive spins on her rear and pulls at the second stocking, met with similar reactions. She stands as gracefully as she can and unzips her bodice, dropping it to the ground. Her bare nipples stand erect as she gives her best shimmy.

"Damn, girl," Cin shouts from her seat. "No pasties? Get it."

"Oh shit." Olive shields herself from the group. "I'm sorry. I didn't know where to get them. I'm sorry. Oh shit." She hurries of the stage, her cheeks blazing.

"No worries," Bunny says, heading up the stairs to gather her things. "If you're all right with it, we won't complain." She brings Olive her clothes. "You're already one of us." She winks and chuckles. "You ready, Julie?"

Olive is dressing in the bathroom for the beginning of Julie's routine. When she comes out, she can see that Julie is clearly rattled. Shaking and missing her steps, then apologizing and asking to start again. She starts three times before giving up in tears. "I'm sorry. I can't do this. Sorry for wasting your time," she says softly as she hurries off the stage into the bathroom. Bunny jumps up quickly and follows her.

"Poor thing. I thought *I* was nervous up there." Susan leans close to Olive with a half whisper.

"Oh, I know. It is so much harder than it looks."

"What are you talking about? You're a natural."

"Really?" Olive snorts her surprise. "I was shaking like mad."

"Didn't show."

"That's good to hear. You were pretty great yourself."

"Oh stop. I appreciate it. This old bird knows better than that though."

"No, really, you were amazing up there."

Susan gives Olive a side-eyed glance and shakes her head with a laugh. "Thank you," she says, twirling her colorful scarf in the air. The door to the bathroom opens. Bunny comes out first, Julie follows close behind wearing her sweats and a relieved smile.

“All right,” Bunny says to the room. “Sophia is next.” She looks around the room then at each one of them. “Is she outside?” Olive shrugs and looks around with the others.

Calvin heads outside, coming back in quickly. “She’s not out there.”

“Oh no. Poor thing,” Bridgette says, holding her hand over her heart. “She must’ve gotten cold feet.”

“If she can’t get up there in front of this audience, how could she with a packed house?” Cin chimes in.

“I know. Still. I feel bad for her.”

“Now, where’s Emily?” Bunny asks, raising both palms to the ceiling.

“Does it matter?” Cin asks flatly.

“We might as well start with interviews. She’d be first.”

“Do you really *need* to interview her?” Calvin slides up behind Bunny. The four friends seem to have forgotten there are others in the room. Olive tries not to eavesdrop, though the conversation is happening right in front of her.

“I want to be fair. And she is an amazing performer,” Bunny says. Cin rolls her eyes and shakes her head. Bridgette sighs and Calvin shrugs.

“Like I said before. It’s your show. Don’t think I’m gonna be in any rush to share a stage with her again,” Cin says. “Either way. You don’t really need us for the interviews. I’m going to the hotel. Call me when you’re done so we can get a drink. You still haven’t told me about your honeymoon.”

“There’s plenty to tell,” Bunny purrs and opens her arms wide. Cin moves in for a hug.

“I’m going too.” Calvin steps up, making it a group hug. “You all did great. You should be proud of yourselves,” he says to the anxious group, awkwardly watching their exchange.

“I’ll stay,” Bridgette says, looking up from her phone at the table.

“Sweet.” Bunny releases Cin and Calvin. “Then I guess we can get started. We’ll work Emily in when she comes back.”

“*If* she comes back.” Cin sneers and gathers her things.

***

Hey this is Vic. Message me when you're done, we can go get that drink.

He checks his phone again, feeling unnaturally rattled. He changes into a pair of gym shorts and his running shoes and heads to his fitness room to run off his unspent energy. Emily's clearly seen the message. *Leaving me on read,* he thinks with some disappointment as he starts on the treadmill. *Must be busy with auditions,* he tells himself as he blasts Pantera on his Bluetooth.

The benefit of having a home gym above a music venue means he can play his music as heavy and loud as he wants. Metal is his favorite for a heavy workout. He skips his warm-up and starts in running as fast and hard as his heart and legs will allow. Once his pulse is racing, he leaves the treadmill for his small punching bag in the corner. His rapid-fire strikes on the rubber bag become part of the music as he punches his way through his physical frustration.

He knows that Emily is bad news. He can feel it in his bones. It's not his bones he's listening to though. His more demanding body parts couldn't care less about the danger she presents. She's exciting for sure. He would be a fool not to want to have her again without the haze of booze. He could show her what he can really do. *I must've done something right for her to come slinking into my office like she did.* He remembers their night together and hits the bag even harder until his arms are jelly and his head soaked with sweat.

No response when he checks his phone on his way to the bathroom. He kicks out of his shoes and peels off his sweaty clothes before the mirror. His chest and arms are taut from his workout. He flexes, appreciating the results of his strict workout regimen, and remembers the first time he stood up to his dad. Stepping between his fist and Mom's face. He'd hoped her bruises would stop that day. He hadn't been quite strong enough. They'd both received the beating of their lives. From that day on he focused on making his body stronger.

His dad would stop hurting Mom if it was the last thing he did. It'd been the summer of junior year when he finally won. His dad's face was swollen beyond recognition, and his mom was screaming through her tears, "You're going to kill him."

He's sure he would have if he hadn't heard the fear in her voice. That was the last time he saw his dad. They packed what little they had and moved in with his grandma. The old man never came to call. He knew where they were, and knew he was not welcome.

Vic had usurped him.

He shakes off the thought and climbs into his steaming shower. Five jets from two angles work their magic on his muscles. He relaxes into the spray. Leaving for college had been one of the most difficult decisions he'd made. He'd felt he was leaving her unprotected. She swore that if he didn't go, she would never forgive herself.

Now, he doesn't worry. His mom is safe and married to a kind and gentle man, which makes Vic's life much easier.

With a towel around his waist, he heads to his walk-in closet and thinks of lighter things. Like if Emily would be interested in dinner along with that drink. Dressing for a casual night out, he towels his hair roughly, then tames the wild curls with a modest amount of product. Something Mike has given him plenty of flack for over the years.

With nothing better to do, he heads downstairs to his office, hoping auditions are almost over so he and Emily can finish what she started. Using his key, he lets himself in the back door and leaves the brick in place in case Emily decides to pop in again. There's no music playing in the theater, though he can hear the hum of several voices around the corner. He feels trapped. It doesn't matter he could go anywhere other than the room next door. That's the room he wants to be in. Until he's allowed back, anywhere else will feel like a cage.

Still no response. Surely, she's had time to send a message.

He sends a message to Bunny, wondering how Emily's audition went as well as Olive's. She may be a bit odd but he's intrigued by her. Despite Emily's unexpected hold on him, he can't seem to forget about Olive's sparkling eyes and her adorably awkward laugh.

How's it going?

You'll never guess who's here auditioning.

***

Olive sits outside on the cement. Susan is inside for her interview. Chris, Julie, and Marty sit along the wall beside her. "How was your interview?" she asks Chris.

"They are such sweet girls," he says of the women who are definitely his elders.

"They really are," Julie says. "Bunny is so understanding. She asked me to stick around for interviews even though I bombed my audition."

"Yeah, she does seem like a real sweetheart. What sort of questions did they ask? Was it a structured interview?" Olive asks, still unsure how she presents herself to the world at large. Ten years of living in it and she still doesn't get all of the unspoken rules of society. She can't count the times she's made ridiculous social blunders over the years. Like earlier this evening when she climbed the fire escape to someone's porch, thinking she was alone. Lucky for her it was Vic.

"It started out structured, then ended up being a pleasant conversation. I even tried to get the dirt on that Emily chick. They weren't budging. All they said was that she was an amazing performer."

"I heard some stuff during her audition. I think they forgot I was sitting there," Marty says. Everyone looks his way. "She performed with a troupe in Minneapolis and did guest spots with A la Mode for a couple shows. Something happened with Cin in Chicago. Something bigger happened in Minneapolis. Her moving here was a total coincidence. She came to one of the A la Mode shows here and weaseled her way into Bunny's heart. Cin's words, not mine."

"Wow. So much drama," Julie says with an innocent grin and a giggle.

"I wonder what she did?" Chris says with dramatic expression.

"She *was* amazing up there," Olive offers. "I wonder where she went?"

"Me too." Chris claps his hands with each word, then steeples his index fingers under his chin.

"Back to the interview though," Olive attempts to steer the conversation away from gossip. "What sort of questions did they ask?"

Chris sighs. "They asked about my stage experience, and my current job. Availability, and my support network. Like if I had a boyfriend or family that supported my choice to do burlesque."

Olive hears his words and considers her own answers to the same questions. Would her family support her if she still had one? What would her mom say about it if she hadn't died years ago of a broken heart in prison? Olive wonders about Eli. Where is he? What is he doing with his life? She hasn't seen him for over three years, since the last time he needed money and a roof over his head.

His years in the foster system broke him. Olive knew it and cried often for the boy he once was. How he loved to dance and sing. That was before, before he was lost in a system that didn't love him. Before he witnessed the violent death of his father and learned the truth about their parents. She shudders and blinks back her tears. Three curious faces watch her. Susan floats out of the Speakeasy with a satisfied grin.

"You're next," she says. Olive stands up, dusting dried leaves and debris from her shorts.

"Wish me luck."

"You don't need it." Susan says with the maternal encouragement Olive craves. "They are going to love you."

"Thanks," she responds before heading through the door. Soft music is playing low. The houselights are up. Bunny and Bridgette are talking at their table with an empty seat across from them. Bunny looks up and grins.

"Hey, Olive," Bridgette calls. "Have a seat."

"Hi." The word has never felt more awkward.

"How'd you feel up there?" Bunny asks.

"Um. Good. I think?" Bridgette and Bunny smile at her and blink. She takes it as a sign to go on. "It felt amazing to be on stage. As far as my performance goes, who knows. I think I did all right. I mean I ended up half nude and that was the goal. So, you know… Sorry about the nipples, by the way, I don't know protocol for something like this."

"No worries," Bunny says, waving her hand in dismissal. "If our theater back home could talk, it would have plenty to say about our naked asses."

"No kidding. You especially," Bridgette teases.

"What do you mean, me especially? What about you and Cin and everyone else for that matter? Hell, I've seen Johnathan naked more often than Mike."

"That's a lie and you know it." Bridgette laughs.

"Okay, that last part, maybe." Bunny looks at Olive and rolls her eyes playfully. "Sorry about that. We have trouble staying on task."

She looks at her clipboard and clears her throat. "Let's talk about your stage experience."

"My brother and I used to put on plays for our folks when we were little."

"Is that it?" Bridgette sounds surprised.

"Pretty much. I was homeschooled, and I didn't get out a lot as a kid. We had tons of family and friends visiting often, so we would put on shows together with the other kids."

"Well, you took to the stage like an old pro," Bunny says. "No dance experience?"

"Only the dancing I did with my family," Olive says, her palms sweating. Remnants of memories from her childhood come and go, random as a dream.

"Hmm." Bunny looks her over, her eyebrows coming together. "Tell me about your family. Do they know you're here? Are they supportive of this endeavor?"

Olive opens her mouth to answer. Her voice cracks. She swallows and shifts in her seat. "I'm an orphan," she says quickly. Knowing that the question was coming and being prepared for it were two very different things. She clears her throat. "I lost both of my parents years ago. I've got a brother, but I haven't seen him for a long time. Honestly, I don't even know where he is." She shrugs and presses her lips together, fighting to keep the tears from falling. Bunny and Bridgette stare at her, looking as if they might cry too.

"Oh honey," Bridgette says with her hand over her heart. "I'm so sorry."

"We don't have to talk about it," Bunny assures. "It's a standard question we ask to see if there are going to be any problems with support from a significant other or overbearing parent. It's happened before. We get a talented performer with loads of potential then lose them shortly after the first show because their small-minded family can't handle it for one reason or another."

"That's terrible," Olive sneers. "My folks would've supported me," she says with a wistful grin. "Dad wouldn't have been comfortable with it. He would've been happy for me, eventually." The two stare back at her from across the table.

"I have so many questions," Bunny says softly.

"Ask away. I'm an open book," Olive responds, leaning back in her chair.

"Why were you homeschooled?" Bunny blurts out then covers her mouth with regret. "I mean, usually it's for some religious reason or something. It doesn't sound like your parents were super religious though."

"They were, and they weren't," Olive says, swaying in her seat. "They were pagan, big back-to-the-land people. We had a self-sufficient farm in Northern Iowa. I never saw a television until I was seventeen years old." She laughs at herself and looks away from Bunny and Bridgette's shocked expressions.

"That's wild," Bunny says. "I thought *I* was country. So, what changed? What made you leave?"

"We had a bad run. Lost my dad. Then it all fell apart," Olive says, controlling her voice. Though she's sure they wouldn't judge for the drugs or the trafficking, she doesn't have the energy to tell the tale.

"That must have been hard for you," Bridgette says as she and Bunny look at her with their faces scrunched up in similar brokenhearted pouts.

"Let's move on," Bunny says, shifting to a kindhearted smile. "Are you available Monday and Wednesday evenings for practice?"

"I am."

"We've got our first show scheduled for October. That gives us three months to make it amazing. What do you think?" Bunny asks with an even bigger grin.

"I think it sounds great. Does that mean you want me?" she asks, butterflies fluttering in her stomach, threatening to fly up and out of her mouth the next time she speaks. It's the best feeling she's had in a long time.

"Of course, we want you. You're amazing," Bridgette gushes before Bunny can speak.

"You really are," Bunny agrees. "I love your energy. You move beautifully on stage. I can't wait to see what you'll do with some direction. How are your sewing skills?"

"I'm competent. My mom and I made a lot of our clothes. It's been years since I've used a sewing machine."

"We can help with that when the time comes. There will be a costume allowance for all accepted routines for our shows. Payment will be based on ticket sales. Which up to this point we have no reason to believe we won't sell out. Our A la Mode shows always have. This will be a debut for our home troupe."

"What's A la Mode?" Olive asks, full of questions about this new, fascinating group of women and men.

"Burlesque A la Mode is our mother troupe in Chicago. Bridgette, Cin, Calvin, and myself all performed together for years until we performed here at the Speakeasy. I ran into an old friend who became my husband. But that's another story for another time." Bunny winks at Bridgette. "My husband and his best friend own this place. We've been bringing A la Mode in for shows for the last two years. They are stretched pretty thin with their own theater, so it's time to start something of my own."

"That's so cool. I'd love to hear all the stories."

"Oh, you will," Bridgette says. "And so much more."

"Welcome to the family," Bunny beams. She stands and walks around the table to wrap Olive in a big warm hug. "So glad you found us."

Olive's heart is in her throat. She can't remember the last time she felt so happy or alive. Bunny and Bridgette are genuine and welcoming. She hugs back and squeezes her eyes against happy tears. "Me too," she squeaks. An indescribably warm feeling of coming home fills her chest. It buzzes under her skin. A brighter future glows on the horizon.

She's been floating aimlessly through her life for a decade, unsure of what to do or where to go. Here in the small, unassuming Speakeasy, in the arms of a veritable stranger, she knows she's found something special.

***

Vic's sitting across the table from Mike. A plate of wing bones lies between them, along with several empty bottles. Music blares over the cacophony of the bustling bar and grill. "I don't get it, man," Vic says, shaking his head. "She came in all hot and heavy. Crawled under my desk for Christ's sake. Then poof. Ghost."

"I don't know what to tell you. Except that girl's trouble," Mike says, finishing his beer.

“Don’t I know it.” Vic catches the attention of their waitress to order another round. “Doesn’t mean I don’t want to get into some of that trouble.”

“I hear you. She might not be the kind of trouble you want though. Amanda’s been talking about her all week.”

“What do you mean?” Vic sits up and leans in, pushing the wing plate to the edge of the table.

“She’s worried about the drama between her and Cin, and the rest, I guess. None of the troupe has anything good to say about her. Amanda likes her, but Amanda likes everyone.”

“What’s the drama?”

“Well, she fucked *one* of Cin’s boyfriends a while ago.”

“One of?”

“Yeah. We both know she’s got plenty.”

“For sure. What else?”

“I think she stole a routine or something from her too. Took it to Minneapolis and performed it as her own. Cin entered it into a festival up there and got a lot of flak from it because they had already seen Emily perform it locally. That’s the real reason she hates her so much. Kinda think she could get over the boyfriend thing otherwise. You know her.”

“Yeah. That’s all *their* drama though. What do I care if she steals routines and boyfriends?”

“I guess you don’t really. I’ve found Amanda’s friends to be pretty accepting of people and their flaws. They don’t offer Emily the same compassion. There has to be more to it than what they’ve told me.”

“I wonder what it is?”

“No clue there. You know what they say though?”

“What’s that?”

“If it looks like a duck, sounds like a duck, it’s probably a bad idea.”

“What the fuck? Nobody says that.”

“It’s true though.” Mike laughs, then drinks the last of his beer.

“Well, I got a taste of that bad idea. I’ll be damned, I’m sure, but I wouldn’t mind another.” Vic peels at the corner of label of his empty bottle.

“I don’t blame you. Have you heard from Amanda? Maybe she’s still tied up with auditions.”

"I did. She asked me if I'd seen Emily. Apparently, she left auditions before her interview."

"See, that's what I'm talking about," Mike says, thanking their waitress who delivered their beers. "Quack."

"You're telling me." They drink in quiet contemplation. "She's so fucking hot though." Vic laments.

"I said my piece." Mike waves his hand in the air. "Now, tell me about the bicycle girl."

Vic huffs. "She climbed the fire escape to my porch to practice for her audition."

"What?"

"I don't know. I went up to my apartment since Amanda wasn't letting me sit in on auditions, and as I'm coming up the stairs, I hear someone moving around. She'd made herself at home up there. She's an odd one. There's your duck." Vic laughs, sipping from his bottle with a smile. A growing warm appreciation for Olive's quirky ways.

"That is strange. Why would she do that?"

"Beats me. She's weird. Cute though," Vic says, remembering the way she moved before she knew he was there. "Small world, isn't it?"

"It really is. What are the chances?" Mike asks.

"I wonder how she did in the auditions." Both their phones sound for a text. It's Amanda.

Hey, fellas, all done. Let's go celebrate.

"I hope she doesn't mind we started without her." Mike gestures to the empties on the table.

"She should know better by now."

Chapter 6

“You sure you won’t come with us?” Bunny asks as the group gathers outside of the Speakeasy.

“I’d like to. I’m beat though,” Olive says, feeling the strain of the day. Her shoulders are heavy, her neck and back muscles tight. “I’ll be back tomorrow same time, if that’s all right?”

“Yep. There are only a couple dancers auditioning. So, if anyone wants to stand in for the group routine, we’d appreciate it.”

“Sounds good. I’ll see you then.” Olive heads to unlock her bike from the light post. “It was great meeting you all,” she calls to the group as they walk past her to the bar down the street to meet Cin and Calvin. They respond in kind. Amanda runs back to give her another hug.

“Call me if you need anything,” she says. “You’ve got my cell.”

“I’ll be all right. Thank you. It’s been a long day. I need to recharge.”

“I hear that. Take care. We’ll see you tomorrow.”

Olive turns her bike on the sidewalk and rides away.

The city takes on a different look after dark. Boisterous people come and go from various bars and restaurants along the pedestrian district. Small trees are strung with bright twinkling lights. Clouds of smoke drift from one group to the next. Security men stand in doorways flexing their bulky arms in skintight t-shirts. Olive pedals quickly past the revelry, heading toward the river. The park is empty except for three men fishing. They stop what they’re doing to turn their attention to Olive.

She’s no stranger to the dark or being alone. Though being alone in the dark in a place so heavily populated is an altogether new experience. Olive puts her head down and pushes harder, hurrying away from the fishing men to the long stretch of the bike path. Then on to the wooded section on the trail. The trees, merely silhouettes against the black sky, are a welcome comfort to her racing heart.

Rock Island is the biggest city she's ever been in. The adventurous feeling that propelled her that afternoon is gone. She can't wait to be home in her bed, being rocked to sleep by the gentle current.

The marina is quiet as she wrestles her bike onto the dock. She chains it to the rails beside her boat and hops to the deck. Inside, familiarity greets her. The dishes and pans her mom packed up to stock the kitchen. Her dad's recliner sitting in the corner of the sleeping area, weighed down with her clothes. She washes her face quickly and strips out of her sweaty shorts and tank, then climbs onto the full-size bed and wraps herself in the quilt she and her mother made. It smells like home, Like the farm and her parents. She cries softly into her pillow.

Leaving Marquette had been surprisingly easy. She hadn't given much thought to it. Part of her believed she would be back quickly. She'd find a new job and stay close to the only home she'd ever known. Something happened at auditions though. Something she couldn't define. It felt like she had opened a door into a new world. A new life. In doing so, she was closing the old one. She'd finally left home, and she knew deep down she was never going back. It should be a joyful moment. Parts of her were ecstatic. Other parts, however, were mortified.

***

Vic and Mike enter the bar. Neon lights glow and blur from the windows and walls; pop music is playing at an obnoxious volume. Vic's wondering if maybe they hadn't had too much to drink at dinner. Amanda is sitting with her friends, new and old. They take up two tables in the middle of the crowded bar. Neither Emily nor Olive are present.

Introductions are made and conversation is easy. People come and go and reappear. Vic watches how the group interacts. The new faces seem starstruck by the veterans. They hang on every word of the stories being shared. Cin talks about when she fell off the stage at an outdoor event. Calvin shares the many experiences he's had as a male dancer in the more conservative towns they've visited. Bridgette tells them about her adventures in New Orleans. Amanda leans into Mike's chest with a content smile.

“Auditions went well, I take it?” he asks when the conversation lulls. “Is this everyone?”

Amanda looks around the table. “We’re missing two.”

“Two?” Cin asks incredulously.

“Yes, two. Emily and Olive.”

“Pfft. How are you going to give that girl a spot in your troupe when she couldn’t even stick around for an interview?”

“She was probably afraid of you,” Bridgette says with a giggle.

“She should be.” Cindy sneers.

“What did she do to you?” Vic asks, leaving polite at the bottom of his last bottle.

“What didn’t she do?” Cindy bites back, teeth flashing. Vic shrugs. “She stole my routine, for one. Took the song, the steps, made her own bastardized version of my costume, and performed it as her own in Minneapolis. Made me look like the fucking thief. That’s one.” Cin holds her index finger in the air. “Not only did she fuck my boyfriend, she fucked him up. I’m not talking showed him such a good time he couldn’t get over her. I’m saying she fucked with his head. Played so many mind games with the poor son of a bitch, I barely recognize him now.”

“Damn. What kind of mind games?” Marty asks, fascinated.

“You name it. She did it. She never even wanted him. She only wanted to know she could have him.”

“You sure about that?” Vic asks. “It’s a pretty terrible allegation.”

“It’s not an allegation if it’s true,” Cin says, squinting at him. “Now, I know you got yourself a whiff of that pussy and you’re hooked on it now. I’m warning you. It’s not worth it.”

“What’s not worth it?” Emily appears beside him, as if magically summoned by Cin’s ill words. She bats her long dark lashes innocently, sipping at her cocktail.

Cin bites her lip and glowers. “I’m calling it a night.” She smiles at Amanda. “I’ve said my piece. I’ll see you tomorrow?”

“Yep.” Amanda nods and stands to hug her. “Love you.”

“Love you too.” She looks around at the new additions to the group, save Emily. “You all did great tonight.” Vic can feel her cool hatred radiating as she passes on her way to the door.

“What’s that all about?” Emily asks.

“You know Cin,” Bunny says.

"I hope she didn't leave on account of me," Emily says with wide-eyed innocence. Amanda smiles awkwardly. The rest of the table looks from one to another with obvious discomfort.

"I'm more curious about where you went?" Vic asks, taking her free hand in his and turning her to him. "I thought you'd ghosted me."

"Why would I do that?" She giggles.

"I don't know. Why didn't you respond to my text?"

"I was on stage when you sent it. Then I got preoccupied. Thought I'd responded." She pouts her delicious lips. "I'm sorry. You still want to buy me that drink?"

"Of course," Vic says smoothly.

"I'm kind of curious what happened to you too," Amanda says crisply from behind her.

"Oh Bunny, I'm sorry. I figured I didn't need the interview since we're already friends."

"You could have told someone you were leaving though," Amanda retorts. Vic rests his hand on the small of Emily's back, his fingers aching to explore her whole body.

"If you still want one, I can come back tomorrow," she offers.

"No, you're right. I already know all your answers to the standard questions. Still, try not to disappear like that in the future. Makes me look bad to the others." Amanda turns her attention to the other people at the table.

"Sure thing, Bunny," Emily coos. She turns to Vic, lips turned up in a suggestive smile. "Now how about that drink?"

Her hands are on him from that moment on. Standing at the bar, she touches his chest, his neck, his cheek. She talks about her audition. He's lost in thought, tortured by memories shouting for attention. Then he takes another shot and forces them away. All he sees is her face. Her lips. He's back at the hotel after the wedding, a haze of sighs and caresses. "Let's get out of here."

***

Monday morning is quiet at the marina. A handful of old men putter around the river's edge with their fishing poles and tackle boxes. Olive hums in the sunlight as she sweeps the deck of her houseboat. The second night with Bunny and friends proved to be as promising as the first. The warm feelings she gets when she's around them spill over into her living space. It sparkles with her newfound feelings of hope. Her weekend is one for cleansing and renewal. She sorts and folds her clothes, clearing the recliner for the first time in months. She strings up brightly colored scarfs as curtains and rearranges her books and trinkets on the shelves covering one wall. Her small closet is more organized than it has ever been. The dishes in her tiny kitchen, which have spent years in rotation from the dirty side of the sink to the clean one, are now nestled in their homes in the cabinets.

On her trip to buy cleaning supplies, she treated herself to a couple of scented candles. They burn while she sifts through her thrift store wardrobe to put together the best outfits for practice nights. She wants to be as colorful and interesting as her new friends. They remind her of the people she used to know, and of the girl she used to be. The one who danced and sang and painted.

She breathes deep, filling her lungs with the sweet summer air. Sunshine and a warm breeze kiss her skin as she sweeps up years of neglect from her home. The bright blue sky and fluttering leaves fill her heart with joy she's not experienced since she left the farm all those years ago.

***

"Welcome back, everyone." Bunny sits on the edge of the stage. Olive sits with the others. Though the second round of auditions didn't bring any more dancers to the group, one more comedian and a magician have joined the ranks. "First off, I have to say how great it is to see you all. I'm looking forward to getting to know you. From what I've learned so far, we've got a great group of people with a lot of talent."

Olive looks around the room at each person. They've filled the space of three tables in the front of the Speakeasy. She and Susan share a small table while Chris, Julie, and Emily share another. Marty with the magician and other comic are at the table next to them.

"For inspiration for our first show, I'd like you all to choose one of the seven deadly sins." The group chatters with excitement. Olive looks around, unsure of the commotion. Her experience with labeling sin has been unpleasant to say the least. Five months in a

Christian foster home had told her that everything in her life had been sin. They'd openly passed judgment on her parents and their way of life, and called them heathens and sinners. The first few weeks she'd gone along to church without argument. A scared child whose world had been turned upside down, she hadn't had the energy to fight. The severe beliefs of their church had been more than she could take. She feigned illness until they caught on. That's when the fighting started. She found her voice after a visit to her mom in prison. From then on, she refused to go to their church anymore. After that she was told to pack her bags. Instead of waiting to be placed in another terrible home, she stole their coin jar after they went to sleep, and one of their many bikes. She rode to the nearby bus station to purchase a ticket to Marquette, where she used the hidden key on the dock to welcome herself home.

"What are you thinking?" Susan's question breaks through her memories.

"I'm sorry, what?" Olive shakes her head and focuses on her.

"What sin are you thinking of doing?"

"I don't know. What are my choices?" Susan looks at her with a raised brow.

Bunny speaks up. "Greed, pride, lust, gluttony, wrath, sloth, and envy are the seven. I'd like to see a routine for each one. Since there's only six of us, I'll have to call in some help. Bridgette and Calvin have already offered to come back for the show. So? What's everyone thinking?" She looks around the room for someone to volunteer. When no one speaks she goes on. "Chris, I was thinking that your audition piece would be great for greed or lust, or even gluttony. A different costume and some added theatrics could take it so many directions."

Chris beams at being called out first. "You're right. I think in three months I could come up with something new too. Maybe a bit darker, considering the theme."

"I believe that. It doesn't have to be dark though. We want some darkness, but we want some lighthearted fun, and sexy takes too."

"How do you make sloth sexy?" Susan asks.

"I believe you can if you're volunteering," Bunny answers.

"I think I could, maybe," Susan responds, her voice trailing.

"Is that your sin then?" Bunny asks.

"Yeah. I think it is." Susan nods.

“How about you, Chris? Greed? Lust?” Bunny asks.

“I’m liking the idea of greed. I think I can have some fun with it.”

“Perfect. Anyone else have any ideas?”

“I’ve got some tricks that I do with fire. And I believe I can get ahold of black doves. If you’d like,” the magician speaks up.

“Perfect, Dave. Could you choreograph it to music? I’d love to see you in a top hat and tails with the Dance Macabre playing.”

“I’ll have to listen. It shouldn’t be a problem though. I’ll put something together and let you know when I’m ready to show it.”

“Awesome. I have no doubt that it’ll be fantastic. How about you three?” Bunny asks, looking from Julie to Emily, then Olive. Julie looks away and bites her lip. Olive looks at Emily, sure that she’ll volunteer for lust. She’s literally sex walking. “Emily. Olive. I have an idea that I’d like to run by you.”

“I’m all ears, boss,” Emily says with a grin.

“Me too.” Olive breathes a sigh of relief. She’ll take any help she can get.

“I’d like to see you do something of a duet with pride and envy.” Olive looks at Emily’s face for her reaction.

“I don’t know how I feel about a duet, Bunny,” Emily says quickly.

“Not an actual duet. More back-to-back bits that play off each other. You would take pride and Olive would take envy. You would each have freedom to do whatever you wanted with a small amount of coordination, be it in costume choice or music. Something that shows the connection.”

“I’m down.” Olive shrugs.

“Of course, I’ll do it,” Emily says, shaking her head and batting her lashes.

“Yes. Thank you. I’ve been playing with the blocking for this show for a while now and wanted to see something like this. It’s going to be brilliant. In all honesty, you could both use your audition pieces with some clever editing and it would work.” Bunny looks from Emily to Olive, then addresses the group. “So, that leaves lust, wrath, and gluttony.” Bunny’s gaze lands on Julie. Julie’s looks surprised.

"I don't think I can do it. We talked about me doing the stage kitten thing for a while, so I could get used to the stage. Right?" Her soft voice trembling. Bunny smiles warmly.

"Yep. I didn't want to leave you out though. Making sure you hadn't changed your mind."

"Maybe someday." Everyone in the room is watching Julie. Olive can see that she's uncomfortable with the attention. She wonders what made someone so shy want to audition for a burlesque troupe.

"I look forward to that day. In the meantime, a good stage kitten can become a stage manager pretty quickly. That would be invaluable." Bunny winks at Julie. "Since no one volunteered, I'm taking gluttony. I've always wanted to make a mess on stage, this is the perfect opportunity. That leaves wrath and lust, and I'm confident Bridgette and Calvin can do something amazing with these. I have a group routine for the opening act we'll start learning tonight. Then we can all start planning for our individuals. I'm here for any questions you might have. Also, I have a group on Facebook to connect us to my A la Mode folks back home. They are happy and excited to help. Make sure you add me on there so I can get you into the group."

Olive is slightly overwhelmed as Bunny chatters on. Olive doesn't have Facebook. Her internet experience has been with Google and YouTube. Once she learned she could carry the internet around in her bag and ask it any question she had, she was hooked. It made navigating the world alone a bit easier.

"Before we move on, I've got to introduce you all to the guys who make this possible for us. Mike and Vic should be here any minute. They own the Speakeasy and have given us the generous costume allowance and the time and space for practice." Olive recognizes their names and understands why Vic hadn't asked her more questions when he found her dancing on his rooftop porch.

"It doesn't hurt you're fucking one of them," Emily teases.

"All day, every day if I could," Bunny says with a wide grin. "Speak of the devils." She hops off the stage as the door opens behind them. Olive turns to see Vic and Mike standing beside the empty bar. Then Bunny's running into Mike's waiting arms. She turns back to the group, one arm still holding him. "This is my husband, Mike. You won't see too much of him. Though he's here when we need him. And this is Vic. He practically lives here. Get used to seeing a lot of him." He fires his dazzling smile around the room. Olive's cheeks warm at the sight. He's a beautiful man. She's embarrassed for having been caught dancing on his roof, for crashing into their truck, for the social blunders she's sure to make in the coming days. He offers her a quick nod of recognition before his gaze lands on someone behind her. She turns to see Emily smiling back with all her natural magnetism.

"Hey, Vicky boy," Emily calls with a familiarity that feels like the pinch to Olive's daydream.

"Hey, Em," he answers, his friendly voice taking a sensual turn as he crosses the room to greet her with a hug. Olive's envious. Vic slides up onto the stage in front of Emily, then he looks Olive's way.

"Good to see you didn't miss your big break," he says with another heart-stopping smile. Fine lines crinkle around his eyes every time he does that.

"Yeah." Olive chuckles at herself, feeling out of place and awkward. He winks and turns his attention to Emily she strokes her long hair over one shoulder and bites her lip. They speak in low voices and Olive turns her attention to Susan, hoping she can't see the red in her cheeks.

***

"Why are we doing this again?" Mike asks as they approach the front door of the Speakeasy.

"Because your wife asked us to," Vic teases. "You know, if you're not careful, I'm going to the board to have you replaced."

"There is no board," Mike says, unamused.

"I think *she* might be the board nowadays." Vic laughs. His heart is light. The troupe is looking great. Amanda's plans for the first show sound fantastic. If she can pull it off, they'll be doing even better than they already are.

"You might be right," Mike agrees with a chuckle. "If that's the case, I'd say I'm not going anywhere any time soon."

They push through the heavy glass door. The familiar smell of the old building greets them. Vic's sight adjusts to the dim houselights as he surveys the room. Amanda comes running at them, wrapping her arms around Mike. He doesn't listen as she introduces them. He's looking over the new faces, finding Emily at once, and crossing the room to her.

"Hey, Vicky boy," Emily purrs as he approaches.

"Hey, Em," he says, wrapping his arms around her before lifting himself to sit on the edge of the stage in front of her. He catches a glance from Olive. "Good to see you didn't miss your big break." He grins. She chuckles awkwardly.

"Yeah," she says, a blush rising in her cheeks. Vic winks and turns his attention to Emily. Though Olive piques his curiosity, Emily is a sure thing. Though she might be the type of woman to get him into a bar fight, she doesn't seem to want more than his body. Olive, on the other hand, seems like a heart-and-soul kind of gal. Bar fights he can handle. After the life he's lived, he's not sure there's a soul left to give.

"I missed you Saturday," he says in a low voice.

"I'm sorry. I was so busy at work. Had some drinks with the girls then went home to crash. Hope you didn't wait up for me?"

"Nah, we had a big crowd for the stand-up show. Didn't get closed until after midnight. I crashed pretty soon after that too," he lies. He didn't close up until after midnight. That much was true. He waited until three, however, for the call she promised and never made. Once the bars had closed, he gave up waiting.

"How about tonight? I can come see you after practice." She bats her lashes and licks her irresistible lips.

"I'll be around," he says with a shrug, ignoring Cin's voice in his head, warning him of what Emily is capable of.

"Good." She grins brightly. "Now stop distracting me with that handsome face. Me and this one have work to do." She points her thumb over her shoulder at Olive. She's chatting with Susan but looks their way as Emily turns to her. She glances at him briefly before giving Emily her full attention. Again he notices Olive's natural beauty. Her sun-bronzed skin looks flawlessly smooth. Her thick coffee-colored hair shines even in the dim light of the Speakeasy. One moment, she seems young and inexperienced, blushing like a child. Then the next, she speaks with the confidence that comes with years of experience. Her age is a mystery. As are many things about her. *What's her story?* he wonders as Emily flashes a gleaming smile his way. "I'll text you later."

"I'll take that as my cue to leave then." He slides off the stage and heads back to where Amanda and Mike are talking by the bar.

"What's up with you and Emily?" Amanda asks.

"What do you mean?" he replies innocently.

"You know what I mean." She crosses her arms over her chest.

"We're hanging out." He shrugs. "Not much really." Amanda stares at him, biting her cheek. She shifts her weight from one foot to the other, looks at Mike then back to him.

"Be careful, Vic. She might be a friend, but that doesn't mean I trust her." Vic looks at Amanda. Though her words are harsh, her expression is kind. He wants to argue, but knows he'll lose. Besides, he knows she's right. Emily is trouble. She's the kind of trouble he likes best. Fast, dangerous, and exciting.

"Don't worry, Amanda. I think I can handle this," he says with some derision.

"It's not you I'm worried about Vic. It's the show." She stares at him with her head tilted to one side, blinking.

"She'll ruin me before I let anything ruin the show."

Chapter 7

"You are such a sweet thing, aren't you?" Emily says as Vic walks away. Her patronizing tone isn't lost on Olive.

"I try." Olive shrugs, shifting her thoughts away from Vic's handsome smile and obvious involvement with Emily. She's thinking of her routine, running through her music catalogue in her mind. *What song?*

"Let's chat," Emily says with false sweetness as she pulls her chair over to their table. "Even though I trust Bunny's vision, you've got to know up front, I don't do duets."

"It's not a duet though, so we should be fine. Do you know what direction you're going in?" Olive asks. Emily narrows her eyes and gives a tight-lipped smile.

"I have some ideas. I hate sharing them so early in the process though. I like to work through them on my own. Get something solid before I start showing it off. Right now, what's floating around could be easily snatched up by someone else."

"You don't have to worry about me snatching at anything." Olive laughs, feeling awkward under Emily's cold stare.

"You sure about that?" she asks with a flutter of her lashes, tilting her chin. She looks to the back of the room at Vic talking with Bunny and Mike. Olive follows her gaze and can't fight the blush that stains her cheeks. Emily answers with a harsh chuckle. "That's what I thought. Snatch away, love. He's not going anywhere." She stands abruptly and looks down at Olive with an overly sweet grin. "Remember, Bunny gave you envy for a reason. You wear it well." She slides by Olive's chair and heads toward Vic, her sweet perfume lingering. Then, she stops and turns back. "I'll give you this. My song is Peaches, 'Boys Wanna Be Her.' Do what you want with that. I'm not going to hold your hand." Olive watches Emily's hips sway as she walks to Vic.

Olive's cheeks are hot with a mix of embarrassment and anger. She regrets agreeing to Bunny's suggestion.

"Damn. She's a piece," Susan says in her deep, slightly graveled voice. Olive turns back to the table.

"You're telling me. What was that all about?"

"Looks like she's intimidated by you." Susan chuckles.

"Me? Why would anyone be intimidated by me? I don't have a clue what I'm doing."

"And yet, you're already better than her."

"What? No. She's amazing. I'm up there dancing like I would in my kitchen."

"You're spellbinding. Not to mention the way her boy toy was looking at you." Susan wags her brow suggestively.

"Now I know you're seeing things. He thinks I'm crazy."

"From the looks of it, he likes crazy," Susan says with a nod in his direction. Emily's hand is tucked tightly in his back pocket. She's whispering something in his ear. He's grinning.

"I think he's got plenty of it already." Olive looks at Susan. They share smiles that turn to laughter.

"You got that right," Susan agrees. "Don't let her get to you though. Focus on the show, on your routine."

"I will. It's going to be a hell of a challenge."

"You'll get it. Any idea of what you're going to do?"

"I'm thinking green," Olive says with a big shrug. "You know, with envy? Is that too literal?"

"I don't think so. It depends on how you do it."

"Well, I need a song before anything, so I'll start there. Do you know what you're doing?"

"I've got twenty years of yoga under my belt, thinking of putting that to use. I'm flexible and there are plenty of poses I can do on the floor. Gotta find the right song too. How about you, Chris?" she calls behind Olive.

"I'm not sure. I'm excited," Chris says happily as he pulls a chair up beside them. "I mean, my gigolo bit would work with greed, but I think I want something darker. It is Halloween after all, and our debut." He's beaming, his energy contagious. Olive feels it bubbling all around.

"Do you have a song in mind?" Olive asks.

"Not yet. How about you?" He looks from Susan to Olive.

“Not a clue. Emily is doing Peaches,” she offers.

“She would,” he huffs, watching her across the room. “I tell you what, I don’t *envy* you.” He cackles and slaps the table. “For real though, I can’t believe Bunny asked you to team up with her.”

Olive shrugs. “She’s got a vision. Who am I to argue?”

“You’re braver than I,” he says and drums the table again. “Have you given any thought to your stage names?” The question hits Olive like a slap in the face.

“Fuck. No. Have you?”

“I’ve been bouncing a couple around,” he says. “I’m not in love with any of them though.”

“How about you, Susan?” Olive asks.

“I like Birdy. I also like Dame… Something. Not sure though.”

“I haven’t thought about it the slightest. I guess I thought someone else came up with that. I mean, I didn’t name myself to begin with. Right?”

“Well, here’s a chance to do it,” Chris says excitedly. “What’s your last name?”

“Meeks.”

“Olive Meeks?” he asks. “If you aren’t the cutest thing.” He holds his hand over his heart.

“Thanks, I think.”

“Oh stop, you know you’re adorable.” He swats at her shoulder playfully. She’s reminded of a friend from years ago, a boy who would spend a few weeks every summer at the farm with his family. His name was Sky, his baby sister Rain. She loved taking them exploring in the woods while the grown-ups did their grown-up things. She wonders about him, where he is now. Then Bunny speaks from the stage.

“Okay, everyone. Are you ready for the opening group routine?” The group cheers their excitement. “It’s going to look silly with me alone. But imagine all of us dressed like sexy little devils with pitchforks, horns, and tails.” She looks up to the sound booth at the back of the room. Vic and Mike are standing behind the board. “Ready?” she calls with a giggle.

A guitar strums, horns blare. “Hell” by the Squirrel Nut Zippers plays. Bunny moves through simple but fast-paced choreography. She’s laughing and talking over the music all the while. Olive cheers with the others as her demonstration ends. Vic and Mike cheer and whistle from the sound booth. Out of breath, Bunny speaks. "What do you guys think?"

"I love it," Chris shouts and claps.

"You get the basic idea anyway." Bunny laughs. "Let's do some stretches and get to work." She shields her eyes from the stage lights and looks to the sound booth. "Will you guys show Marty how to run the sound? That way we've always got someone here who can."

"Sure thing," Vic answers. Marty hurries across the room and up the ladder to the booth.

***

"You're a lucky guy, Marty," Vic says, standing behind him, watching as he quickly figures out more about the soundboard than he or Mike has ever known.

"Huh? Yeah," Marty says, distracted by the lights and switches on the soundboard and the women stretching on the floor. Vic doesn't appreciate his dismissal. He doesn't appreciate how this guy gets to sit in the sound booth and watch the dancers stretch, warm up, and eventually strip with a bird's-eye view.

"That's all you got?" he asks, standing with his arms crossed over his chest, challenging him. Mike stands beside him, watching his wife stretch and move with the others, oblivious to the exchange.

"I'm sorry," Marty says with a quick look over his shoulder to Vic. "I am lucky. You're right. How many guys get to spend their time doing this?" He gestures to the women all bending at the waist, touching their toes.

"You know, Mike, maybe we should see about bringing John in for practices too. He'd probably have a lot to offer the production from up here. No one knows this board and lights like he does."

"Hmm?" Mike asks, his gaze still set on Amanda.

"John? You think we should bring him in for practices? It would cost some. I don't think he's working nights right now."

"Sure. If he's available. I don't see why not."

Marty shifts uneasily in his seat and clears his throat. "In the meantime, I can take care of it." He shrugs. "It's a pretty simple setup. Pushing start and hitting stop."

"Yeah, but don't you have some work to do yourself? Aren't you supposed to be writing comedy?" Vic makes no attempt to hide his objection to Marty in the booth.

"That's what I'm here for," Marty says with more confidence than Vic wants to hear. He should be squirming under his glare. "If you guys weren't up here, James could sit with me. We could write while we watched." He pulls his glasses off his face and cleans them with the bottom of his t-shirt, looking from Vic to Mike. Vic feels a twitch in his jaw. He doesn't like the way Marty's talking. He doesn't care for the familiarity or the attitude.

Mike nods. "He's right. We do take up a lot of space up here. I wouldn't mind getting something to eat." He moves to slip behind Vic to descend the ladder. "I'll get ahold of John, see if he's available on Mondays and Wednesdays."

Vic watches as Mike walks over and stands at a polite distance from the group, waiting for Amanda's attention. She's bent in another revealing pose, along with the others. Emily's breasts, though held in place with some serious elastic, threaten to pop out. Olive's long, lean back peeks out of her baggy t-shirt as she reaches for her toes again. Marty's stare moves from one woman to the next. He makes no attempt to hide his appreciative smile from Vic.

"Well, Amanda seems to like you," Vic says, his attempt at being cordial.

"Amanda?"

"Jesus Christ, her real name's not Bunny." He grinds his teeth and shakes his head. "Don't get too comfortable up here," he growls before descending the ladder.

***

The city is quiet, as Monday night in the District tends to be. Vic stands in the alley between his building and the theater. The two are connected in front creating a small, private alcove. It's a perfect place for stretching before a run, and a run is exactly what he needs. The music from practice stopped over an hour ago. Emily still hasn't messaged him. He's waited all evening, watching TV, listening to music, feeling trapped again by her promise to visit. If she hadn't said she was coming, he could have gone out. He could have found something to do with his night. Instead, he spent it waiting on a call that he was now sure wasn't coming.

On the off chance she's still hanging around inside with Amanda, he decides to check before he heads out. The lights are still on down the short hallway. He hears the soft cadence of female voices. Amanda spots him and smiles while talking with the only other person in the room. Her back is to him, but he knows it's Olive. She's relaxed in her seat, her long legs stretched out onto the chair beside her, crossed at the ankles. Her bare toes pointed. Geez, she's pretty. Her beauty is effortless. She turns to see who Amanda is smiling at and offers her own beaming welcome. He can't deny how that smile makes him feel. Yet, that same feeling worries him. Unlike Emily, who eats people for breakfast, Olive is almost too gentle for the world. Vic doesn't want to be a protector anymore. He wants uncomplicated. He wants someone who won't expect anything from him.

"Hey, ladies," he says, approaching the table. "Thought I'd see how things were going before I took off."

"Where are you taking off to?" Amanda asks.

"It's a beautiful night for a run. Everyone else gone then?" He scans the clearly empty room.

"Yep. We got caught up in conversation. This girl has the most amazing story." Amanda points at Olive.

"I don't know about amazing." Olive shakes her head, avoiding Vic's gaze. He wonders why she looks away when only moments ago she'd dazzled him with her hundred-watt smile.

"Oh, come on," Amanda scoffs. "It's fucking amazing, and I'm so happy it brought you here."

"Me too," Olive says, giving Amanda her full attention. As he surmised, she must be shy. Lots of performers are, but they carry a mega smile in their back pockets.

"Well, you ladies seem to have things under control here," Vic says, watching as silent communication takes place between them. He doesn't feel so much unwelcome as he does unnecessary. Women tend to have a language all their own, and they don't share it with men. Besides, he came in looking for Emily and she isn't here. "I locked up in back already," he calls as he heads to the front door. "See you on Wednesday." He pushes through the glass door into the mild night air. His sneakers hit the pavement in a steady beat as he jogs to the riverfront.

What is Emily's deal? Cin's warnings ring loud as he knows Emily's mind games have begun. He runs faster as he hits the bike path, his deep breaths expanding his lungs and making his heart race. Low lamps cast pools of light on the cement path. The river ripples beside him. He pushes harder, as fast as he can. Sweat streams down his back and chest, and thoughts of Emily fade. He's a man running, doing what his body was meant to do, pushing the limits of his endurance, his speed, his strength. He runs until he's weightless, feet springing back from the pavement in a steady rhythm. Totally in the zone.

He hits his two-mile marker and stops to catch his breath, pleased with his performance. He shifts to jogging pace as he runs back along the way he came. The bike path is empty, save for a lone bicyclist in the distance. His next goal is to catch up and pass. From the looks of her progress, it should be no problem. He picks up his pace, closing the distance between them easily. As he nears, he recognizes the long, lean legs pushing the pedals. Olive is riding at a leisurely pace down the empty bike path. *I can't run up on her. She'll think I'm following her. Maybe I should be. What's she doing riding alone out here after dark?*

He's struck with a sudden compulsion to keep her safe. What would happen with the show if something happened to her? How could Amanda let her ride off alone like this into the night?

"Hey," he calls, out of breath from running. She picks up speed, without looking back. "Olive," he shouts. "Wait up." She slows and steals a quick glance over her shoulder before stopping fully.

Chapter 8

"I feel like I've known you forever," Olive says to Bunny. They sit together in the Speakeasy. Vic has recently come and gone. She has a feeling he was looking for Emily. She's beginning to get the feeling Cin's assessment may be accurate.

"I feel the same way. Like we were meant to meet. The universe has a funny way about it." She smiles. "I can't believe you ran into Mike's truck like that. It's such a wild coincidence."

"You're telling me. Then when Vic found me on the roof, I didn't recognize him at first. Then once I did, I was mortified."

"He's a good guy. Been Mike's best friend for years. He was there for him when I wasn't," Bunny says with a sorrowful expression, which makes Olive curious about her story.

"What do you mean?" she asks, immediately regretting it. Bunny looks her way with a small smile.

"Mike and I grew up together, got engaged young. Then I left him to find the life I'd always dreamed of. The universe brought us back together. I honestly don't know how I ever thought I could live without him. I did it for twelve years." Her laugh is barely more than breath. She blinks away tears and clears her throat. "Now, I can't imagine a day without him." Shaking her head, she smiles broadly. "So how about you? Do you have someone special in your life? Someone you can't imagine a day without?"

"Not really." Olive shrugs, feeling an emptiness in her heart. "I've been alone for a long time. Never had a relationship really. I mean, there have been guys around. I've dated some. I don't know." She shrugs again and shakes her head. "I guess I don't have a lot of trust in people." Her voice quavers.

"Oh honey." Bunny's voice trembles some too. "I'm here for you always. You're part of my family now." She stands and walks around the table, wrapping Olive in her arms from behind. She's warm and soft. Olive drops her head and places one hand over Bunny's. She stifles the sobs rising in her chest.

"Thank you," she responds softly, forcing her voice to stay calm. "I've been out there floating for a long time. It's good to hear those words. I've been missing my family."

"Do you want to stay with us tonight? We've got a spare room." Bunny lets her go and stands up straight.

"No." Olive dabs at the tears she wouldn't let fall. "I'll be all right. Thanks for the offer, though. Being alone isn't so bad. It's peaceful."

"You sure?" Bunny asks, sitting back down.

"Yep. In fact, I think I'm going to head out. I've kept you long enough and it's a long ride back."

"I can give you a lift."

"No. Don't worry about it. I like the ride. It calms me."

"Okay. Be safe." Bunny stands with her. Olive slings her bag on her back. "Text me when you get there."

"I will." Olive smiles, her heart filling with a warmth she hasn't known for a long time.

***

On the bike path, Olive pays little mind to the world around her. She's happily wrapped up in the feelings of love and appreciation she'd gotten from her talk with Bunny. It's been years since she felt a part of something. As a child she grew up with the knowledge of interconnectedness between her and the natural world. Her parents taught her that her family was as broad as the night sky. That all things were one. She believed it too. Until it all fell apart. Bunny's words made her feel connected again.

The night is beautifully mild, warm with a gentle breeze. The river runs softly beside her. She breathes in the sweet muddy air and thinks of what the future holds. Then she hears steps approaching fast. She's been on this path several times already, and though the first night had been overwhelming, she's come to feel safe here.

"Hey," a man's voice calls from behind. Without looking back, she starts pedaling faster. Her heart races with fear at what this man has in mind. She's moving fast as he gains on her. "Olive," he pants her name. She slows to look over her shoulder. "Wait up." Vic is standing with his hands on his hips, covered in sweat. She stops to wait for him to catch up. "Where are you off to?" he asks through heavy breaths.

"I'm going home," she answers. "What are you doing?"

"I said I was going for a run. Where do you live?" he asks, pulling one foot up behind him to stretch.

"Wouldn't you like to know," she teases.

"Come on. There is nothing down this way."

"There is actually."

"Isn't there a better path to your place? Seems out of your way to get anywhere from here." He continues stretching as he talks, now twisting at the waist. His white t-shirt clings to his chest, soaked with sweat. His face glistens.

"Do you want a towel?" she offers, swinging her bag off her shoulders. "I bring one for practice. We really don't sweat that much though. You on the other hand…" She smiles, holding the small pink hand towel out to him.

"Thanks." He takes it and wipes at his face and neck. "I didn't think I was going to see anyone out here. Can I walk with you?"

"I guess." She shifts her bag back into place and climbs off the bike, holding it between her and Vic.

"I don't know if it's really safe for you to be riding this way at night," he says, talking easily now.

"What do you mean? I've ridden this way twice already after dark, no problems whatsoever."

"It only takes one time, one person. Does Amanda know you come this way?"

"Why would she?" Olive asks.

"I don't know. Maybe because she should know if one of her dancers is putting themselves in danger to get to and from practice," Vic says shortly. Olive can hear the irritation in his voice.

"I don't think I'm putting myself in danger." Olive shakes her head, feeling her irritation rise at his insinuation she's incapable of knowing what's good for her. "I've been taking care of myself for a long time. I can manage a bike ride after dark," she snaps.

"Can you? Seems to me like you can't manage one in broad daylight without running into the side of a truck," he shoots back, and he's not teasing.

"That was the first and only accident I've ever been in. Hey, it scored me this new bike, so I think I managed it pretty well," she quips.

"Yeah, with the help of me and Mike. What would you do if you ran into real trouble out here with no one to help you out of it? This isn't Marquette, sweetheart." The tone of his voice is acrid, nothing like the smooth sweetness she's come to expect from him.

"Don't call me sweetheart," she shoots back. "I appreciate you being there. Though I would've been fine without you." She picks up her pace, tempted to hop on her bike and pedal away. He could try to keep up if he wanted.

"Sorry." He matches her pace. "I'm sure you would've been. Out here though, not so much." He's back with the smooth sweetness.

"What's the worst that could happen?" she asks, gesturing to the empty bike path in both directions. It's lined on both sides with high fences. In the spots where the fences are low, the wide, desolate lots don't offer a lot of opportunity for sneaking up on someone. "It gets a little sketchy around the train tracks, but for the most part, it feels pretty safe and secluded."

"What if I hadn't been me?" he says with urgency. "Then safe is out the window. Secluded is all that's left." Olive slows down and stops; he does the same, raking his hand through his thick curls. They look at one another, blinking. She thinks of the fear in her heart before she recognized him, the fear from her first night on the path with the men fishing. She shakes her head. Living alone, fear becomes a constant companion.

"You're right," she says quietly and nods. "I'm not used to having people looking out for me." Vic raises one brow and looks like he wants to say something. It's his turn to shake his head.

"Well, get used to it." He smiles his adorable smile. "Can I walk you home?" he asks earnestly.

"Sure." She shrugs and starts walking again. He follows.

"Where are we headed? There's nothing down this way except old industrial buildings and the marina."

"Yep." She nods her head, looking forward.

"Don't tell me you're squatting in one of these abandoned buildings," he says with some desperation, gesturing to the sprawling brick structures with their broken windows.

"What? No. That's too much, even for me." She laughs and stops pushing her bike again. "Do I strike you as someone who would squat in an abandoned warehouse?" she asks.

"I don't know what you strike me as." He stops and shakes his head. "I know you're full of surprises." He smiles again, dazzling even in the dark. Olive hopes her blushing cheeks aren't as bright. There is something irresistible about him. Something beyond his beautiful face, golden curls, and Adonis build. She's intrigued, enamored even. But he's with Emily.

"I'm not all that interesting." She laughs at herself and starts walking again. "I live in a houseboat. That's where I'm headed. Until I know the city a little better, this is the quickest way for me to get from here to there and back."

He teases her, "I'm not that interesting. By the way I live on a houseboat." Vic chuckles and walks alongside her. "I've met more squatters in my life than I have people who live in houseboats. In fact, you're the only person I've ever met who does."

"Congratulations," she says with false enthusiasm. "Aside from my living situation, I'm about as dull as they come."

"I don't believe that for a second." Olive notices the tenderness in his voice.

"Well, believe it." They walk in silence as the path opens gradually to a point on the river. The buildings and fences loom behind and ahead of them. A lone bench sits on an outcrop with nothing but a rocky flood wall separating them from the rippling black water. "I love this spot," she says as they pass by. "The river is so wide here, beautiful."

"It is," he agrees. She turns back to say something and sees Vic watching her instead of the river. "What *is* your story?" he asks.

"It's long," she says, embarrassed by his attention.

"We've got a way to go before the marina."

"I suppose we do." She walks slowly, looking down at her handlebars. "It's sad too," she says softly.

"You don't have to tell me. I am curious though," he says quietly.

"No, I can. I didn't think I would be telling it twice tonight, is all." Olive sighs heavily and straightens her back. "I grew up on a farm not far from Marquette. My folks were big-time hippies. Free love, back-to-the-land kind of people. I didn't go to school, didn't have a TV or a computer. I didn't know those things were even out there. We had music, and art, and the woods. I never knew anything was missing."

"That sounds awesome," Vic says wistfully.

"It was," she agrees, "until it wasn't. I learned when I was seventeen that they were growing and distributing marijuana all over the country. We would have big parties a few times a year. Harvest season was the biggest one. Go figure. The people I thought were my family and friends were my parents' drug runners."

"That's not so bad though," Vic scoffs. "I mean, it's legal or decriminalized in over half the country. Who doesn't smoke a little weed every now and then?"

"Not in Iowa, and not back then. It's not the weed. That's not the bad part. What did I care if they were breaking the law? Up to that point, I had no understanding of it." She shrugs. "No, it was the punishment." Memories of her father being gunned down, her mother wailing, her brother screaming. She shivers. "The DEA shot and killed my dad during the raid. My mom went to prison and died there. They took my brother away, and he lived in foster care until he was eighteen. They kept us apart. He was different when we were finally reunited. He came and went randomly. I haven't seen him for years. He wasn't doing well. I don't even know if he's alive." The tears she'd fought so well while telling Bunny her story spill freely down her cheeks. She wipes at them with one hand, holding her bike up with the other. Vic takes the bike. Olive wraps her arms around her middle, taking several deep breaths to calm herself.

"Olive, I'm sorry. I shouldn't have pried. I never would've guessed."

"No." She sniffs, shaking her head vigorously. "It's fine. How could you know? I'm okay."

He stares steadily at her, his brow furrowed. "Are you sure?"

"Yeah. It hits hard sometimes. What am I going to do? This is my life." She shrugs and sniffs, reaching for her bike. Her hand comes down on top of Vic's. A shock runs up her arm. His skin is warm. His knuckles wide and masculine. She wonders what it would be like to lace her fingers with his. To wrap them in his rough warmth. "Oops. Sorry," she says, pulling her hand away quickly.

"For what?" he asks.

"I didn't see your hand there. I'll take this," she says, taking her bike back gently.

***

My God, her hand is soft. Vic rubs the knuckles of his hand where she touched him with his rough fingertips. He clears his throat, settling the feelings stirring in his heart. "So, how did you end up here?" he asks.

"It's funny actually. The night I met you, my friend at the casino found an ad in the paper. She told me I should audition. I didn't think anything of it. Things happened and I lost my job. I remembered the ad, and figured it seemed like a fun change of pace. What good is living on a boat if you don't take it on adventures like this?"

"Your douchebag boss fired you?"

"Oh no. I quit. Kyle was a fucking creep," Olive says with a small shudder.

"Yeah?" Vic feels the familiar fire in his chest upon seeing her shiver like she's trying to shake off the memory. "What did he do to you?" he asks darkly, knowing he should've smashed in the asshole's face that night.

Olive looks his way and shakes her head with an awkward smile. "Nothing, really. He made a pass at me. I put him in his place and left that night."

"I knew I didn't like that little prick." Vic's insides burn with rage. He wants to drive north right now to find the little fucker and put him in his place for real. Surely Olive took it easy on him. He wouldn't. "How would he think he had a chance with a woman like you?" he asks.

"Who knows." Olive shrugs. "Hey, in the grand scheme of things, I owe him one. I would never have made the trip without him doing it."

"You don't owe him shit," he says flatly, still seething over the idea of the shitheel doing whatever "it" was.

"You're right. I am happy to be here. I'm happy I finally left Marquette." Her wide, genuine smile returns to her lips. Vic can't help but appreciate the curve of her cheek, her long neck, and the shadows of her collarbone as her loose t-shirt slides off her shoulder.

He wonders if her shoulder is as soft and smooth as her hand is. He imagines what it would be like to nuzzle his face there, where her shoulder meets her neck.

"Me too. I know Amanda loves you already," he says as they descend the last small hill before the marina's empty parking lots spread out before them. Orange and white lights twinkle on the black water as the walk along the open bike path. The industry of downtown is behind them. Black silhouettes of trees reach for the milky dark sky.

"That's good to know. She's been great."

"She is pretty great," Vic agrees, taking in their surroundings. The marina is quiet. "I've never been down here after dark," he says. "It's peaceful."

"It is. Not as quiet as up in Marquette. There are so many more stars up there. Probably what I miss the most. Here I feel like I'll be lucky to see the moon." She laughs.

"Yeah, I remember the stars out at Yellow River that weekend we met. It was like a different world."

"Sometimes I take the boat out to the middle of the river and find the darkest place I can with no cities or bridges around and stargaze. It's hard to find since there are cities up and down the river. There are pockets of darkness though."

"I'd love to see that sometime." Vic stares at the hazy night sky. The light cloud cover glows with an odd yellow-orange light of the city.

"I'll take you," Olive offers. Her innocence is refreshing and frightening. Clearly, she can take care of herself, but he worries about how trusting she is. How can she offer to take a stranger out on a late-night boat trip to the middle of nowhere on the river? "Well, not tonight obviously," she says as though she read his thoughts. "Sometime though. It's really amazing. Especially during a new moon." She smiles like a child. Vic's heart warms. He's never wanted to keep someone safe as much as he does with her.

"It sounds like it." They approach the docks. Dozens of boats float silently in their places, mostly oversize speed boats and pontoons. She stops in front of one that's half the size and looks like a rickety steamboat from an old black-and-white cartoon.

"This is it," she says with a wide flourish. "I'd invite you in, but I haven't had company in a really long time though." She lifts her bike onto the boat and turns to him. "Besides there isn't really much to see." She laughs. "Thanks for walking with me."

"Yeah. No problem." Vic nods and feels awkward for the first time in a long time. After spending this much time with a beautiful woman at her front door, he should be holding her, making promises, and kissing her face. He should be easing his way into her bed. But he doesn't. He can't. The space separating them seems insurmountable. As she stands with her sweet, innocent smile an arm's length away, she's untouchable.

"All right." She nods. "I'm gonna go inside now. Thanks again." She hops over to the deck. "I'll see you on Wednesday."

"I'll be there." Vic waits for her to go inside.

She looks at him, raising one brow. "Are you going to stay here all night?" she asks slowly.

"No. I was waiting for you to go inside," he answers quickly, feeling even more out of place. How many times has she come and gone from that boat without his protection?

"Are you worried the bats are going to carry me away?" she teases.

"No. You're right. You're fine," he stammers, searching for his confidence. "I'll see you Wednesday. Stay safe." He nods and turns to leave, walking at first, then jogging once he hits the pavement. He's halfway home before he realizes he's still holding her towel. Swiping at the sweat on his face, he smells her earthy feminine scent, like flowers and patchouli oil. It's Olive and he wants more.

Chapter 9

"I think I want to do a fan dance with green fans," Olive says to Chris. They're sitting on the pavement in front of the Speakeasy, waiting for Bunny to arrive. The sticky heat leaves them with little energy. She's sweaty and worn out from her bike ride.

"Ooh. I like it. Do you know what song you are using yet?"

"No, but I really like the idea of using fans. I listened to Emily's song and it's pretty heavy. I don't imagine she'll be using fans. It seems appropriate since I was so envious of her with her fans at auditions."

"That makes sense. Do you think she'll accuse you of stealing the idea?" he asks.

"She might. But does that mean each fan dance is stolen from the one before it?"

"That's a solid point. You know her though."

"Yeah, and I know Bunny. Bunny gets it."

"She does. I'm thinking of doing Pink Floyd's 'Money' for mine."

"Oh, fuck yeah. That's a good one. I like it."

"Thanks. I was thinking of monochromatic too. Not green though. Maybe gold, or purple…"

"What about silver *and* gold?"

"I like that," Chris says, clapping his hands.

"You should really have green in there too. I mean it's the color of money, and the song is called 'Money.' And you're representing greed," Olive offers. "It won't bother me at all."

"No?" Chris asks and studies her face. "You sure? I don't want to step on your toes."

"Chris, if I can't share the color green, I've got serious problems." Olive laughs. "I suppose I do have problems though, since I can't think of a song."

"Oh, it'll come to you." Chris swats at the air in dismissal. "What about your name?"

"There's another problem. I can't think of one for the life of me. How about you?"

"I keep thinking Rock Studson." He laughs wildly. "But I hate it. It's literally the only name I can come up with though."

Olive snickers. "I kind of like it though. Did you tell Bunny?"

"Not yet. I was hoping to come up with something better."

"I don't know. The more I think about it, the more I like it."

Chris rolls his eyes. "We'll see." He shakes his head. They sit in silence.

"Hey," Olive says suddenly, "I've got a silly favor to ask."

"What's that?"

"Can you help me with Facebook? I don't have an account and I know Bunny wants us all on there. I'm not media savvy." Olive grimaces.

"Oh honey. How are you such an old lady? I would understand this from Susan. But you?" He laughs. Olive shifts, embarrassed.

"You're right. I've never had any reason to be on there." She shrugs.

"Okay. Well, first you need a profile pic. Let's see what you've got." He gestures for her to hand over her phone.

"Um, I don't have any."

"What. How is someone as lovely as you not taking selfies all day every day?" he asks incredulously.

"I don't know. I guess I never thought of it." She shrugs again.

"Okay, whatever. Give me your phone, I'll take a picture for you. You do have an email account, right?" he asks, raising his brows.

"Yes, I have an email account." Chris snaps a picture as she's mocking him and laughs hysterically before showing her the shot. It's not a flattering expression.

"You know, for looking so mean and angry in this pic, you still look hot as fuck," he says.

"Okay, good. Use it. Let's get me on Facebook so I can be connected like everyone else."

"Let's take a few more," Chris encourages, then starts snapping photos. Olive looks away, her cheeks red. She hasn't had her picture taken in years. It's an awkward feeling. She smiles, laughs, and rolls her eyes.

"Are you done?" she asks with a serious glare. Chris snaps a couple more.

"Damn you are sexy when you're mad," he says with a smile. The door opens behind him. Vic pops his head out and looks down at them. Olive's heart seems to stop beating as he offers one of his beautiful smiles.

"Hey. Amanda called and said she's running late. You two want to come out of the heat?" He steps out of the Speakeasy, holding the door open. He's in gym shorts and no shirt, sweat beading on his sculpted chest. He catches Olive's appreciative stare before she can look away. "Sorry, I was working out when she called, hurried down here. Guess I could have grabbed a shirt. You guys come on in. I'll get out of the way."

"No apologies necessary," Chris offers with a brazen stare as he walks through the door.

"Right." Vic smiles at Chris then Olive. "Just the same, I'll head back upstairs. Amanda should be here soon."

"Thanks for letting us in," Olive says, gathering her bag from the ground. Though she hasn't seen him since Monday night, he's been on her mind. A lot. Heat radiates from his frame as she walks past.

"No problem." He lets the door shut behind him. "See ya later," he says as he heads to the back door. Olive notices the appreciative look on Chris's face as they both watch Vic leaving.

"Ooh boy. If I weren't already taken," Chris says once Vic is gone. "That one would be in real trouble." Olive scrunches up her nose and giggles, glad her daydreams are her own. "Did you see those calves? He's like a damn jungle cat."

"How could I not?" Their laughter fills the room. Bunny hurries through the front door.

"What's so funny?" she asks, looking from one to the other with a curious grin.

"Your pet jungle cat passed through," Chris chirps. Bunny looks confused.

"He's talking about Vic. He came down to let us in, and must've been working out. He was shirtless," Olive offers.

"Shirtless?" Chris interjects. "Girl, the only thing between him and us was a pair of tiny shorts and some sneakers."

Bunny shakes her head. “He would do that. How are you guys?” she asks, changing the subject.

“Chris is doing great,” Olive says. “He’s got his song and his stage name picked out.”

“Olive, why?” he laments.

“What? Tell me,” Bunny says excitedly.

“Rock Studson,” he mumbles.

Bunny looks at him, silently processing. “I love it.”

“Really?” he asks, sitting down with a big sigh. “You don’t think it’s dumb?”

“No, I don’t. You’ll want to make sure it’s not already taken. If it isn’t, it should be. What’s your song?”

“‘Money.’ Pink Floyd.”

“Love that too. How about you, Olive?”

“All I’ve got is green.” She shrugs. “And maybe fans?” Bunny nods. “I can’t think of a name or a song though.”

“It’ll come to you. I know Susan and Emily have their songs and names picked out. We can brainstorm after group practice. Are you on Facebook yet? You’re the only one not on the group page. You’ve got to get on there. It’s such a great resource.”

“We were working on that when Vic came to let us in.”

“Let’s get that done while we wait for the others.”

***

Facebook is an assault on her senses. After spending fifteen minutes learning the basics, she finds herself friends with people from Chicago to New Orleans. There are more strange faces than familiar ones, and they all have opinions. She spends her down-time at practice reading through past posts, watching the shared videos, and responding to the warm messages of welcome from the wide-reaching burlesque family. Her messenger alert pings. It’s from Cin.

Bunny told me what she asked you to do. Not sure why she paired you with that viper. I’ll help any way I can.

Olive thinks long and hard about how to respond. She types several messages and deletes them all. She can’t believe Bunny paired her with Emily either. She knows better than to say anything negative in print.

She's got a vision. I'm excited to see how the show turns out. It's an interesting theme. Thanks for the offer. I'm sure I'll be needing loads of help.

She reads the message one more time before sending then lays her phone on the table to

focus on the people around her. It pings again.

I was there for Bunny when she was a burlesque baby. Now, I'll be here for you. She says you're having trouble coming up with a name. What do you think of Ollie Would? I figured since you showed us all your bare titties you're probably down for anything. So, Olive Will, Ollie Would. Like Hollywood.

She cringes at the name. The only person in her life that's ever called her Ollie is Eli. Even reading it written stirs up all the emotions. Though it's the best she's got at the moment. She'll try it on for size. It's been years after all.

It's the best I've heard yet. Thanks for helping. I'll see what Bunny thinks.

She switches her phone to silent and tucks it in her bag, amazed at how easily

distracted she's become. *It's time to focus.*

"Looks like Susan is running late. We're going to open the stage for anyone who wants to start working on their individual routine," Bunny says from the front of the room. Chris volunteers quickly; in a matter of minutes he's pacing on the stage while his song plays over the speakers. Bunny sits next to her and watches.

"Cin gave me a name," Olive mutters.

"Yeah? What is it?" she asks while still watching Chris.

"Ollie Would." Olive grimaces and waits for Bunny's reaction.

"What do you think?" She looks away from the stage.

Olive shrugs. "I don't hate it. I don't love it either. It's growing on me, I guess."

Bunny squints at her, "If you don't love it, it's not right. Clever, but meh."

"That's what I thought too. It is clever. Not me though."

"Okay then, find a better one," Bunny says with a smile before turning her attention back to Chris.

"Hey, Vicky," Emily squeals from her table behind them. She runs across the room to Vic, who's returned, fully clothed and freshly showered. He catches Olive's gaze with a quick smile over

Emily's head. Olive looks away, her face feels hot. She has no right to be jealous. He walked her home. No big deal. So what if she couldn't get him out of her mind? So what if his bare rippling pecs were going to be in her dreams? So what if she already dreamed of his dimples and his eyes? She's got nothing over Emily, who's pure sex walking.

***

Vic looks over Emily's head at Olive. *Is that disappointment?* Emily wraps her arms around his neck and stands on her tiptoes to nip at his ear.

"I'm sorry about Monday night. I got a call I wasn't expecting. I should've messaged you."

There's a flash of irritation over another of her lame excuses. "Hey, no big deal," he responds quickly as he peels her arms away from his neck. "You're busy, I get it. Maybe next time." He's done waiting around for a woman who never calls or keeps her promises.

"You're mad at me, aren't you?" Emily pouts. He looks down into her big blue eyes, her dark lashes flutter. She purses her lips then sticks out the bottom one. "I'll make it up to you, I swear." He feels a momentary hesitation in his resolve to be done with her. This woman knows how to play him.

"We'll see, Em. Actually, I'm here to talk to Amanda. Text me later." He gives her a smile and a nod, and leaves her standing by the wall alone. "Hey." He takes a seat at the table with Olive and Amanda.

"Hey," Olive responds quietly, still watching Chris.

"What's up?" Amanda says, turning to him.

"I wanted to talk to you both, actually." Olive looks his way.

"Well, you've got us both. What do you need?" Amanda asks.

"Two things." He looks from Amanda to Olive, then back to Amanda. "First off, do you know where she's living and how she gets home every night?" Olive looks like she's about to speak. Amanda beats her to it.

"Yeah. She rides her bike. A hell of a lot healthier than the rest of us."

"Healthy, yeah, not safe. Anything could happen to her on that bike path after dark."

"Oh, please, Vic," Olive interjects. "We talked about this on Monday. If I hadn't recognized you, I would've been long gone. There's no way you could have caught up to me on my bike."

"That's if you saw me coming. I swear, Olive," he lowers his voice to hide his irritation. "I've been worried about you since I left you Monday. This really isn't Marquette. There are a lot of people in this city. A lot of bad ones."

"I told you. I'm fine," Olive insists.

Amanda holds a hand up. "Wait a minute. What happened on Monday?"

Vic looks at Olive. Her long legs are crossed, and she's bouncing one foot, her arms wrapped around her chest. "Vic walked me home Monday night. He came up on me on the bike path," Olive says while staring him down.

"Well, that's nice," Amanda says.

"No, Amanda, it's not nice. She rides down the bike path, alone, after dark. Literally anything could happen down there and no one would know." He's still looking at Olive. The flush in her cheeks is not the same as the innocent blush he's come to adore. It's anger. It's red hot, and he's worried he may have overstepped.

"Bunny, I have been up and down that bike path over a dozen times already. I'm perfectly safe," Olive says, still leveling her cold stare on Vic. "I'm not a child."

"All right, you two." Amanda stands. "Let's take this outside." Olive stands too and starts walking immediately. Vic follows in a lovely cloud of patchouli and flowers. Outside the air is thick. The mugginess pulls at his clothes. He can feel it working its way into his hair. Olive shoots him a look as sharp as daggers before Amanda joins them.

"I can't believe you did that," she snaps. "What are you trying to accomplish?"

"You'll see," he offers, wishing she wasn't so angry yet somewhat enjoying seeing her with her feathers ruffled. "I don't bring problems unless I have a solution." Her face softens into a more curious look.

"Okay, guys," Amanda says as she pushes through the door. "What the fuck is going on?"

"I'm concerned for Olive's safety," Vic offers. "I don't think it's a good idea to have one of your dancers riding around after dark and living at the marina. What if something happened to her?"

"Nothing is going to happen to me," she insists.

Amanda looks at them, her brow knit. "I don't know, Olive. Maybe Vic is right. I guess I hadn't thought of your ride being dangerous. I figured you weren't far from the Speakeasy."

"It's fine, Bunny, it really is," Olive says. "I've been riding my bike alone for a long time."

"I know that, but not here," Amanda tells her. "Not in Rock Island."

"That's exactly what I've been trying to say." Vic nods. "I have a solution. We've got the empty apartment upstairs the theater rents out for directors for their touring productions. They're running a local show all summer so it's empty right now."

"I don't want to live in an empty apartment," Olive argues.

"It's fully furnished," Vic says.

"Well, I don't want to move." She crosses her arms over her chest again.

"You don't have to. You can stay there on the nights you have practice so we aren't worried about you getting home safely."

"That's a great idea," Amanda says with relief.

"That, or I can walk you home every night," Vic says with a half-smile. He hadn't planned on the second offer. He'd enjoyed their walk on Monday. He'd enjoyed getting to know her and seeing where she lived. It might not be so bad to walk with her every night. Maybe, someday, she'd invite him in.

Olive drops her hands to her hips and sighs. She looks from Vic to Amanda. "I understand you're concerned for my safety. I appreciate it. I truly do. However," she shakes her head, "I'm not going to stay here. I've got my home. Unconventional as it may be, it's my home and I'm not comfortable staying anywhere else."

"Looks like I'll be getting some exercise then," Vic says with a hopeful smile.

"Maybe you should get a bike," Olive offers with a hint of challenge.

"Okay, perfect," Amanda says. "We've solved that then. What's number two?" "Hmm?" Vic asks, having almost forgotten she was there.

"The second thing you wanted to talk about. I'm assuming Olive's living situation wasn't it."

"Oh yeah. I was wondering if Olive wanted a job," he says to Amanda first then turning to Olive. "What do you say? I know you've got cocktail experience. We don't only do burlesque here. We've got comedy and bands most weekends. We could always use an extra set of hands."

"That would be awesome," Olive says with a bright smile. "I was going to have to start looking for a job pretty soon. So, yeah. I would love to."

"Perfect," Amanda says. "Now will you let us work?"

"Sure thing," Vic replies, feeling surprisingly light. He'd known what he wanted when he came down. Although Olive won't be moving in down the hall anytime soon, she'll be working here, and he'll be walking her home after all of her shifts.

She'll be safe.

Chapter 10

"Really?" Olive looks at Vic. He's standing beside a bike that looks older than the one she totaled in her accident and half the size it should be. "Did you steal that from a child?" She laughs.

"C'mon. I could barely keep up with you Wednesday. I had to get something." His smile is irresistible.

"Okay, but is there a little boy somewhere crying because you stole his bike?" she teases.

"If the little boy is me. I got this from my mom's place. What do you think? It's my old bike." He puffs up his chest with childish pride.

"I think you might need a new bike." Olive laughs. "Let's see if you can keep up." She hops on hers and takes off quickly through the intersection. She glances over her shoulder to see Vic struggling to mount the small dirt bike, then hurrying to catch up.

"See, I got this," he says, looking up from his low seat and grinning, despite the wobbling to and fro. He stands on the pedals and races forward as fast as he can. Olive does the same, quickly overtaking him with her superior bike. Laughter bubbles up from her belly. The kind she hasn't felt for more years than she can count. She's swinging on a rope swing. She's splashing in a stream catching crawdads. She's running through an open meadow. Her heart is singing as Vic appears beside her, keeping pace with some effort.

"I'm not even trying," she says quickly before racing away faster than Vic's little bike can possibly go.

"Okay. Okay. You win." he shouts from far behind. She hits the brakes and turns to see him struggling with the small bicycle. He dismounts and walks it the rest of the way. "You're the winner. Happy?" he asks with a humble smile.

"That's right. Don't forget it."

"I'll have to get a better bike is all."

"You know what they say about a man who blames his tools." She dismounts and begins walking alongside hers.

"Oh, come on. Give me a break. You said it yourself, it's a child's bike."

"I bet I could beat you with it. Wanna trade?"

"Really?" Vic asks with a one-dimpled grin.

"Yeah, really." She drops the kickstand of her bike and steps away.

"Let's do it."

Taking the low handlebars in her hands, she eases her legs over the small seat. Vic stands beside her bike, stifling his laughter. Her knees hit the bars as she attempts to pedal away.

"Is there a problem?" he asks sarcastically.

"I've got this. Have to acclimate myself is all." She nods and rides forward with an awkward swerve. "Give me a minute." The wheel wiggles as she stands on the pedals. She's bent at an odd angle to reach the handlebars, quickly losing her resolve to prove him wrong.

"Let's see what you've got," he calls from behind.

Olive hits the top of a small hill and picks up speed, exactly what she needs. The hill allows for her to get control of the small bike and she races up to the next high point. She hits the brakes and swerves around to see Vic standing several yards away at the top of the other hill. "See?" she exclaims proudly. He mounts her bike and follows smoothly.

"Are we racing then?" he asks, pulling up beside her.

"Let's do it. To the next sign, on three. One…" She straightens the small bike, looking at the level stretch ahead. "Two…" She steadies her foot on the pedal ready to push off. "Three," she shouts and springs off, pedaling quickly and steering the bike with some difficulty. Vic eases up beside her on her bike. She pushes harder, barely making a difference. Then he zooms past her, making it to the next sign with time to spare.

"You were right," he agrees, dropping her kickstand. "I do need a new bike." He laughs.

"Now the question is, do I walk that hunk of junk all the way back to my apartment or throw it in that dumpster?"

"Don't throw it away. There's a kid somewhere who'll want it."

"I'm sure." He reaches for his bike as she dismounts. "You got any paper at your place? I want to make a free sign and leave it at the park by the dock."

"I do."

"You were right. It's a much quicker trip on two wheels."

"Told you."

"I still don't think it's safe. What about after your shifts? You'll be riding home after midnight."

"True. I'll have my escort though, won't I? With a better bike," she teases.

"You will," Vic agrees with a nod. He's looking straight ahead. Olive sneaks a glance at his profile. His chin juts out under full lips and a nearly perfect Roman nose. He fits the description of the hero in every story she's ever read. "I am surprised we made such good time. We're almost there."

"Yep," Olive agrees. She looks away to the river, her heart racing. Not from the physical exertion, though. It's Vic's presence. His assurance he'll be there to make sure she gets home safely. The last time she felt so cared for was with her family. There had never been a night her parents didn't say "I love you." Until there were no more nights together. If she'd known it was going to end so abruptly, she would've treasured those moments more. Would've committed them to her memory. Instead, they blended with all the other memories, fading with time.

"You all right?" Vic asks gently.

"Yeah. Why?"

"You were somewhere else," he says.

"I was. Sorry. It happens sometimes. Memories, you know." She waves her free hand in the air. They walk in silence, stepping up onto the dock. He leaves his old bike leaning against the fence. "Looks like I made it safely, again," she says in the direction of her boat. "Thank you. I appreciate it."

"Hey, I'll race you any night." He smiles.

"Maybe once you get a better bike." Olive laughs.

"I'm serious, Olive. Bike or no. I'm here whether you want me or not." He steps closer; only her bike separates them. He places his hand on the bars, his fingers brushing hers. Her cheeks blaze, her stomach flips.

“What about Emily?” she asks quickly. “What does she think about it?”

“Why would she care?” He looks confused.

“Aren’t you two a thing?” His hand slips from the bars, and he steps away.

“I don’t know what Emily thinks about anything. We’re not a thing though. At least I don’t think we are.”

“She seems plenty interested to me,” Olive says, moving to lift her bike onto the boat deck and quickly following it. She looks at Vic from the safety of her boat.

“She does, doesn’t she?” He narrows his eyes and nods. “I wish I knew what she was up to.”

“So, you aren’t together?” Olive asks, attempting to sound disinterested while her heart soars at the prospect of a free and available Vic.

“I guess you could say it’s complicated,” he says with a hint of anger. Olive’s heart drops again. Complicated is worse than together.

“I hope you figure it out,” she offers with little energy. She realizes she was about to invite him in under the guise of making a sign. “Wait here, I’ll get you a sign for your bike.” Inside she flips the light on, pulls out some scissors, a thick permanent marker, and a cereal box. She cuts out a panel and scrawls the word FREE on the blank side. Then, she rushes out to Vic. He’s standing on the dock, looking out over the mass of boats.

***

He watches as she hurries through the door. The lights through the small window flip on, lighting a flurry of activity on the other side of colorful curtains. Then, she appears through the door with the sign and a pleased look. “Here it is,” she says brightly. “See you Wednesday.”

“Thanks.” He takes the sign. “Yeah, see ya.”

“No, thank you for everything.” She grins.

“Anytime.” He watches until she’s safely through the door, then shuffles away, looking at Olive’s bold printed sign. It’s perfectly spaced with a delicate curve to each letter. He admires her clear and lovely handwriting then chances a sniff at the cardboard. It smells mostly of the fruity sugar crisps the box once held. There’s a hint of patchouli, which makes him smile as he looks for the best place to leave the bike with its sign.

He leans it against a tree near the playground, tempted to hold on to the sign. *Don't be dumb,* he thinks with one last look at it. Then, he glances over his shoulder to the light glowing from the window of her boat. He wonders what it's like inside, imagining the inside of a genie's lamp or something equally ethereal. *Maybe someday she'll invite me in.*

He starts jogging, following the bike path. The path he and Olive had raced down moments before. It's more than empty without her. Dark and forbidding. The absence of her laughter is almost painful. *You shouldn't have touched her like that,* he reprimands himself. *She's not like the girls you run with.* He picks up the pace, moving as fast as his heart and lungs will allow. Running as fast as he can away from the damage he would surely do someone as pure as Olive. He pushes on, until his rushing pulse forces her name out of his heart.

He's feeling alive and focused as he turns down the alley. A good workout always clears the mind. He's jogging now, ready to stretch and relax. No emails, no phone calls. He rounds the corner to his stairway.

"Hey, handsome," Emily purrs from the fire escape. She's sitting on the stairs, her breasts barely covered by the sheer fabric of her dress. Vic's body responds instantly. "I messaged you and you didn't answer. I got worried and came over. Where have you been?" She stands and slinks toward him. Her dress skims her thighs on the short side of indecent. It's black and trimmed with lace. Not a dress at all.

"What are you doing dressed like that in a dark alley?" Vic snaps, his irritation fading quickly as his appreciation for her physical attributes rises. He knows exactly what she's doing there.

"Like I said, I was worried. I wanted to make sure you were okay."

"So you came over here in your pajamas?" he asks. She looks down at her gown.

"It's not pajamas, silly. It's a slip. I have a dress upstairs. I was trying to surprise you. You were taking so long though. I was on the roof and saw you coming, so I snuck down to meet you." She bats her thick lashes. "You're still mad about last week, aren't you?" she pouts.

"I'm not mad," he says quickly. She's so near to him now, the sweet scent of vanilla and cigarettes engulfs him.

"I thought we could have a drink," she offers. "I brought a bottle of wine." Her breasts are against his chest, soft and enticing. She grimaces and pulls away. "You're sweaty."

"Yeah, I went for a run. Wasn't expecting company. Left my phone here."

"That explains why you didn't answer." She smiles and turns to walk back to the stairway. Her ass wiggles with every step. Vic's resolve to stay away melts with each one. "I was worried you were mad at me."

"I wasn't happy to be left hanging two nights in a row." He follows her up the stairs.

"Why don't you take a shower and I'll open this bottle for us?" she says from his doorway, holding a bottle of red wine in the air. Her dress is draped on the chair beside the door.

"I don't know. I was planning on turning in early tonight." He thinks of Olive grinning as she handed him the cardboard sign, her innocence refreshing. She's too good for him.

"One glass?" she tempts. "Then you can let me apologize for leaving you alone." She moves subtly while she waits. Her breaths are slow and measured, her breasts rising and falling seductively. "Or you could forget about the shower and fuck me right here," she offers, pulling at the hem of her slip. The animal in him breaks free. He's on her in an instant. The satin of her slip sticks to his sweat-soaked t-shirt. He grinds against her soft frame, covering her face and neck with rough, angry kisses. She moans into them. He hurries to unlock the door behind her and pushes it open. She stumbles back. He gathers her yielding body to his in the hallway and kicks the door shut behind him, ignoring the alarms going off in his mind. The clarity he'd felt from his run is muddled in the sweet, smoky, seductive cloud Emily has woven.

***

Lucinda Williams's low and dreamy voice sings from Olive's phone while she sways in her hammock. She's floating on the water away from the marina among the river islands and trees. The cloudless sky is impossibly blue. She's remembering her mom, dancing to old records and dusting. How she would throw open all the windows and doors to let the sweet freshness into the house. How she had loved the summer. She'd passed that love down to Olive. The warm air and glowing sun, the plants thriving and reaching to the heavens. She breathes deep and relaxes into the lovely memories. Instead of pushing them away, she holds them close and lets the tears fall. Her heart breaks free from years of not feeling, and from being wrapped in emptiness. Instead, there's acceptance, excitement, and dreams for the future. Dreams of Vic.

Though she's tried to deny it, he's become a permanent fixture in her mind. Their nighttime walks are the thing she looks forward to the most. Was he going to kiss her Monday night? If she had leaned in when his fingers brushed hers, would her night have ended differently? If she had invited him in, would he have stayed and lit her space with his dazzling smile? Warmed her skin with his hands? "I Envy the Wind" begins playing as she imagines what could have been. She sees Vic's hair fluffed and blown by the wind, then his body wet with rain, and finally his smiling face in the warm sunshine. She laughs at herself, at her childish crush, and then realizes the song is perfect for her routine. It's haunting, full of longing and sad beauty. She stands and starts the song again to begin choreographing her dance.

***

"Your fans are here," Bunny says, holding up a long leather bag with handles and a zipper. She lays it on the table in front of Olive.

"I can't believe these came the day I found my song." She runs her hand over the leather case.

"Open it," Bunny demands with a wide grin.

Olive holds her breath and pulls the zipper slowly. "Oh my god," she exhales, "they're beautiful." The long emerald-green ostrich feathers spring to life, fluttering and shimmering as she pulls them from the case.

"Open them." Bunny watches with glee as Olive shakes the fans open.

"These are amazing." Olive dances in place, spinning in small circles, the fans floating around her. "Do you want to hear my song?"

"Sure. Do you want to try them out on stage?"

"I do." Olive's heart races at the thought of dancing across the stage with the beautiful fans.

"Marty is up in the booth. Give him your song so you can hear it over the speakers."

Moments later, she's on stage in her bare feet and street clothes waiting for Marty to find her song. "I'm seeing a long sheer, glittering, green halter under the fans. One that will drop easily when I untie it," she says to Bunny and Chris, who appeared from nowhere and is seated next to Bunny in front of the stage. Bunny nods and the music starts playing.

Olive is carried away on the gentle guitar. Moving with Lucinda's voice, she sees Vic in her mind. She's dancing for him. The lyrics pull at her heart and imagination. She feels the words in her bones as she spins under the warm stage lights. The fans move fluidly, extensions of her arms and her emotions. The song ends and she's met with silence. Instantly embarrassed, she feels like it must've been the most boring three minutes of Bunny and Chris's lives. Their stunned faces say otherwise.

"That was beautiful," Chris says slowly as Bunny dabs at the corner of her eye.

"It was. It really was. You are such a natural." Bunny shakes her head and claps her hands. "It's perfect."

"She's like the green fairy up there. You know the absinthe fairy?"

"She is," Bunny agrees. "Wait a minute." She picks up her phone and starts typing. "I've got it. I've got your stage name," Bunny exclaims.

"Really?" Olive hurries down the steps to the table, placing her fans gently beside her as she sits.

"You ready for it?" Bunny squeals.

"Yes," Chris shouts before Olive can respond.

"*La Fae Verte*," she cries with a grand flourish.

Goosebumps spring up all over Olive's body. She's stunned by the simple beauty of it. It's magical and perfect. It's exactly who she wants to be on stage.

"I love it," Chris sings. "It's so very you, Olive."

"It really is," Bunny agrees. "We've got *La Fae Verte*, Rock Studson, Dame Monroe, Bunny Demure, Poppy Jones, and Philina

Fatale. We're starting to sound like a bona fide burlesque troupe. Make way for Burlesque A la Mode Quad Cities."

Olive is beaming along with Chris and Bunny while they discuss small details for the show: costume pieces, hair and makeup. Bunny shows them pictures of their devil costumes for the opening act. The feeling of happy belonging settles around Olive. She feels at home in the most wonderful way. As Bunny and Chris chatter on, Olive daydreams about her walk home with Vic later that evening. She can't wait to tell him about her routine and her name.

As she's picturing his handsome face, he walks through the front door. The butterflies in her stomach take flight. She fights the urge to run to him, to throw her arms around him and thank him for his smile. The smile that inspired her routine and, in turn, inspired her stage name. Then Emily follows behind him.

"Thanks for the lift, Vicky," she says loud enough for all the room to hear.

"Yeah, no problem. Want me to bring the mirror in now?" he asks.

"If you would, please," she says in a baby voice.

Olive's heart sinks. Her face grows warm and all the butterflies seem to drop dead, turning into dried husks in her gut. Vic heads back outside. Emily walks toward them with a wide grin. She finds Olive and levels her proud stare directly on her.

"There's something about having a big strong guy wrapped around your finger. Isn't there, Bunny?" she says with a chuckle, her gaze never leaving Olive.

Bunny, oblivious to the exchange, barely looks away from her conversation with Chris. "You're telling me."

"What did I miss?" Emily asks, taking a seat next to Bunny. Then without waiting for a response she goes on. "I found the perfect mirror for my routine at the thrift store this afternoon, and called Vic to come help me get it. He said it could stay backstage 'til the show."

"Awesome," Bunny says. "The show is really coming together."

Olive watches as Vic carries in a large standing mirror, beautifully carved. It looks heavy as he hefts it onto the stage with ease. He scans the room. His gaze meets Olive's. He gives her a small, tight-lipped smile then looks away. The dead butterflies turn to rocks.

"I'll be in back if anyone needs me," he says, coming down the stairs.

"Thanks, Vicky," Emily sings.

"No problem," he responds brightly. The rocks catch fire as she swallows the bitter taste in her mouth.

"Isn't he the best?" Emily says as he turns down the hall. "I can't get enough of him." She smiles, her cold stare on Olive.

"He's pretty great," Bunny agrees. She's watching their exchange with a curious look. Her gaze meets Olive's and Bunny squints. Olive shrugs and turns her attention to the fans lying on the table. "How's your routine coming along?" Bunny asks Emily.

"It's great now that I have the mirror. I'm waiting on the leather corset. I've already got the boots. I only need the little things now. Fishnets and pasties."

"You're going with leather then?" Bunny asks.

"Seems appropriate with the song, right?" Emily twirls her hair around her finger.

"It does. Though it really doesn't go with my original vision," Bunny says, looking from Emily to Olive. "I love both ideas…" She glances at her notebook, open on the table, full of words, scribbles, and doodles. "It actually frees up the lineup. I can put either of you anywhere now." She makes some quick, illegible notes in the book. "I still want to open with you, Emily. It's a strong song, with a good beat. I think it'll set the pace perfectly."

"Isn't that what the opening group is for?" Emily snaps. Olive looks at Chris, shocked. Bunny clears her throat and taps her pen on the notebook.

"The opening group is to set the mood. The opening individual sets the pace," Bunny answers with an air of finality.

"It seems like a waste to have me at the beginning, don't you think?" Emily asks. Bunny inhales deep and slow, never looking away from Emily. She stops tapping her pen.

"Which sin do you think would be the first in line to be seen?" Bunny looks from Chris to Olive, then Emily. "Surely not gluttony," she gestures to herself, "or sloth, or envy, or even greed." She gestures to Olive and Chris. Olive does her best to hide the joy she feels at seeing Emily be put in her place. "Maybe wrath or lust. But they are coming all the way from Chicago and New Orleans. Seems to me like they deserve to close the show." Chris covers his mouth and fakes a cough to hide his smirk. Emily blinks and crosses her arms over her chest. "Right?" Bunny asks.

"You're right." Emily nods.

"I'm glad you agree," Bunny says brightly. "The opening individual is one of the best placements in a show. Look at it this way, you won't have to be in the group routine. I know how you hate those." Bunny shifts to look at Chris and Olive as if Emily disappeared. "I'm thinking about changing the choreography for the group. Once Susan gets here, we can get to work."

An hour later, Olive is panting on stage as they run through the group routine for the fifth time. She's paired with Chris, who is a much better dancer. Though he says he's taking it easy on her, she doesn't believe him. Fast steps and high kicks aren't her strength.

"Looks great from up here," Marty calls down from the sound booth.

"It really does," Julie agrees. She's sitting near the stage watching with James. Emily sits on the other side, looking at her phone. She stands up suddenly and heads down the hall. The only thing that way is Vic's office. Olive's heart drops. She looks at Bunny, who looks less than happy.

"Thanks," Bunny says, panting. "It's a lot easier in my head." She laughs and bends at the waist, dangling her arms and head with theatrical exhaustion. "I think that's good for this one tonight. Let's take five."

They all sigh their relief and leave the stage. Olive struggles with her emotions as she takes her place at the table. She looks at Emily's empty seat and tortures herself with images of what's happening in Vic's office.

"Why the long face?" Susan asks as she sits beside her.

Olive sighs and shakes her head. "Just zoning out," Olive responds as lighthearted as she can manage. "Hey, Bunny, I think I'm gonna call it a night, if that's okay?"

"You all right?" she asks.

"Yeah, I've got cramps," she lies. "That opening routine kicked my ass."

"Okay," Bunny says brightly. "Take care of yourself. You are starting your new job on Friday."

"I'm looking forward to it," Olive lies again. She gathers her things and heads out the door with a heavy heart. Another night of watching Vic from afar while he fawns over Emily.

Chapter 11

The music is down, voices are quiet. Vic heads out to the alley to collect his new bike from its home chained on the fire escape. He feels like a kid, ready to race Olive again. He can't wait to challenge her to an evenly matched one. As he rounds the corner from the alley, expecting to meet her for their ride, he finds an empty sidewalk. No Olive, no bike. He heads inside to find Amanda talking with Marty and James.

"Hey, did Olive take off already?" he asks from the doorway. Amanda looks up from her conversation.

"She left early today, after group. Said she wasn't feeling well."

"How long ago was that?" he asks, attempting to sound unconcerned and failing.

"I don't know." Amanda shrugs. "It was still light out." She excuses herself from the table and crosses the room to him. He steps back behind the sound booth, away from the curious stares of Marty and James. "What are you doing?" she asks in a loud whisper, joining him behind the booth.

"What do you mean?"

"What do you mean what do I mean? What are you doing with Olive and Emily?"

Vic's throat goes dry. He swallows hard over the lump forming there. "What I do with Emily is my business, and I'm looking out for Olive's well-being. Which is more than I can say for you," he snaps with immediate regret.

Amanda crosses her arms over her chest and cocks her chin. Her suspicious stare bores through him. "Don't give me that bullshit, Vic." She steps forward. "Haven't you always said you don't mix business with pleasure? It looks like you've forgotten that rule lately. You've got Emily pawing at you every chance she gets, rubbing Olive's nose in it. Then poor Olive, stammering and blushing when your names are mentioned." She takes another step closer. Vic steps back and hits the wall. "You know I don't give a fuck what you and Emily are up to. Would you do me a favor, though, and leave Olive out of it? She's had enough drama in her life. She doesn't need yours."

Vic stands against the wall, his ears and cheeks burning. Amanda's normally smiling face is set with an intense anger he's never seen. She stands, waiting for his response. He can't find any words of defense. He thinks of his failed resolve to leave Emily be. He remembers his attempt at testing the waters with Olive. The way she hurried to put distance between them. "You're right," he agrees. "She deserves a whole lot better than I have to offer."

Amanda's countenance softens. "That's not what I said." She shakes her head. "I said she doesn't need the drama. It's not your drama, either. It's Emily's. She brings it wherever she goes. Though I accepted her and her drama years ago, it doesn't mean I want her spreading it to others. You asked for it, Olive didn't."

"You're right," he agrees.

"I knew I would regret bringing her on," Amanda says. "I didn't realize it would happen this fast." She leans against the ladder.

"I don't know what to do." Vic relaxes. "She's got me all mixed up."

"Yeah?" Amanda asks. They stand in silence, watching one another.

"Cin was right," he says, studying the stark contrast of his white sneakers on the dark carpet. "I'm not sure what kind of game Emily is playing. I do know I'm right in the middle of it."

"I can see that," Amanda huffs.

"I don't even want her when she's gone. Like, I can think of a million and one reasons to avoid her. Then she's there in front of me and I can't resist. You ever been on a diet and been offered your favorite dessert?" Amanda blinks at him. "It's like that. I know she's bad for me, but I can't say no when it's offered up on a platter."

Amanda shifts. "I would think you would have more self-control than that." Her voice is flat, no gentle words, no pleasant laughter. Vic risks a glance in her direction. Her face matches her voice. Absent her normal good humor. "Besides, I'm not worried about what you do with your irresistible dessert," she sneers. "I'm worried about Olive. She doesn't deserve this."

"Deserve what?" Vic asks quickly, making no attempt to hide his irritation. "All I'm doing is walking her home."

"Don't play dumb, Vic. You've been around long enough to know when a woman is sweet on you. I've been around long enough to know when *you're* sweet on someone."

"It's not like that. I'm looking out for her," he says with little conviction. Amanda raises one brow, holding his gaze. Vic sighs, accepting defeat in their silent face-off. "Okay," he agrees. Despite his failure to avoid Emily, Olive has been on his mind nonstop. She's refreshing. A mix of bold and innocent, exotic and humble. He feels lighter when she's around. Women like her don't fall from the sky, or run into the side of your best friend's truck for that matter.

"Whatever you and Emily have is whatever it is." Amanda shakes her head. "But it's going to fuck up what you could have with Olive. You might want to decide what it is you really want." She stands straight, offering him a small smile. "Until you figure that out, you should leave Olive alone."

"Yeah, thanks for the advice," he responds with little energy. His heart aches over the accuracy of her words.

"I adore you, Vic. You know that. I want to see you happy." She steps close and wraps her arms around his shoulders. He hugs her back, reveling in the chaste affection.

"Mike's a lucky guy," he says with a squeeze.

"Thanks," she says with a genuine smile. "Now, I gotta get back to work."

"Don't let me keep you." He smiles back and pushes through the door. The muted orange light of the streetlamps greet him along with the empty sidewalk. Olive's absence hurts more than he cares to admit. He climbs on his bike and heads for the bike path. He's got to know she's home safe. Once he sees her bike on the dock, he'll leave. She won't even know he's there.

Riding blindly down the familiar path, his has his mind on Olive. The way she moves like she's dancing. How her words spill like song from her lips. She's poetry incarnate, art walking, breathing, laughing. Shadowy old buildings glide by as he moves swiftly over hills, around curves. He bumps over the railroad tracks. The nearer he gets to the marina, the faster he pedals.

Amanda's right. I've got to stop with Emily. She's no good for me.

He approaches the dock. Yellow light glows from Olive's boat. Her bike is parked safely on the deck, chained in place. Soft music floats through the open window. Vic straddles his bike, listening, hoping she walks past the window so he can catch a glimpse of her before riding home.

As he decides to take his leave, she appears on the deck. Not through the door, but as if she materialized there. She squints in his direction. "Vic?" she calls, barely loud enough for him to hear. "What are you doing here?"

"You weren't at practice," he answers. "I wanted to make sure you got home all right."

Olive hops from her boat to the dock and walks to him, her long t-shirt and short shorts revealing the sleek lines of her lovely figure. With her thick glasses and loose ponytail, she reminds him of the day they first met. "Well, I'm here. I'm safe," she says. As she nears the end of the dock she stops and crosses her arms over her chest.

Vic stands, straddling his bike. He offers a small smile. "I'm glad to see it." They stare at one another for what feels like eternity. Olive leans her hip against the railing, her arms still crossed.

"Thanks for checking on me. I think you can stop worrying about me though. As you can see, I manage fine on my own. You're a busy guy," she says with a coolness that cuts him deep. "I'd hate to keep you."

"You aren't keeping me from anything. I wanted to show off my new bike," he says, attempting to lighten the mood. She glances at the bike. A tiny smile plays on her lips. He's amazed at the joy it inspires in him. The only other woman whose smile held his heart that way was his mom's on the rare occasion he saw it—when his dad was gone and they were free to laugh and be themselves.

"You did," Olive's playful voice interrupts his thoughts. "Wanna beat me fair and square I see." She chuckles and steps down from the dock, approaching him. "Let's see it."

Vic drops his kickstand and steps away to give Olive space. He catches her patchouli scent as she steps closer. "What do you think?" he asks.

"It's a good-looking bike. I think mine's faster though," she teases. Vic's thankful for the shift in her countenance. She's close enough to touch. All he has to do is step forward and reach out. He could brush the errant strand of hair off her face, tuck it behind her ear. What would she do? How would she react? Would she let him stroke her cheek and whisper his feelings in her ear? Or would she hurry away as suddenly as she appeared on the deck of her boat?

"It probably is," he agrees dreamily, still imagining what it would be like to touch her. To really touch her, not an accidental bumping of hands, or an exploratory brushing of knuckles. What it would be like to truly hold her in his arms, to touch every inch of her.

"Are you okay?" Olive is looking at him with a concerned expression. He looks back, Amanda's words echoing in his mind. Emily's hold on him loosening its grip.

"I am," he responds. "Better than I've been for a while I'd say. You want to get a drink?"

"I don't drink," she says, shaking her head.

"Really?" Vic asks, unsurprised.

"Really. I hate hangovers. I've got some tea," she offers.

"Are you inviting me onboard?" He raises a brow.

"You did ride all this way to check on me. It's the least I could do." She turns to walk away. "Bring your bike," she says over her shoulder. "Hope you like iced chamomile."

***

"I was attempting to stargaze," Olive says, pointing to her hammock filled with pillows. "Have a seat, I'll get you that tea." She goes inside to fill a cup with ice and tea. Emotionally, she's a wreck. Moments ago, she was mourning the loss of her imaginary relationship with Vic, lamenting all that would never be. Now, he's making himself at home in her hammock, the first person she's allowed into her personal space, ever. Is it a dream come true or a terrible mistake in the making?

As she heads out with his tea, she sees him trying his best to sit up in a hammock made for lounging. He smiles up at her as he takes the drink in his hand. Olive takes her cup from the small wooden table beside him and pulls it away to a safe distance to sit.

"You should sit here," Vic says, standing awkwardly. The hammock and constant rocking seem to rob him of his physical prowess. Olive giggles and stands to trade. Their proximity as they shift their way around one another is almost too much. He smells like a fresh summer breeze, sweet and warm. She lingers for a moment before sinking easily onto her hammock, arranging the pillows for maximum support while sitting. Vic lowers himself gingerly onto the small table. "Gotta get my sea legs," he jokes.

"You get used to it," she responds, sipping her tea.

He takes a long sip of his and winces. "This is chamomile?" He holds the pale beverage to the light.

"You don't like it?"

He looks at her and back at the glass. "It's…" He holds the glass near his mouth but doesn't drink, "interesting."

"It's my favorite. I think it tastes like sunshine." She smiles broadly and takes a hearty swallow, reveling in the cool, refreshing flavor.

"It tastes like grass," he says flatly.

She chuckles. "Try it again. Close your eyes and imagine a sun-warmed meadow full of wildflowers." He does as she says and brings the glass to his lips. She watches his throat as he swallows, taking full advantage of the moment, admiring his masculine bone structure, the smoothness of his skin, the curl of his golden hair. As he brings the cup away from his full lips, he smiles a dreamy smile. His blue eyes open slowly.

"I get it." He nods, lowering his glass, and gazes her way.

She sways in her hammock with the gentle rocking of the boat, grateful for the distance between them. "Do you really?" she asks from behind her own cup.

"I do," he says. "Still tastes like grass. But I get it." He chuckles.

"I suppose that's something." She shakes her head and lowers her cup. "Thanks for checking on me. I appreciate it. Sorry if you were worried. I'm still getting used to having folks looking out for me. I figured since you'd given Emily a ride to practice, you would be taking her home."

Vic rests his cup on his knee and tilts his head slightly. "I didn't give her a ride. I met her at the thrift store and picked up the mirror. She followed in her car."

"Oh, well, she made it sound like you rode together. Then she dipped out of practice and headed to your office. I figured you were busy." Olive shrugs, trying to dismiss the sinking feeling in her stomach at the mention of him being busy with Emily. "Didn't want to bother you."

Vic sets his cup on the ground beside him and leans forward. “You will never bother me,” he says with such conviction, Olive shifts in her seat. His steady gaze holds her own. “I said I’d be here for you and I meant it. Whether Emily is around doesn’t make a difference.” He sighs and sits up straight, looking away. Silence falls between them as the waves ripple beneath the boat. “I don’t know what to do about her,” he says finally, as if thinking out loud. Olive wonders if she should respond. She sips her tea and looks at the worn wooden boards of the deck. “I mean if I would have known…” he says softly. Olive looks up. He’s still looking away, slouching with his hands clasped in his lap. His thumbs twitch.

“Known what?” she asks. He looks back to her with an expression of confused sadness. Opening his mouth to speak, he closes it and blinks slowly then offers a small smile.

“If I would have known you.” He shakes his head slowly and looks at his hands in his lap. “If you would have been at that wedding dancing and laughing the way you do, you would have eclipsed every woman in that room and I…” He looks at her again. “I wouldn’t have seen Emily, or anyone else for that matter. I would have fallen. I would have fallen hard.” He shakes his head.

Olive fights the urge to spring into his arms as the dead butterflies from earlier are resurrected. They flutter about her stomach, and her cheeks grow warm. His confession confirms she’s not a foolish girl with a silly crush. There is something there. Something that could grow.

It also confirms that his complicated relationship with Emily is exactly what Olive had presumed it is: a relationship. “But I wasn’t. She was,” Olive says quietly. Their silence is less awkward than it is full. They stare, blinking unspoken words. She longs to stand and wrap him in her arms. To hold him close and breathe in his fresh air scent. To feel his arms around her. She wants to comfort him and kiss his lips. Something stops her. She sways in her hammock, watching as the look on his face turns from sadness to acceptance.

“I should get out of here,” he says softly, standing.

“Wait,” she calls and stands to join him. They’re face-to-face, nothing separating them except for the muddy Mississippi air. “I wish I’d been there,” she says, barely more than a whisper. He steps closer, looking down at her. His eyes glisten in the low light. He’s so near she can feel his energy radiating, warm and gentle. She steps closer still, taking his hand in hers, holding his fingertips lightly.

The sensation from the simple touch vibrates up her arm. It tingles throughout her body. She leans up on tiptoes and presses her lips against his, tender yet shocking. He kisses back with gentle urgency, moving his free hand to her cheek. He pulls his lips away, resting his forehead against hers.

"You're here now," he says, "and I'm going to make this right." He places another satiny kiss on her open lips and brushes the hair from her cheek. Smiling, she leans into his open hand. He smiles back. "I'll see you tomorrow." He kisses her one more time, gentle and sweet, then slowly makes his way off the boat. Olive stands motionless while shuddering wildly on the inside. Three small kisses and she is utterly lost.

Chapter 12

"You can't do this to me, Vic." Emily is sitting at his kitchen counter; two glasses of red wine remain untouched between them. Her shirt is open dangerously low, revealing red lace and soft, pale skin.

"C'mon, Em. What are we really doing here?" he asks, taking his glass and not drinking it. "You show up, we fuck, you disappear. It's not what I want."

"You sure it's not what you want?" she asks, uncrossing and crossing her legs suggestively for the express purpose of allowing him a peek of her matching red lace panties.

"Yes, I'm sure. You don't call when you say you're going to. You leave me hanging all the time. You show up when you want to." He takes a long sip from the wine.

"I didn't leave you hanging tonight," she offers, running her finger along the stem of the wineglass.

"No, you didn't. And I was shocked. Since when do you answer my first text, or any text for that matter?"

"I was nearby. You seemed like you needed to see me." She bats her lashes.

"You were right. That's the problem, don't you see? You were nearby. Is that the only way I'm going to see you? If you're near?"

Emily takes her first drink of wine. She clears her throat. "I'm sorry, Vicky," she pouts. "It's only, I like you so much. I'm afraid of what will happen if we get too close. I like to keep a safe distance."

"If what we've been doing is a safe distance, I'd be amazed to see what up close and personal is," Vic jokes, not believing her act for a moment.

"You know what I mean. Sex is one thing. Personal stuff is too much."

"Exactly. I want the personal stuff."

Emily's laughter rings from the high ceilings. Somewhere between hysterical and wicked. "That's rich, coming from you," she quips darkly.

"What's that supposed to mean?"

"You know you didn't even ask my name that night at the wedding?" Vic looks over the counter at her, his hands griping the edge. "When I tried to say anything personal, you would cut me off with kisses and gropes. I understand you were drunk and depressed, looking for some 'no strings attached' fun at your best friend's wedding. That set the precedent for our relationship from day one."

"I don't remember you asking for my name," he says quickly.

"I knew your name. You were the best man."

"Well, we were drunk," he defends.

"No. *You* were drunk. I had to be at work in the morning. I'd only had a couple drinks all night." Vic stares at the wine stain ring on the counter, his throat growing tighter by the minute, all his thoughts and opinions about Emily crumbling around him. He realizes as he stands there under her gaze that he knows nothing about her. All he thought he knew was someone else's gossip or his own assumption. All the bad things he believed to be true hadn't kept him from fucking her every chance he got.

"Em." He swallows the lump in his throat. "I'm so sorry. I had no idea. I thought we were on the same page. I thought you wanted the random anonymity."

"I thought that's what you wanted," she says softly, tapping her finger on the base of her glass. "I know what this is about." She takes another sip of her wine. "It's Olive, isn't it?" she asks. "You were fine with things as they were with me. But you want her now. And she doesn't want to be a random woman in your bed. She wants to be the only one. So here I am, getting pushed out." She takes another drink, almost finishing her glass. "How many more calls do you have to make tonight?" She stares at him, holding the wineglass over her angry smirk, raising one brow.

Vic opens his mouth, then closes it. She's the only person he's been seeing.

"You know what?" she says, standing with her last swallow. "I'm done. I thought we had something good. I can see I was wrong. I was only here to keep your bed warm." She pushes the wineglass across the counter with more force than Vic expects, it topples and shatters in front of him. He stares at the shards gleaming in the light and looks at Emily.

"Emily, it's not like that. It was never like that. I thought you wanted it this way. I had no idea. I'm sorry. I don't know what to say."

"Say that you want me. Say you want me to stay."

She's beautiful. Her pale cheeks flushed with anger, her eyes wet with unshed tears. Vic's heart aches for what he's done to her, how he never gave her a chance. He feels like he's seeing her for the first time. She not the heartless maneater he took her to be. She's fragile, sensitive, and thanks to him, heartbroken.

He steps away from the broken glass, around the counter to where she stands, nearly a foot shorter than him. He lowers himself onto a barstool. He looks her over, trembling and anxious, ready to fall into his arms. He's looking at her but sees Olive and the tender moment they shared. The guilt weighs heavy in his chest as he considers his next move.

He should wrap her in his arms and tell her to stay. He should give them the chance they never had, make things right with her. But when he closes his eyes, he sees Olive looking back at him.

"I'm sorry, Emily. I can't." He shakes his head. "I wish I could. I wish we'd communicated better. In the end, I don't know if it would've ever worked."

"That's not what you said last time I was here," she hisses.

"I barely said anything the last time you were here."

"You barely say anything at all. You're just a fat dick looking for a wet hole. I can find that anywhere," she snarls. "Have fun cleaning up your mess." She looks at the broken glass on the counter and steps around him, slamming the door behind her on the way out.

Vic stared at the broken glass again. The last bit of wine had splattered on the white countertop, the shards and dust gleaming around it. He feels like an asshole. Emily's words ring in his mind.

She's right.

He has little to offer her and even less to offer someone like Olive.

***

"You okay?" Simone, Olive's dainty new coworker, asks from the other side of the beer cooler. She raises one stark brow and steps toward Olive. The small crowd is gathered in seats near the stage. The first comedian of the night is starting his set.

"Yeah. I'm okay. Sorry if I spaced out there. I've got some stuff on my mind is all." Olive waves her hand in dismissal and offers a smile.

"I've seen that look before," Simone says, leaning her small frame against the counter.

"What look?" Olive feigns ignorance.

"It hasn't happened much these last couple years, but I've seen it enough to recognize it. New cocktail waitress watching the front door and the back hall, looking all over the room, waiting for someone. It used to be Mike they were looking for. But, since he went and got hooked up with Bunny, it pretty much stopped. She adores you, so it couldn't be Mike." She stares at Olive, waiting for a response. Olive shifts uncomfortably.

"Where is Bunny anyway? I thought she would be here tonight." Olive attempts to change the subject.

"She was in earlier, before you got here. Said you shouldn't have any problems with the work but told me to look after you."

"She did?"

"Yeah, said she'd stay if she could but that Mike had made plans for them and tonight's show isn't going to be a big one." Simone stands to serve a customer who approaches. "So, what am I looking after you for?" she asks as she crosses to the beer cooler for three bottles. She opens and hands them off, still looking at Olive.

"I don't know." She shrugs. "It's my first night on a new job. You tell me." She wonders if Bunny knows about Vic. Did he tell her anything? He didn't come back yesterday like he said he would. She didn't have his number. She'd waited, half hopeful, half heartbroken. Until the night came and heartbreak won. She'd hoped he would be here when she arrived with apologies and reasons for not showing up.

Simone crosses her arms and leans back against the counter. She gives a little laugh and shakes her head. Her short dark hair is motionless, plastered in place with more than enough gel. "So, where you from?"

"Marquette. Born and raised," Olive says. "Small town, farm life." She offers little of her story. Though she likes Simone, it's exhausting to tell it, and she doesn't have the energy. "How about you?"

"Not much to say either, born and raised here. I've known Vic since we were kids. Had this job since they opened. You should have seen this place in the beginning." She chuckles.

"What do you mean?" Olive asks, suddenly more interested in what Simone has to say.

"It was so run-down. It was an improv club before it closed, if you can imagine." She smirks. "When the guys got it, they started booking local bands, mostly metal. We had pretty good turnouts for those. Enough to keep us up and running anyway. Then they booked a cover band one night, sold out for the first time. That's when they realized the local metal scene wasn't where the money was. They started booking more mainstream stuff and putting money back into the building. It's grown a lot since those days."

Olive looks around the Speakeasy, the well-lit stage with its deep red curtain, the pressed-tin ceiling overhead, the low lights mounted along the dark green walls. She can't imagine it as Simone describes it.

"You should have seen the guys too. Mike hasn't changed all that much. But Vic, he was something else."

"Really? How?" Olive asks, trying to seem indifferent. Simone raises her pierced brow and serves another round of beers at the counter.

"He was always looking for a fight. Was the first to throw someone out on their ass. We almost lost our liquor license on account of the police being called too often."

"What?" Olive tries to imagine sweet, charming Vic picking fights with strangers. *No one with a smile like his could possibly want to hurt someone.* Then she remembers him shirtless and covered in sweat. The way his muscles twitched as if having a mind of their own. He was built for fighting.

"Oh yeah. He's always been like that. Even when we were kids. He would be so proud of his bruised face and broken lip."

"Wow," Olive says with a chuckle. "I would've never guessed."

"I think he grew up a bit once the city threatened to shut us down. The police were called in almost every weekend. He realized he couldn't keep acting out his *Road House* fantasies here if he wanted to keep the business. He's still the first one there if someone's causing trouble," Simone says with a shrug. "Speaking of trouble." She nods toward the back hallway. Vic is walking their way. Olive's heart jumps. He's looking at her, the line of his jaw tight and grim.

"Hey, ladies." He sounds cheerful, but Olive isn't buying it. "Can I borrow Olive for a moment? She's got some paperwork to do."

"Sure." Simone shrugs. "I think I can manage." She gestures to the empty bar and small crowd near the stage.

"Thanks. It won't be long." He smiles and turns away, walking back to the office. Olive tiptoes through the crowd, her heart in her throat, beating wildly. The kisses they'd shared two nights before still linger on her lips. She's dreamed of his touch and his smile. Even after she accepted he wasn't coming yesterday, she chose to believe it was for good reasons. She's ready to hear them.

***

Vic swallows the lump in his throat and drops the positive pregnancy test in his drawer as Olive enters the office with a timid smile. "Hey," he says softly, pushing the drawer shut.

"Hey," she responds.

"Sorry about yesterday. I know I said I was coming. But something came up. I…" He wants to say that he fucked up. That he's in a terrible mess. That he made big mistakes and even bigger problems for himself. He stops. "I don't have your number." He remembers how Emily showed up the day before, dropping the positive test on his desktop.

"It's okay. I figured as much." She sits in the chair across from him, her smile bright and innocent. "I can give it to you now." She plucks a pen from his desk and twirls it.

"Yeah. Good," he stammers and slides a small stack of official paperwork her way. "I'll need copies of your ID and social security card too, when you get a chance. No rush." She looks at him with a wrinkled brow and lowers the pen to the desk.

"What's up?" she asks. The heavy ache in Vic's chest won't go away.

"Turns out, I'm in deeper with Emily than I thought," he says, leaning back in his chair.

"What does that mean?" she asks.

"She's pregnant," he says quickly, nearly choking on the words.

"Really?" Olive's smile fades. Whatever happy energy she brought to the room evaporates.

"Yeah. I thought we'd always used protection. She says there was one time we didn't have anything and we were drinking. I don't remember. There's a lot I don't remember," he says, shaking his head, rubbing the back of his neck. "I don't know what to do."

"Hey, it's okay. You'll figure it out," she says sadly, looking down at the documents on the desk.

"I'm in shock, honestly."

"It's not like you don't know how it happened," she says flatly, focusing on the paperwork.

Vic sits, feeling like he's being reprimanded. She steals a glance his way and blinks before starting on the next form. It's silent in the office. Laughter and applause float through the open door. Vic's never felt lower, sitting across from one of the sweetest, most genuine people he's ever known, whining about an avoidable predicament he's gotten himself into. He can't imagine what she thinks of him. She drops the pen onto the papers and stands. "All done," she says with an impersonal nod, making it clear what she thinks of him.

"Olive, wait," he says. Her eyes widen, her lips are pressed together tightly. "I called her as soon as I left your place Wednesday. I called to tell her it was over. She left angry. She didn't mention anything about being pregnant or thinking she might be. Then yesterday morning she hits me with this text then shows up here." He shakes his head and looks up at her.

She takes a deep breath. "It's okay. I understand. You're a good guy. You'll do what's right. But you should probably focus on her now. No more escorting me home." She gives another quick nod and a sad smile before walking out.

Vic watches from his chair, his heart a lead weight in his chest.

Chapter 13

"I'm worried about you," Chris says from across the table.

Olive's pineapple fried rice sits in front of her, its fragrant steam enveloping her senses. "Why?" she asks, her fork poised to dive into her first-ever plate of Thai food. It's been over a week since she learned about Vic and Emily's baby. Though she's the only one who knows, Chris isn't the first to notice something was up.

"You don't seem like yourself lately," he says, covering his mouth while he chews.

"I'm myself." She shakes head and takes her first bite of heavenly, savory sweetness. "My god this is amazing," she says upon swallowing. "I can't believe I lived this long without it."

"I told you." He smiles. "Really though. I'm serious. You seem so sad lately."

"I'm fine," she insists. "It's been a hell of a transition, moving here and joining a burlesque troupe. I've never done anything like this in my life. I'm adjusting. At first, I was riding high on the excitement of it all. Now I've settled into a routine, and I've started to realize I'm never going back." She shrugs and takes another bite. Though what she says is true, it's not what's bothering her. It's Vic. Vic and Emily's business is theirs. They haven't made any announcements. She won't be the one to start blabbing.

Chris watches her skeptically, then seems to accept she's not in the mood to reveal her innermost heartaches. "Well, whatever you left behind, I'm glad you're here. If you ever need to talk, I'm here for you." He smiles and continues with his lunch. "I was thinking we would start with some thrift stores first. You never know what you're going to find. With your figure, there might be the perfect gown for twelve bucks that fits like a glove. If not, we can go to the fabric store. Then we can head back to my place. Wait 'til you see my craft room."

Olive swallows another delicious bite. "I love thrift stores," she says between bites. "And I can't wait to see your place."

"Tyler is working late today, so we'll have the whole place to ourselves. We could get a bottle of wine and have a sleepover," he says excitedly.

"Okay," Olive agrees, welcoming the distraction. It seems the only thing she can do lately is daydream about what would never be, reliving the handful of kisses she and Vic shared before the news dropped like a guillotine on their burgeoning romance.

Hours later, with several giant bags over their shoulders, Chris and Olive enter his apartment. Chris flips on the lights. Olive is shocked by the plain neutrality of the living room. It's tastefully decorated in several shades of gray and taupe. Through a large window cut out in the wall, she can see an equally dull kitchen. "Are we in the right place?" she asks with a light chuckle as Chris drops his bags on the couch.

"Of course we are." He crosses the room to open heavy, dark shades, letting in the sunlight. "This is Tyler." He gestures to the cold, modern décor. Then, gathering his bags, he leads her down the hallway. Pushing open the first door on the right, he steps aside to let her in. "*This* is me." He flips on the light. Olive is assaulted by every color imaginable. Sequined starlets in gilded frames smile down at her. Quirky cross stitches, small tapestries, plaster animal heads, pinups, and several small oil paintings adorn the walls. Strings of crystals and gems hang from the ceiling light. The space is otherwise tidy with a dress form in one corner and a sewing machine and serger set up on a worktable. Several glittering gowns hang in the open closet.

"This makes more sense," Olive teases. "I really had thought we were in the wrong apartment for a minute there."

"Oh, stop. Tyler is far more serious than me. He pays all the bills so he gets to decorate." Chris shrugs and dumps his newfound treasures on the pink futon by the door. "I get to do whatever I want in here."

Olive sets down her bags and crosses the room to examine the dresses in the closet. "These are beautiful."

"Thank you. I do costume work for some of the local queens. It's good money, but the demand isn't too high in these parts, if you know what I mean."

Olive lifts her brow. "I don't," she says, stroking the purple silk of one of the gowns.

"We've got about a dozen in the area that can afford to commission work, and like three venues for them to perform in." He stops looking through his newfound treasures and gazes at the open closet. "Tyler says I should start a website or something. Try to tap into the Chicago market."

Olive pulls the purple gown out and holds it against her chest in the mirror on the wall. "You should. This is beautiful." She examines the seams and the shape of the garment. "Your work is impeccable. I know my way around a machine, and this, this is art," she says, hanging up the purple gown and pulling out a bright orange and pink one. "I wish I could afford to hire you." She hangs up the orange dress and continues to admire each lovely gown.

"Oh stop," Chris gushes. "You don't have to hire me. I told you, I'm here to help."

"These are amazing. You must have hours in each one."

He smirks and crosses the room. "I do. I won't even say how many I have in this one." He swings the closet door closed. Hanging on the back is a tuxedo made of lustrous black satin with glittering silver and gold piping. Its buttons shine like mirrors.

Olive reaches out to stroke the shining silver braid on the lapel. "This is amazing."

"Thank you. I'm super proud. The costume budget made all the difference. It wouldn't look this good made from thrift store finds."

"Where did you learn to sew like this?"

"My mom wanted a girl." He laughs. "Also two years at the Art Institute of Chicago." He takes the pants from the hanger and pulls them apart quickly. "Check it out. The pants are tear away and I made the bow tie and thong to match."

"You're amazing," she says with breathless appreciation, still admiring the fine details of the suit.

"I'm okay." He shakes his head and hangs the suit back on its hook. Olive notices the subtle blush on his freckled cheeks. "Now. Let's see what you've got."

It isn't long before Olive is standing in the middle of Chris's craft room while he's holding shimmering pale green organza in place on her rib cage with one hand, and pinning with the other. She admires the look of total concentration on his face. He's barely said a word since he started pinning. “I really appreciate your help,” she says.

“It’s no problem. You’ve got a shape for dressing, and this is such a simple design,” he says through the pins held in his teeth. “You *have* to share a bottle of wine with me later. I won’t take no for an answer.”

“I don’t really drink,” Olive confesses, remembering the handful of times she let alcohol take away her pain. She’d never felt so sick. Then again, she was drinking her dad’s whiskey that she found on the boat. She’d been so young then. “I suppose one glass won’t hurt though.”

Chris looks up with a wide smile. “That’s what I want to hear,” he says brightly, stepping back to admire her in the pinned-together gown. “This color was made for you.”

She turns to see her reflection. The dress isn’t much more than several yards of fabric pinned and tied in place. She does love the color against her skin. “This is going to be perfect,” she sighs.

“It is,” Chris agrees. “Now shimmy out of it so we can finish it.” He motions for her to lift her arms and tugs gently at the dress, careful not to poke her with any pins. He lays it out on his table and hands her a brightly colored robe. “Here, put this on. Let’s go get that wine.”

***

Vic sits alone in the brightly colored waiting room. Women and nurses eye him curiously. He checks his phone. Emily is late. She said ten o clock sharp, he’s been sitting here since nine forty-five. He smiles awkwardly as a young woman sits beside him with a newborn in a car seat.

The tiny baby sleeps soundly in its carrier. Its little hand rests on its chest. Its plump lower lip hangs slack. The young mother smiles at the baby then at Vic, her expression full of love for the little one.

“How old?” he asks quietly.

“He’s six weeks today,” she says proudly.

“Congratulations,” he offers before turning his attention back to his phone, peeking at the sleeping baby from time to time, watching the door for Emily. He allows himself to imagine what it will be like to look down at a tiny version of himself. Will the child have his hair or hers? Their eyes will be blue for sure. He imagines a little girl with golden curls and large blue eyes. His heart skips a joyful beat at the thought of her smiling face turned up to his, tiny feet standing on his while her hands hold on to his fingers and they dance. For the first time since he heard the news, he's happy for it, excited even.

Sure, he'd never imagined Emily as the mother of his children. Never imagined children in his future. She *is* lovely and a generous lover. Men have killed and died for lesser women. Given time, their mutual attraction could grow into something more. Maybe even love. Vic peeks at the sleeping baby again. The absolute dread he'd felt for days dissolves into something much more pleasant.

Then Olive's picture is there on his phone. His heart aches for what would never be. Facebook tells him she's someone he may know. She's half smiling, half snarling. A curious choice for a profile picture. But everything about her was curious. Floating up and down the Mississippi on a houseboat, riding her bike everywhere. Joining a burlesque troupe on a whim. As much as he longed to know her better, to connect and understand her curious ways, there was nothing to tie her here. She could be gone the next day if she chose to leave. Knowing that, why does he continue to entertain his fantasies about her?

Another glance at the little bundle sleeping beside him. Amanda always says the universe has a way of making things happen. Maybe the universe wants him to be the dad he never had. He swipes Olive off his screen and checks the time. Ten after. *Where is Emily?* As if on cue she pushes through the door beside the nurse's window. Her pale cheeks are flushed, she's wearing a loose sundress, her thick, shining hair lays smoothly on her shoulders. She smiles.

"I thought you stood me up," she says, crossing the room to him. He stands to meet her, and she's in his arms, pressing her soft frame against his.

"I was thinking the same thing. Been here since a quarter-till."

"You were late."

"You said ten o'clock sharp." She steps back and looks up, shaking her head.

"Nope, nine thirty." She chuckles and steps away. "Let's get out of here."

"Is everything all right? What did I miss? What did they say?" He follows her out into the warm sunshine.

"Everything is fine. It's still too early, no heartbeat yet," she says over her shoulder. "They said I'm healthy as long as I quit smoking." She pulls a cigarette from her purse and lights it. Vic's cheeks blaze, he fights the urge to snatch the burning cigarette from her lips.

"And?" He makes no attempt to hide his irritation. She rolls her eyes, inhaling deeply.

"They say it can cause more stress for the baby for me to quit cold turkey. I'm going to wean myself off, slowly."

"This is weaning?" he asks angrily.

"Yes," she says, stopping beside her car. "I smoke a pack a day, sometimes more. It's going to be a process. Don't think because I'm carrying your baby that you can tell me what to do."

"I thought you might be a bit more concerned with the well-being of *our* baby," he responds quickly.

"Fine," she scoffs, tossing the cigarette away and opening her door. "I won't buy any more once this pack is gone." Her face softens as she steps closer to him. "Thanks for coming today. I really didn't expect to see you. It means a lot."

"Hey, I'm here for this." He rests his hand on her shoulder and squeezes. "It's unexpected, but I'm here for you, for the baby. We're going to make it work." She smiles and bats her lashes, then steps closer, wrapping her arms around his waist.

"That means a lot, Vicky." She steps away and sits in her car. "I work this afternoon. Maybe I'll swing by after. We can have a late dinner." She pulls the door shut and rolls the window down. "I'll call you when I'm off." She smiles and backs out of her spot. Vic watches as she pulls away, slipping on dark sunglasses. He walks to his car and sees her at the intersection, lighting another cigarette.

***

"You know what we should do?" Olive asks from behind her wineglass, swirling the clear, pale liquid with a smile. Chris sits across from her, his feet resting on the railing of the porch. The sun sets on the trees in the courtyard, casting stark shadows with golden light. Her cheeks are warm and her head floats on a joyful cloud of abandon. It feels nothing like the heaviness of whiskey, no broken tears and heaving sobs. She feels light and playful.

"What should we do?" Chris asks, pouring himself another glass.

"Let's get dressed up in our finest thrift store finds and go to the Speakeasy. Marty and James are both doing sets for the open mic. We should go support them."

"You had me at dressed up," Chris says, standing with his glass and bottle in hand. "Let's go."

Laughter fills the air of the Speakeasy. Olive and Chris were happy to find Bunny had the same idea. She and Mike welcomed them to join their table. At the back of a packed house, they watch and laugh with the crowd. Olive sips the Moscato Chris bought her. It's far sweeter than the wine they shared at his place, but delicious nonetheless. The dark room is hazy and joyful as she enjoys her new friends. Bunny and Mike sit as close as a pair can sit on barstools, their contact never breaking. Bunny's hand on Mike's knee, Mike's on Bunny's shoulder. They whisper and laugh as if they're the only two in the room full of people. Chris grins in his brightly colored printed blazer with his low-cut vee-neck t-shirt revealing the sprinkle of freckles and light hair over his chest. She looks down at her skintight, bright green tank dress and blushes. It was an impulse buy, strongly encouraged by Chris, who decked her out in more jingling bangles and dangling necklaces than she's ever worn. He'd scoffed at her black flip-flops and made her promise to shop for shoes next time they went out. She stands to go to the restroom, tugging at the bottom of her dress. The room spins suddenly. She catches herself on the back of her chair and waits for the spinning to stop.

"You okay?" Bunny asks, standing quickly.

"Yeah." Olive giggles. "I'm fine. Walking, you know. On my feet." She shrugs and steps away from the table, taking slow, measured steps.

"Let's get you some water," Bunny says, following a step behind.

"Yes, water." She shifts her direction from the bathroom to the bar. "Hi, Simone," she calls upon seeing her at the bar. "I like Simone. She's feisty," she says to Bunny, who steps beside her. "Feisty Simone." Olive giggles as she approaches.

"Hey, ladies." Simone smiles, shaking her head. "Got us a lightweight, I see."

"I would like some water, please," Olive says, tugging at the long chain that dangles on her chest. "Thank you," she calls primly as Simone walks to retrieve her water. "Do you think he's here?" she asks Bunny with a loud whisper.

"Who?" Bunny asks.

"Vic. I haven't seen him since…" With a quick intake of breath, she covers her mouth with one hand. "Since I saw him," she says, slowly sidestepping away from Bunny. Simone offers her a plastic cup of icy cold water. She drinks it thirstily, realizing how dry her mouth had become. "Thank you." She leans her weight on the bar.

"Anytime, lush," Simone teases.

"You okay?" Bunny asks.

"I'm fine. I don't drink," Olive responds with an air of confidence. "Typically." She shakes her head. "This wine is delicious." She takes a long drink from her water.

"That's water, dear," Simone says with a wry smile.

"Well, it's the most delicious water I've ever tasted."

"Nothing but the finest from the Rock Island tap for you, milady."

"Why thank you." She takes another big drink of the cool water. It dribbles down her chin. She wipes at it with the back of her hand. "Now, I really have to pee," she says before hurrying away.

Bunny follows her into the bathroom. "How are you getting home?" she asks from the other side of the stall.

Olive sits on the toilet, the dim lights buzzing around her. She focuses on the words scratched into the metal door, then looks down at her bare toes and dirty flip-flops. The room seems to slant and rock like her boat on a windy day. She stands slowly. "Chris and I got an Uber." Her words float out of her mouth.

"You aren't planning on riding your bike then?"

"Nope." She pushes the door open.

Bunny is leaning against the sink. "You sure you're all right?"

"Yeah. I said I don't drink. The wine went right to my head."

"I'm not talking about the wine. What were you saying about Vic? What did he do?" The gentle, pleasant haze from the wine evaporates instantly.

"What do you mean?" Olive asks.

"You said you hadn't seen him since…" Bunny stands to make room for her. "Since what? What happened?"

"Nothing." Olive washes her hands and looks at Bunny in the mirror. "It's him and Emily. I told him I didn't need him walking me home from now on." She shrugs and hopes that Bunny assumes the color in her cheeks is from the wine. "I don't think she likes it much."

"No, I don't imagine she does. So, nothing happened?"

"Not to me," Olive says with a tight smile. "The rest is Vic's business."

"What does that mean?" Bunny asks.

"You can ask him. Like I said, it's not my business." She pushes through the heavy bathroom door.

Back in her seat, she can feel Bunny's gaze on her as she tries to enjoy the rest of the show. Marty takes the stage and has the drunken crowd rolling with his self-deprecating act. He tells one failed dating story after another. Soon, Olive forgets about her awkward exchange with Bunny. She forgets about Vic and Emily. She laughs along with her friends and accepts the offered refill of cool, sweet Moscato.

After Marty's set, he joins their table, sitting next to Olive. "What'd ya think, boss?" he asks Bunny.

"You did good, Marty." Bunny laughs.

"How about you?" Marty turns to Olive, eying the low neckline of her dress.

"You were funny. I liked it," Olive answers, sipping her wine.

"Good. Can I buy you another?" he asks, nodding to her nearly empty drink.

"Sure." She shrugs. James joins their table and the rest of the comics do their sets. Eventually the lights are up and the crowd is gone. Simone joins their small group. The conversations are wide and varied. The wine begins to pull heavily on Olive. She rests her chin on her hand and listens with her eyes closed. The rise and fall of their voices remind her of home. Of the hours she spent listening to adults conversing down the hall, late into the evening.

"Hey, stranger," she hears Mike call out over the lull of voices. She sits up and looks around. Vic's approaching the table.

"Hey, guys. Thought I heard people down here. Little after-hours party?"

"I've been trying to kick them out for a while," Simone jokes. "You know this one, when he doesn't want to move, no one is moving him." She gestures to Mike with his arm around Bunny.

"Oh, I can get him moving," Bunny teases.

"Damn right you can," he agrees, finishing his beer. "Was that an offer?"

"You know it was," Bunny purrs. "Are you all safe for driving?" she asks as she and Mike stand to leave, her gaze lands on Olive specifically.

"I'm good. I'll call an Uber. No bike tonight." Olive shrugs and yawns.

"Okay, good. Love you guys. Great job tonight, you two," she says to Marty and James. Mike follows her to the door, saying his good-byes. James offers Chris a ride home. Simone finishes her closing work. Olive stands, between Marty and Vic.

"I feel like I shut the party down," Vic says, grinning.

"Ah, it was ending anyway. At least for me, that is," Olive says with another yawn and a big stretch. Her bangles jingle down her arms.

***

Vic watches as Olive stretches her arms to the ceiling. Her skintight dress creeps up her thighs as she rocks at her waist. "I need to call for a ride," she says, her voice sleepy. He tries his best not to stare, but her long, lean legs seem to go on forever. The bright green clings to her curves. The tan swell of her cleavage draped with gold chains is beyond enticing. She turns to get her phone. Her dress barely covers her ass as she reaches for her bag. Vic catches Marty watching her.

"I can give you a ride," Marty offers.

Vic clenches his teeth. His hands form fists involuntarily. He imagines pummeling Marty's smug face. Emily was a no-show again. He'd spent the evening waiting on a call that never came. The last thing he wants to do is watch Olive ride away with this slimeball and then spend the rest of the evening imagining what happened. The idea of her alone in a car with him, half drunk and barely covered... He's about to say something when Simone speaks up.

"I can too, Olive. Pretty sure we're going the same way."

Vic breathes a sigh of relief. Olive turns and looks from Marty to Simone, then to him. The alcohol shows ruddy in her cheeks. "Thanks, guys. I appreciate it. I don't even have the app on my phone." She laughs. "I was going to have to download it and set up an account. Super prepared, huh?" More laughter.

"I thought you didn't drink," Vic says softly, watching her as she drinks the last of her wine from a plastic cup.

"I don't," she says, stacking the cup with the other empties from the table and crossing to the trash can. "Not usually. You can blame Chris. He started it."

Marty stands, awkwardly forgotten. He speaks up. "Well, I'm taking off if you want to ride with me," he offers. Vic shoots him a look that says back off.

"I think I'm going to help Simone clean up. You go. I'll see you Monday. Good job tonight."

"Yeah. Thanks." Marty looks crestfallen. Vic stands with his arms crossed over his chest, glaring. Olive shuffles, dragging the garbage can to the table. Simone counts the cash from the drawer. "See ya," he says to no one in particular before leaving alone.

"Glad you didn't go with him," Vic says, helping her clear the table.

"What does it matter to you?" she asks.

"It matters plenty. That guy's a creep. I can throw him farther than I trust him."

"Yeah?" she challenges.

"Especially with you dressed like that."

"What's wrong with the way I'm dressed?" She spreads her arms wide and looks down at her body. "I look good." She smiles. "Right, Simone?"

"You look fly as hell, girl," Simone calls from the bar. "In fact, Vic should be more worried about me taking you home." Blush rises to Olive's cheeks instantly, her expression one of amused shock. Vic smiles at her innocence.

"Watch yourself, Simone," he says with a playful tone.

"Shit." She approaches with a bank bag, slapping it against his chest. "You don't scare me. I beat you every time."

He takes the bag. "Only because I let you win."

"You don't let me win shit. I'm better, plain and simple."

"We haven't boxed for years," Vic says, relaxing.

"Yeah, because you don't like losing." Simone laughs wildly. "Come on, Olive. You'll be safe with me. I promise." Simone gives him a knowing smile.

"Okay. I appreciate it." She reaches for her bag again. Vic steals a glimpse at her thighs as her dress creeps recklessly high. "See ya, Vic," she calls with a wine-soaked smile that seems to have forgotten their kisses and his broken promise.

"See ya, girls," he calls as they leave through the front door. The relief he feels knowing she's with Simone is stronger than it should be. It shouldn't matter to him who she leaves with. If she had left with Marty, though, there's no way he would sleep.

Chapter 14

"Are you ready?" Chris asks, pulling a garment bag out of his trunk.

Olive stands in front of the Speakeasy with Susan, waiting for Bunny to arrive. Her weekend had been uneventful. Aside from the massive headache on Saturday morning reminding her why she didn't drink, not much had happened. Work had been slow. Vic made an appearance and they chatted comfortably enough. As Chris unzips the bag, revealing her gown, she feels guilty for having spent her Sunday doing little more than swing in her hammock. The gown spills out of the bag shimmering and fine. "I can't believe you finished it already," she says, touching it gingerly.

"It was easy. Honestly, like two seams and a hemline." He pulls it from its hanger and hands it to her. "I may have added some embellishments here and there. It was a super-simple design otherwise."

Olive holds the finished dress to her chest. The embellishments he's referring to are hundreds of hand-sewn sequins gathered in a bunch at the neckline then sprinkling throughout the gown. "Some embellishments?" Olive asks, running her hands over a mass of sparkling disks. "There must be hundreds." She's in awe.

"Well." Chris shrugs. "Tyler watches the most boring documentaries on the weekends. It's the only way I can stay awake with him. I can't wait to see it on you."

"Me either," Olive squeals. "Thank you so much, Chris. I can't even begin to tell you what this means to me."

"Stop. It was fun. You're like my own personal Barbie doll."

"Yeah right." Olive snorts a laugh and admires her reflection in the window with the dress held to her chest. "I can't wait to dance in this."

Inside, Olive looks at herself in the mirror. The dress is far more than two seams and a hemline. It fits her like a dream, ruched at her waist with a slit up to her hip. Cascades of emerald green sequins in varying sizes sparkle like bursts of fairy dust. Instead of a halter, the thin spaghetti straps are secured with snap buttons that release with a gentle tug. The ruching hides another series of quick-release snaps so that the entire garment can be torn off effortlessly. She pushes through the heavy bathroom door, beaming. "Chris this is perfection," she calls, without looking first.

She's met by a commotion of congratulations and cheers. Vic and Emily are standing near the stage. He's wearing a ridiculous grin, with his arm resting on Emily's shoulders. Her hand is over her stomach protectively. "What'd I miss?" Olive asks, knowing the answer.

"We've announced our baby," Emily says with a large false smile. "Like I said, before Olive interrupted, we'd like to keep it secret, until after the show. But we knew we couldn't keep it from you guys. We're family after all," she says, turning her attention back to the group.

Olive stands, with bare feet on the sticky carpet, looking down at her gown. Knowing about the pregnancy and seeing them announce it together are quite different. As long as it was secret, she could pretend on some level, it wasn't true. Watching Emily be swarmed by the eager group asking all the standard questions about duc dates and doctor's appointments left her feeling small and foolish. Despite the pain, she steals a glimpse at Vic. He's looking at her, void of expression. Then he offers a sad smile. Olive smiles back, emotions welling as she thinks of all that will never be. Emily notices and jabs Vic in the ribs. He looks down at her and gives her a squeeze as the group closes in on the happy couple.

Olive feels awkward, standing alone behind the group. She doesn't know what to do. Does she change back into her street clothes? Does she stay in the gown until practice officially starts? As much as she would love to run through her routine with her full costume, she feels downright silly in the gown. Not to mention painfully exposed. As beautiful as the gown is, it does little to hide her bare breasts and panties from the world.

Chris breaks away from the crowd and walks her way. "Talk about a surprise," he whispers.

"Yeah," Olive attempts to sound disinterested.

"You look like an absolute dream," he says, pulling and adjusting her straps. Sequins, expertly placed, settle over her nipples, like pasties. "Now it's perfect."

"I honestly don't know how you did this so quickly."

"Idle hands." He laughs and wiggles his fingers in the air. "Now turn around, I want to see the back." Olive twirls, the hem of the dress floating above the floor.

***

Goddamn she's perfect. Vic watches as Chris fawns over Olive in the sheer gown, made to display her shape beautifully. It's some sort of gossamer magic, clinging and floating in tandem. The fit is nothing short of miraculous. She smiles as Chris spins her in circles. Amanda is watching from her chair. She didn't rise to congratulate him and Emily along with the rest. She sits and watches and says nothing. Emily pays her no mind. She stands among the others, drinking up the attention. Vic gives Emily's shoulder a squeeze and excuses himself from the group.

Moments later Amanda pushes through the door without knocking. "So, that's it?" she says, closing the door behind her.

"What?" he fires back.

"That's what's been going on with Olive?"

"No," he says with a hint of anger. "It's what's been going on with *Emily*. Nothing has been going on with Olive."

"You know what I mean." Amanda moves across the small office and drops herself onto the couch.

"If you're asking if Emily's pregnancy is why I stopped walking Olive home, the answer is yes." They sit in silence. Amanda looks like she has something to say. "And if you're here to throw shade or accusations, I can stop you right there." He pulls the positive test out of his desk drawer and tosses it beside her. She looks at it with disdain. "For Christ's sake, it's fucking clean. It's been in my desk for days."

"That's positive," she says without picking it up. Then leans forward, resting her elbows on her knees. "Are you?"

"Yep. We've already been to the doctor."

"So, what's your plan?" she asks.

"I don't know. Take it one day at a time, I guess. She's got a lot of great qualities. I know folks don't trust her. Maybe that's part of the problem. I want to give her the benefit of the doubt. I've got to make it work. You and I both know what having a shitty father can do to a kid. I'll be damned if I let it happen to mine."

"Yeah." Amanda breathes deep, staring at her feet. They sit together in the awkward silence that exists around hard truths. "What about Olive?"

Vic leans back in his chair. "I think she'll be all right. What did we have? A few moonlit bike rides? A couple of kisses? Kid's stuff." He shakes his head. What he felt, or was beginning to feel, for Olive was far beyond kid's stuff. He had fallen for her hard. Harder than he ever thought he could fall. But in light of Emily's pregnancy, it has to be over. If there had been a choice to be made, the universe went ahead and made it. Olive was not the one for him. "I'm going to do whatever I have to do to make sure my kid has a happy life. If that means no Olive, I'll have to live with that. My primary focus from here on is making Emily happy, and being a good dad to my kid."

"I suppose." Amanda watches him for a moment then stands. "Well, congratulations." She leans in and wraps him in her arms. Her voice is anything but congratulatory. It's laced with sad acceptance. Or pity. Probably both.

"You know, I'm surprised to say it. I'm actually kind of excited."

"That's good to hear." She lets him go and smiles a genuine smile before leaving. Vic sits in his office, staring vacantly at two blue lines that now define his future.

"God, she's such an attention whore," Emily says loudly, pushing through the door that Amanda had left open. She plops herself on the couch.

"Amanda?" Vic asks, shocked.

"No. Your little girlfriend. Didn't you see her out there parading around practically naked in that fucking dress?"

"You're a burlesque dancer. Seems to me you should be used to naked women by now."

She huffs and crosses her arms over her chest, slouching back into the cushions. "I should've known you'd defend her. You and Bunny have your heads so far up her ass you can't see straight." She shakes her head and bites her cheek.

"I'm not defending her. I don't see what the big deal is, though. She was trying on her costume. Don't you all run around topless out there?"

Emily relaxes with a sigh. "You're right. I still don't like you looking at her. I guess maybe I'm a little jealous," she says, looking down at her hands in her lap. "Eww, Vicky. Why is this still lying around?" She plucks the pregnancy test from the couch and tosses it in the trash. "Are you getting sentimental on me?" she asks, standing and wrapping her arms around his neck.

Lowering herself into his lap, she kisses his face. Planting her luscious lips on his cheeks, ears, and neck. Working her fingers into his hair.

***

Emily beams from the stage. "I'm so glad this corset still fits." She runs her hand over her flattened stomach in front of the standing mirror. "It took so long for it to get here." She admires her reflection then turns to the group. "Good thing the show's only a week away. I don't know how much longer I'll be able to squeeze into this." She looks to the sound booth. "Ready when you are, Marty," she calls before stepping backstage. Drumbeats lead into heavy guitar. Emily reappears through the curtains. She moves with smooth grace in her tall, high-heeled, black leather boots. Though the song is fast-paced she's slow, sensual, practically making love to herself in the mirror. She is the definition of pride and arrogance, perfectly suited for the role. After four minutes of garish self-love, Emily steps down the stairs among cheers and applause, cupping her bare breasts in her hands. "I wonder if these will ever stop aching," she laments as she takes a seat next to Bunny, still cupping her bare breasts.

"If I have to hear one more word about her being pregnant, I'm going to scream," Chris says under his breath, leaning in close.

"I know what you mean," Olive agrees, forcing a smile.

"You know, I was surprised when they made their announcement. I thought for sure that you and Vic were becoming a thing."

"Why would you think that? He and Emily have been together since I met him."

"Oh, come on," he scoffs. "He was walking you home every night after practice. He gave you a job. And that one night after the open mic? He looked like he wanted to strangle Marty for even offering you a ride."

Olive responds, holding a finger up as she counters each one of Chris's points supporting her involvement with Vic. "He wanted to know I was safe. He needed a cocktail server. I have experience and needed a job. I can't say I would've been thrilled to ride home with Marty that night, and I guess Vic knew it."

"How do you explain him showing up every time your song starts?"

"What?" she asks, feeling the color rise in her cheeks. "He does that?"

"Not every time. It happens often though. He'll wander out of his office to talk to Bunny or check something at the bar. I've seen him open and close that empty register more times than I can count. He's watching you the whole time."

"You're serious?" Olive says, feeling a warm glow around her. "I haven't noticed."

"That's because he's gone before you come off stage. I think Emily must've said something. She cut him off in the hall last week. He hasn't done it since." Chris shrugs. "Poor guy." He shakes his head.

"Poor guy? He knows where babies come from," Olive snaps.

"Hm." Chris watches her for a long pause then clicks his tongue. "You're right," he says, shaking his head. "Reap what you sow, I suppose."

"Yep. I'm sure you're imagining all that about him coming out when my song plays. He and Emily seem happy together."

"I don't know about that. I think he seems sad," Chris says as Susan takes her place on stage. Marty mistakenly plays Olive's song. Before he has time to turn it off, Vic appears in the hallway. He sees Olive sitting and looks confused then hurries to Bunny's table. "I told you," Chris says with a knowing grin.

Olive watches from her seat as Vic sits beside Emily, who's relaxing with her bare breasts on display. He's grinning broadly and talking excitedly. Then he settles back, draping an arm over Emily's shoulder. She leans in, whispering something in his ear. Bunny smiles and stands. "Hey, folks, listen up. Vic brought us some great news. We're sold out for all four nights." The room erupts with cheers and whistles.

Olive joins the group in the celebration before the reality settles in. Four sold-out nights. Instead of dancing for a handful of friends and fellow performers, she'll be dancing in front of hundreds of people. Her stomach churns. She looks around the room and doesn't see a single concerned face. Even Susan, standing in her costume on stage, waiting for her song, comes down to celebrate.

"I knew ticket sales were good. I didn't expect us to sell out all four nights," Chris says to Olive. "This is amazing."

"It is. Aren't you nervous?" she asks.

"Not really." He shrugs. "I'm excited. Can't believe next Friday is opening night. Seems like yesterday that we were auditioning. Where did the months go?"

"Time flies when you're having fun, right?" Olive responds halfheartedly. She looks around the room, watching as the troupe talks excitedly. Everyone except for Vic. He's sitting across the room, his arm resting on Emily's bare shoulder as she chats with Bunny, paying him no mind. His gaze is on Olive; a sad smile touches his lips as their eyes meet. The sound of the room falls away. For the moment, they are the only two there. She remembers his words from that night. When he told her how he felt and promised to make it right, how his lips felt against hers. He looks away and the spell is broken.

"I saw that," Chris says, leaning close. Olive turns to face him, sure that her ears are burning red.

"Saw what?" she asks, flipping her hair over her shoulder and turning away from Vic completely. "Do you know how to make pasties?" she asks quickly.

"Yeah. You don't have yours yet?"

"I thought I could buy them. Turns out that's not the case."

"Oh Olive, my sweet summer child. What am I going to do with you?" Chris asks, shaking his head.

"You're going to teach me how to make pasties this weekend."

"Sure." He shrugs. "We'll make a day out of it. And maybe you'll tell me what's really going on with you and Vicky over there."

"It's nothing," she says with solemn conviction.

“You keep telling yourself that,” he says, shaking his head. “But you might want to let him know too.” He nods toward Vic walking back to his office. “He was staring a hole through you the whole time he was out here.”

“You’re imagining things.”

“I suppose Emily is too,” he whispers.

She can feel Emily’s cold stare on her back.

***

There is that haunting music again. Vic moves quickly through the door and down the hall. Weeks ago, he had stumbled into practice while Olive danced on stage. It had been by chance the first night, intentional every one after that. She moved across the stage with a wild grace that could only be described as magic. Her long fluid steps on bare pointed toes, spinning and twirling with emerald green feather fans fluttering around her. She was like a dream floating on the gentle melody of her song. The lyrics like a spell. He had found himself stuck on heavy feet, unable to move, his jaw slack, his head in a daze. It wasn’t until he felt Emily’s elbow in his rib cage that he realized he was staring the way he was. It had taken hours of coddling that night for Emily to forgive him.

He’d learned to be more careful about watching Olive after that. Though he’d chosen to be with Emily and to do whatever it would take to make her and their baby happy, it didn’t mean he couldn’t watch a beautiful woman dance an enchanting dance from time to time. There was no harm in it.

He follows the music and sees Olive is sitting with Chris. Susan’s on stage. Vic does his best to mask his surprise and continues to Amanda’s table, where Emily sits with her full pale breasts exposed above a black leather under-bust corset. Her hair, almost as black as the corset, is roughed and tousled. Her full lips glisten with clear gloss. *There are worse situations to have to make the best of,* he thinks to himself as he takes the seat beside her. He smells her sweet vanilla smell, makes note of the cigarette smoke with some irritation. Brushing it off, he leans in. “Ask me how many tickets are available for opening weekend,” he says to Amanda and Emily.

Amanda grins. “How many?”

"None. Now, ask about the second weekend."

"Are you serious?" Amanda says with a rolling giggle.

"I am."

"That's awesome," Emily coos. Vic leans back, wrapping an arm around her shoulder, stroking her silky skin.

"It is, isn't it? Maybe we should schedule a third weekend."

"That would be amazing. But it wouldn't work. Bridgette and Calvin both have shows later in the month."

"We'll have to keep it in mind for the next show. I wonder if we could run a full month?"

"It would be incredible if we could," Amanda agrees, before standing for her announcement.

Emily leans in close. Her sticky lips brush his earlobe. "We should celebrate later," she says, her hand running up his thigh. "It seems like it's been forever since I visited."

"It does," Vic agrees, the familiar tremor of arousal rising from where her hand rests on his upper thigh.

"I'll come back when we're done here." She nips his ear with her teeth before shifting her attention back to Amanda.

Vic sits, his neck and ear cold where she left her trail of kisses. Directly in front of him is Olive, chatting comfortably with Chris, her face alight with pure joy, then worry and concern. He can't hear what she's saying, but all of it's obvious by the look of her face. Delight makes way for trepidation as she realizes what a sold-out show means for her. Vic smiles at her innocence. She's not the one for him. A lovely dream for another lifetime. She glances his way. For a moment he's living in that imaginary lifetime where she's his and he's hers and there is no one else. The soft, warm skin under his hand is a reminder and tether pulling him back to earth. In this life it's Emily and their baby.

"Hey, come find me when you're done," he says to Emily, giving her shoulder a squeeze. "Let's order in and watch a movie or something."

"Okay, I shouldn't be much longer."

"Good." Vic's feeling emotional. Though he wouldn't have considered a life with Emily in the past, the idea of his child growing in her belly changes all of it. She's softer than people know, kinder too. Over the weeks he's seen a gentler side. One that he can imagine a life with. If only she would open up, let him in. They might have something beautiful. If she would make herself available. It seems, however, her time is even tighter than it had been. Getting her to visit or spend the night is more difficult than before. He's read plenty about pregnancy in recent weeks and learned that it can be an incredibly emotional time. He hopes that she's merely sorting out her emotions and will eventually open up and let him in. Despite his attraction to Olive, he wants to make Emily happy. He wants to embrace their burgeoning family and everything that comes with it.

Emily gives him a puzzled look. "Are you okay, Vicky?" she asks slowly.

"Yeah. Yeah, I'm fine. Looking forward to spending some time with you is all."

"Good." She chuckles. "I'll see you later."

***

"She's gone again, isn't she?" Vic says to Amanda, who's packing up after practice. The Speakeasy is quiet, empty save for Amanda and Vic.

"Everyone's gone. Emily left early. I thought she was with you."

"Nope." Vic shakes his head. Amanda drops her bag on the table.

"I'm sorry. You want some company? Mike's out at his parents' place. I'm going home to an empty apartment. We could get a drink or something." She shrugs.

He sighs and smiles. "No. I think I'm going to go for a run. Maybe she'll get ahold of me later. She keeps weird hours, you know?"

"Yeah she does." Amanda hefts her bag back onto her shoulder. "Come here. Give me a hug." He steps into her open arms. For a brief moment, there's a shudder in his chest. A painful weight that threatens to turn into tears if he stands still for too long. Vic sighs and steps out of her embrace.

"Thanks. I'm really hoping she comes around and lets me take care of her. I keep telling myself she must be afraid of losing her independence, and that's why it seems like she's pushing me away."

"I'm sure you two will work it out. If you need to talk, Mike and I are only a phone call away."

"I know. Thanks. See you later." He leaves through the front door.

The night is cool and crisp. Though summer is holding on under the sun, fall creeps into the evening hours. He zips his hoodie and starts his all-too-familiar route. Along the river, on the bike path, to the marina. To watch the yellow light glowing from a tiny window on a boat. To hear the music play.

Chapter 15

"Are you all ready for this?" Susan asks. Olive stands with her and the others outside of the Speakeasy. They wait in the unseasonably warm sunshine for Bunny to arrive and open the doors for dress rehearsal.

"I can't wait." Chris claps his hands. "Seriously can't believe it's already here."

"I can't either," Olive says. "Where did summer go?"

"I'd say you discovered Moscato." Chris laughs.

"Whatever. Who's been feeding it to me?" Olive asks and lightly elbows him in the ribs.

"I'm pretty sure you'd manage without me."

"I'm a little disappointed I haven't been invited to one of your wine nights," Susan interjects with a playful lilt.

"Oh Susan, Dame Monroe," Chris says with a grand flourish. "I can't think of anything I would love more than to include you in our wine nights. They always happen spontaneously. I will be sure to call you next time."

"Well, I've got a hell of a wine cellar. I would love to share it with you all."

"That would be amazing." Chris beams. "I bet you have the most beautiful house."

"I enjoy it." Susan smiles. "I'd love to have you all. In fact, we should have a wine night at my house after the show, everyone," Susan says, looking around the group of performers. "It would be lovely to have you come by. I mean it. My house is empty as fuck these days. I would love to fill it with you wonderful people."

Olive smiles brightly at Susan and Chris. They have become the best part of her life over her months in Rock Island. Susan reminds her of her mom in a way, and Chris is like no one she's ever known. Olive finds herself moved almost to tears at the thought of how they've affected her life. As she looks around the group of new friends gathered in the alcove of the Speakeasy display window, she dabs at her eyes. Except for one person, she's felt an acceptance she hasn't known since childhood. Bunny is wonderfully kind. Chris is pure sunshine. Susan is full of knowledge and grace. Julie is sweetness defined. Marty and James are always entertaining. And Vic… Though he's not there at the moment, he's been the most prominent in her mind. She can't shake him. No matter how hard she tries. He's there in her thoughts every night, his lips on hers, his hand on her cheek. She dreams of all that will never be.

As they chat and reminisce about the months they've been working together on the show, Bunny, Calvin, Bridgette, Cin, and Dave the magician round the corner laughing and carrying on. Aside from Bunny, Olive hasn't seen any of them since auditions. She's forgotten how intimidating they all seem together. Their confidence draws attention from anyone passing by, not to mention their glamorous beauty.

"Are you guys excited?" Bunny calls as they cross the street. She's met with collective cheers and whistles. "Looks like we're only missing one," she says as she approaches.

"Big surprise," Cin says with a look of disdain.

"Oh stop," Bunny says. "Look, there's her car." She points down the road and steps up to unlock the door.

"I can't wait to see this. Bunny can't say enough about how great you all are." Cin smiles as she moves through the group, hugging each person. Calvin and Bridgette do the same. Though they've been elsewhere throughout the production process, they've been available online for support since the beginning, forming friendships remotely.

Once inside, they start unpacking their sparkling costumes across many tables. Bunny speaks from the front of the room. "We've got to mix up the lineup tonight for Dave. He's got somewhere to be later so he'll be doing his bit first. I'm so excited to see it. After that we'll take it from the top. Starting with the opening. Olive, Susan, and Chris, I want you in costume. We've got to make sure you have time to get changed for your individuals. It'll be a rush for you, Susan, but I'm pretty sure with Marty and James's opening, Emily's routine, and their bit after that should give you enough time. If not, they'll have to stall for you. The lineup is Little Devils, Emily, Susan, Olive, intermission. Then Dave, Chris, me, Calvin, and Bridgette. You all ready?"

The group sounds their readiness. "Stage is yours, Dave. John is running late, Marty. Could you take care of sound 'til he gets here? Should be any minute."

The houselights go down. Violins pierce the air. Dave enters through the curtains with a pointed moustache and goatee in a tuxedo with tails. He does tricks with fire and smoke, flowers and handkerchiefs. He makes playing cards float. Then pulls a rolling cart from backstage with a large box and a birdcage on top. He fills the cage with black doves that he pulls from his coat. Once there are six doves in the cage, he lifts it off the cart and lowers it into the ominous-looking black and gold box. Draping the box with a black sheet, he waves his hands over it several time and slams his hand down. The sheet goes flat: the box, the doves, the cage are all gone. Waving his hands once more over the flattened sheet, he lifts it from the cart to reveal a black bunny with shining eyes and a wiggling nose. He hugs it to his chest and bows as his music fades. Olive cheers along with the rest of the room. He bows and thanks them, rolling his cart backstage and appearing moments later with the doves in their cage and the bunny still tucked under his arm. "I'll see you all tomorrow. Break all the legs," he says as he heads out the front door.

"That was epic," Olive says to no one in particular. Bunny follows Dave out the door in her little devil costume.

"Get ready, guys," she calls over her shoulder. "We'll start as soon as I'm back."

Olive moves her costume pieces to the backstage area. It's a tight fit. As she hangs her gown and fans on the garment rack, she catches her reflection in Emily's standing mirror. The woman looking back at her is a stranger. Her hair is gathered on the top of her head in a messy bun. Sparkling devil horns rise up out of the tousled mess. Her satin corset squeezes her waist to an unbelievably small size. A pointed tail dangles from her short red tutu. Fishnet tights and high heels finish the look. Susan follows in the same costume. Chris is next, decked out in his own variation of the look: hot pants, vest, bowtie, fishnets, and dance flats.

"Looks like we made it," Susan says, reaching for their dainty, glittering pitchforks and handing one to each of them.

"Looks like," Olive agrees.

Bunny pushes through the curtains. “You ready?” she asks, taking her own pitchfork. They see the houselights go down through the curtain. The stage lights come up and the music starts. First the strings then on the beginning horn note they prance onto the stage. After months of practice, the routine is second nature to Olive. She moves through the fast-paced steps with ease. The small group cheers from darkness beyond the stage lights. The song ends as quickly as it began. Olive’s heart races as she runs off stage to hurry into her costume. Julie is there to set the stage for Emily’s routine. She drags the mirror out through the curtain as Marty and James begin their introductions. Emily is there, preening in one of the mirrors on the wall. She’s decked out in her black leather, looking somehow voluptuous and sleek. Olive wonders when she will start showing her pregnancy as she avoids eye contact. She helps Susan out of one costume and into another as Emily stands at the curtain for her big entrance.

Olive hears Marty’s and James’s voices. Then Emily’s music starts. She realizes what little time she has to change into her own costume. She rushes to the mirror, removing her horns and corset, then kicking out of her shoes and peeling off her tights. She’s completely bare when Emily comes back from her routine. Their eyes meet in the mirror, Olive’s wide with nerves, Emily’s full of disdain. She sneers and says nothing as she passes through to the back door and exits the dressing room.

“Don’t mind her. She’s a harpy,” Susan says as she waits for her cue.

“I try not to.” Olive shrugs and shakes her head as she pulls her sparkling green thong into place.

“Let me know if you need anything,” Julie says as she pushes the standing mirror against the back wall, dropping Emily’s bra and gloves on the vanity table.

“Thanks.” Olive smiles, snapping her gown in place. She lets her hair down and shakes it loose.

“Here goes nothing.” Susan grins and pushes the curtains aside to the sound of the gentle rhythmic tones of her soothing song choice. It’s a beautiful trance-like melody with bells, chimes, and soft chanting.

Olive peeks through the curtain. There’s a voyeuristic feel to watching this way. Though she’s seen the routine dozens of times, it's never been from behind the scenes. She's taken back to many years ago during a party at her family's spring equinox celebration. The adults would herd the children into the house before dusk, stating that the fairies were known to steal children away after dark on the eve of Beltane. For years she behaved and stayed in the house, wondering what life would be like with the fairies, until the year when she and Sky, the oldest, decided they were too grown for the kiddie games and nonsense. They waited until the little ones slept and snuck out of the house to the garden, hiding themselves behind trees and bushes.

What they saw was shocking and exciting. The adults danced naked around the raging bonfire. The red and orange light cast haunting shadows on the darkened grass. Though most only danced and frolicked, many lay on blankets in the light of the flames. Some blankets held couples lost in love's embrace. Others had several people all tangled in passionate puddles. It was hard for Olive's pubescent mind to fully understand what was happening.

Nudity had been a constant in her life. She bathed with her mother often and saw her dad nude without thought. He would pass through the hall on his way to the bathroom or dive into the pond bare as the day he was born. The human body was no source of shame. Though sex and nudity weren't exclusive, what she saw that night with her lifelong friend felt dirty and thrilling.

They watched for a long while before running back to the house as quickly and silently as possible. As they lay panting on the porch, watching the stars and catching their breath, their laughter rose into the starry night sky. It wasn't long before they were kissing and petting. Then awkwardly attempting to mimic what they had seen. It ended rather innocently with more laughter as they realized their bodies didn't quite work that way yet.

As the years passed, they would sneak away from the little children and play their adult games under the stars. Until Sky realized his arousal had more to do with the men sharing blankets than Olive's feminine frame.

Applause emerges from the darkness and Susan brushes past in pasties and panties. Olive shakes the memories from her mind. "That was amazing, Susan."

Susan grins at her and laughs a hearty laugh. "It felt amazing. You ready?"

"As I'll ever be."

***

Vic sits beside Emily, watching as Susan moves through a series of impressive yoga poses. She's added sultry choreography and floor work, which makes him simultaneously sleepy and aroused. Her rendition of sloth is perfect. Emily had been unsurprisingly perfect during her routine, letting everyone know she was the one they all came to see. Despite his reluctance to like Marty, he and James have an easy candor that's entertaining to say the least. Up next is Olive. Emily shifts, uneasy in her seat next to him.

"Welcome to the stage *La Fae Verte*," James exclaims before he and Marty hurry to their seats. Emily shifts again, looking uncomfortable.

"I'm not feeling great. I think I need to step outside," Emily says, louder than necessary. Bunny shoots a glance Vic's way. He takes his cue and escorts Emily out, disappointed he'll be missing Olive's routine. The soft music floats behind him as he follows Emily. Stealing a glimpse to the stage as he leaves, he feels his heart skip a beat. Olive is glorious with her tousled locks, sparkling gown, fluttering feathers, and bare feet. Her natural beauty shines under the golden stage lights like it had the night of auditions when he caught her dancing on his roof in the setting sun.

"Vicky?" Emily calls from the open door.

Outside, she leans against the window, pulling a cigarette out of her purse. "I thought you were quitting," Vic says.

"I am. It's hard, okay? Especially when I'm stressed out about my baby daddy lusting after his little tramp."

"She's not a tramp," Vic defends, his anger about to boil over as she lights her cigarette.

"Hm," she huffs, inhaling deeply. "I don't get what you see in that scrawny little bumpkin." She blows out a cloud of smoke and looks at her feet.

"She's a friend." Vic watches cars pass on the street.

"Yeah right." She takes another deep drag and blows the smoke in his direction. They stand in silence, her staring at her feet. Him watching the road. The same silver sedan passes by slowly. He glares at the man behind the wheel, who stares back with a look of disgust.

"Come on. Put that out. Let's go back inside." He watches as the sedan turns the corner.

"I'm not going back in until she's done. You do whatever you want. I don't give a fuck," she snaps.

"Em, stop."

"I'm not doing anything."

"You're acting like a spoiled brat."

"Am I?" She squints her eyes at him and opens her mouth to speak. Then, the color drains from her face. She flicks her cigarette on the ground and hurries to the door. Vic turns around. The silver sedan pulls to a stop across the street. The man driving steps out, slamming the door behind him. He's tall and thin with a thick black beard and gray streaks in his pompadour. He crosses the street without looking.

"Can I help you?" Vic asks, ignoring his first instinct to tell the hipster lumberjack to keep walking.

"Yeah, you can step aside," the man says with unmasked anger.

"Sorry, buddy. That I can't do. It's a closed rehearsal for a sold-out show. You'll have to wait until next time." Vic steps in front of the door, blocking the man's way.

"Well, that's my fucking wife you were just talking to, and I'd appreciate it if you'd let me by." The man's words hit Vic like a punch in the gut. The anger he felt at this guy's intrusion is replaced by something he doesn't recognize.

"Your wife?" he asks as the door opens behind him and the entire troupe spills out for their intermission break.

"Yeah," the man answers, pressing his lips together, looking for Emily in the crowd.

Everyone watches their standoff awkwardly. "Looks like they're on a break now," Vic offers, "let me make sure everyone is out." He backs through the door, watching Emily's husband as the glass door swings shut. "Emily. What the fuck is going on?" he asks. She's packing up her things and looking wildly around the room.

"What?" she shouts back. "What does it look like?"

"I don't fucking know, but I want some answers. What about the baby? Is it even mine?" he asks, feeling another sucker punch as he realizes the child he'd been imagining and falling in love with all these weeks was slipping quickly away.

"What baby?" Emily's husband asks from the doorway. Amanda and several others follow him in. Emily looks from Vic to her husband and the group gathered behind him. She says nothing. Her eyes are wet with unshed tears. "She's not pregnant," he says with disgust. "She had her tubes tied six years ago when our son was born." There's a collective gasp from the doorway.

Vic's shoulders slump. "Is this true, Em?"

"What do you fucking care?" she snaps.

"You made me care, Emily. What the fuck were you planning? What was your end game? I'm not the brightest man in the world, but I feel like I would have figured it out pretty soon." He's never been this angry with a woman. As he watches her struggle with what to say, he realizes what she was going to do to him. That she would eventually make him grieve the loss of a child that never existed. His chest and throat constrict. The rage and pain roiling through him is like nothing he's ever known. If she were a man, he'd know exactly what to do. Then he looks at her husband standing beside him. His gaunt face and tortured eyes. Vic turns and storms out of the room, the blood rushing in his ears muting the excited chatter behind him.

He passes his office and heads directly up the fire escape to his apartment. He has to punch something. He pummels his punching bag in silence until he hears a knock at his door. He takes a towel from the shelf and wipes the sweat from his face, expecting Amanda. He's shocked to find Olive's big green eyes staring back at him.

"Are you okay?" she asks softly.

"I don't know what I am," he responds flatly. "Come on in." He opens the door. She steps into the kitchen and takes a seat on one of the stools.

"Do you want to talk about it?"

Vic watches her sit, then lean one elbow on the counter, filling up the room with her light. "No."

"Are you sure? I mean, what happened down there was extreme. I can only imagine what you're feeling right now."

Vic sighs, crossing to the fridge for his pitcher. He pours himself a glass of chamomile tea. "You want some?" he asks, holding the glass up.

"Is that my tea?" she asks.

"It grew on me." He shrugs. The truth is he hates the flavor. Despite it he drank a glass daily and closed his eyes, imagining a sun-warmed field of wildflowers with Olive standing in the middle. "Tastes like sunshine." He hands her the glass and fills one of his own. The cool drink is refreshing after his unexpected workout.

"Bunny wanted me to tell you not to worry about the show. She said Jonathon is bringing a costume for Cin tomorrow. They were already coming for opening night. Cin said she is happy to do it." Vic listens as he sips his tea. "That's what I came to tell you." She bounces her head from side to side and chuckles nervously. She sips her tea and stands, turning to leave. "Since you seem okay, I'm going to go back down there."

"Wait," he calls.

She stops and turns back to him with a halfhearted smile. "I'm glad you're okay. Maybe you can walk me home later. If you feel like it, that is."

"I'd like that."

Chapter 16

"I fucking told him so," Cin says from across the table. Rehearsals are over. Bridgette, Calvin, and Cin are staying in the empty apartment upstairs, and the rest of the troupe are too excited for tomorrow to call it a night. Instead, they'd grabbed some wine from the corner store and headed back to the Speakeasy to gossip. "That woman is the most toxic person I've ever known. Who knew she was married with a kid?"

"Right?" Bridgette says, shaking her head. "How did she hide it from everyone?"

"Who knows? I feel bad for Vic, though, and her husband. Poor guys," Calvin adds.

"I wouldn't worry about Vic too much," Chris interjects, "he's got someone to help him lick his wounds." Olive feels her cheeks blaze. Cin, Bridgette, and Calvin turn to her.

"Whatever, Chris." She rolls her eyes and looks away.

"Now that makes sense." Cin points at Olive, then back toward Vic's office. "She'd be good for him. He could use a levelheaded sweetheart like you."

"Is that a thing? You and Vic?" Bridgette asks.

"No. Not really. I mean, we may have started to maybe have a thing before he found out about the baby. But it wasn't anything. A couple kisses and some sweet nothings. You know." She shrugs.

Cin raises her eyebrow. "I didn't think that man was capable of sweet nothings."

Olive blushes again. "It wasn't anything really." She shakes her head as Vic appears in the back hallway, leaning on the wall, his gaze on her.

"I swear he knows the second you say there's nothing going on between you two," Chris half whispers. Everyone on the other side of the table turns to see what she's blushing about. Vic offers the room a brilliant smile and saunters to the table.

"I thought I heard something going on down here. How's everyone doing?" he asks as he takes a seat next to Calvin. The group hesitates to continue their conversation, considering the subject matter has joined the table. "Oh, come on, guys. I know you're talking about what happened tonight. Lord knows I'm thinking about it."

"It was pretty crazy," Bunny says with a relieved sigh. "I had no idea she was married. We've known her for how long?" she asks her original troupe-mates.

"Years," Cin says with an irritated look. "I always knew she was a snake. Sorry she had you all fucked up, Vic."

"Yeah, me too," he responds. "So, what happened after I left?"

"Chad, Emily's husband, confronted her about sleeping around," Bunny says. "He said he should've known it was happening again when she got back into burlesque. I tried not to listen too closely, but he wasn't using a lot of tact. Sounds like she pulled something similar when they lived in Minnesota, except the guy she was sleeping with then was married to a lady who's pretty big in the burlesque scene up there. That's why they ended up moving here."

Olive listens to Bunny recount the events of the evening. She watches Vic. Though he seems to be carrying himself lighter than she's seen in a long time, there's a sadness about him too. *He must be so heartbroken.* Suddenly her wine tastes sour. She wants nothing more than to be home in her bed away from the drama and gossip.

"I think I'm going to head out," she says, standing up. "I can leave all my stuff here for tonight, right?"

"Yep." Bunny nods.

Everyone in the room says their good-byes as she pulls on her jacket. "Can't wait for tomorrow, you guys. It's going to be amazing. I can feel it." Her words bubble with excitement.

As she exits the Speakeasy, she's met by the cool October night, and is thankful she thought to bring a jacket despite the warmth of the afternoon. The smell in the air takes her back to her younger days, to harvest celebrations and bonfires. They weren't always drunken naked debauchery. Many were family friendly, filled with spiced cider, roasted meats, and baked goods, and dancing in costumes and telling spooky stories. There was laughter and friendship and happiness. All were feelings that seemed lost to her, until she found her way to Burlesque A la Mode.

She fills her lungs with the crisp sweet air and unlocks her bike from its place on the streetlight. "Hey." Vic's unmistakable voice startles her. He stands a few paces away, holding his bike beside him. "You never did get to see how fast my new bike is."

"Are you challenging me to another race?" She grins.

"That depends. Are you feeling up for the challenge?"

"I'm ready to smoke you, if that's what you're saying."

"We'll see about that," Vic says as he takes off on his bike toward the river.

Olive hurries to catch up, meeting him on the bike path. "How far are we going?"

"You tell me," he says with a grin and a lightness she hasn't heard in his voice for a while.

"Want to go all the way to the train tracks?"

"That's a hell of a race."

"Don't have it in you?" she taunts.

"Oh, we'll see who doesn't have it. On three." Vic prepares for his takeoff. Olive does the same. "One… Two… Three." He springs ahead of her quickly, pushing off as he says three. Olive hurries to recover the lost ground. They're neck and neck in no time. She pedals harder and faster than necessary and flies past him. They glide over the trail, up and down hills and around curves. Bare trees stretch her limbs under the black night sky, their fallen leaves blowing across the path. The crescent moon shines as crisp as the air itself. Olive is invigorated. Her heart pumping with the joy of the ride. Or is it the man she's racing? It feels like they are racing away from something dark, away from wicked intentions and lies meant to keep them apart. She'd accepted his circumstance with a heavy heart, resigned herself to hold him at arm's length. Now, as they race toward her boat, he doesn't have to remain at a distance. There's nothing keeping him from wrapping her in his arms and finishing what they had started so many nights ago.

Olive brakes suddenly, skidding to a halt as Vic shoots to victory, reaching the train tracks with many feet between them. "You win," she says, catching her breath.

"What's the deal? You were going to win. Why'd you stop?"

"I thought I saw a stick," she lies. The truth is she's not ready for what might happen if they make it all the way to her boat. If she welcomes him aboard.

Hours ago, he was starting a family with another woman. Now they are racing to her house like teenagers with no parental supervision.

"Huh," Vic says, scanning the path for sign of a stick or crack. "I don't see anything."

"Must have been a shadow," Olive replies as she rides to meet him.

"It's no fun winning that way," he says playfully.

"It's probably the only way you'll win," she teases.

"What are you getting at?"

"Only that the last time you beat me, I was riding an inferior bike. This time, I was distracted," she says.

"By what, imaginary sticks?"

"Or something. I think I can make it from here, though, if you wanted to head back home. It's not such a pleasant ride now that it's getting colder."

"I'm not going to leave you here on the train tracks."

"No, I suppose you aren't." Olive smiles and swallows her trepidation. All she has to do is not invite him in. It's as simple as that. Get to the dock. Thank him for his time. Wish him well and be on her way to safety. "Want to walk the rest of the way?"

"Sure." He shrugs and steps off his bike. She does the same, positioning the bike between them.

"How are you really doing?" she asks after they share a comfortable silence.

"I'm not sure," he says, looking out over the river with a sigh. "On one hand, I'm relieved. Emily had some good qualities, but the bad outweighed them. The only reason I was staying with her was the baby. Then to find out that there never was a baby… It's surreal. I was conned." He turns his gaze to his feet as they walk along the path. "What was she going to do once it became obvious she wasn't pregnant? I can't figure out why was she trying to keep me when she's already married. I don't understand any of it." He's quiet again. Olive walks beside him, unsure of what to say. "On the other hand, I was starting to think about the baby, she was becoming a real person in my mind, with tiny hands and big sweet eyes. I was starting to pick out names. And now…" His voice catches in his throat. "Now, I'm a fool. It's over," he snaps his fingers, "like that."

"I don't think you're a fool," Olive says. "I didn't know this kind of thing happened in real life."

"Yeah," he huffs.

They come upon the dock, black water rippling in empty spaces left by boats spending their winters in driveways and garages. It's time to turn him away. "Thanks for getting me home safe," she says gently.

"Thanks for listening," he responds with little energy.

Time to say good night, Olive tells herself as she watches Vic stare at his feet, looking like a lost little boy. She knows she should send him home. She should wait at least a day or two for the shock to wear off, but she's been waiting and watching for so long. Each day she's spent watching him with Emily was torture. She thinks of the moments she and Vic could've shared, of the boat ride she offered what seems like forever ago. If Emily hadn't lied, Vic would've made good on his promises. He would've been there the following morning.

She knows more than most how quickly life can change, how suddenly someone can be lost. She doesn't want to waste another minute. "You want to come in? I can make you some hot tea, or a grilled cheese. Sorry, I don't have much else."

"Some tea might be nice. It gets pretty chilly out here once you stop moving."

Once inside, Olive does her best to keep her distance. His body fills up the space of her small kitchen. His energy creeps into every corner until she feels the whole boat might burst. Leaning against the small table, he watches her put the water on. "Welcome aboard, I guess."

"It's exactly how I imagined it," he says with one of his smiles that spreads to his eyes.

"You've imagined what it looks like in here?" She snorts. "Let me give you the grand tour. Here's the kitchen. There's the rest." She points through the door to her living quarters: a bed and a chair all crammed into a tiny space.

"It suits you."

"Thanks," she says with another snort.

"I mean it. It's eclectic and unexpected. Like you."

"Pretty sure you have to be rich to be eclectic. I'm poor, so crazy is the word you're looking for."

"You're not crazy." His voice softens.

The change in his tone turns the air into electricity. Olive reaches for her basket of assorted teas. She straightens her back. "I've got all kinds of tea here. What flavor do you want?" she asks, turning to face him. He stands up and steps to her.

"I don't want tea, Olive." He takes another step and stands near enough she can feel his heat. "I want to hold you. Every day since I left this little boat with my promise to make things right, I've dreamed of holding you."

"Vic, I…" she stammers, her heart beating wildly. She breathes in his fresh air scent and steps back, bumping into the counter. "I don't know. It feels rushed. Not even five hours ago, you were expecting a baby with another woman."

"Not five hours ago I was being manipulated as a victim of circumstance. You haven't left my mind this whole time. I can't tell you how many nights I ran here, the only purpose to see the light in your window."

Olive looks down at the basket of tea in her hand. The single, solitary thing between them. "You did that?"

"I did, for weeks, until I realized what a creep I was being." He shakes his head.

"I don't think it's creepy," she says, still holding the basket, looking into his earnest face.

"No?"

"I think it's kind of sweet actually." She turns her gaze back to the basket.

"Olive, will you put that basket down?"

"I promised you tea. And I don't know if it's the best idea…"

"Let me pick out a flavor then." He takes the basket from her hands and sets it on the counter, sliding it away without so much as a glance. Then he rests his hands on the counter on either side of her. She can feel the heat rise in her face. Her body responds to his nearness, screaming to be touched, to be even nearer. She might feel trapped if it was anyone else standing this close, blocking her escape. But there's no desire to run from him.

"Vic, I don't know."

"Say the word and I'm gone," he says as they stare at each other. She swears she can hear her heart beating, or maybe his. She reaches out, running her hand over the rough stubble of his cheek. His skin warms her cold hand.

"I don't want you to go."

His arms are around her in an instant, crushing her to his chest. She turns her face into his neck. Her lips find his pulse; it beats rapidly against them. She kisses there again and again. Then down his neck, relishing the rough stubble against her nose and mouth.

"I don't ever want to let you go," he breathes into her hair. She tilts her face to his. His mouth is on hers, pressing, urgent. He squeezes her body then releases her from his iron grip, only to run his hand up and down the length of her back. Then he cups her face in both hands and continues to kiss her hungrily. His tongue plays at her lips until she responds with her own. His fingers slip away from her face, working their way into her hair, gripping slightly at the roots. Her body is alight with passionate fire. His cock prods at her belly through their clothes. A groan rumbles in his chest.

"Vic, stop," she whispers against his mouth. He pulls away and unravels his hands from her hair, resting his forehead against hers. "This is happening too fast. I've never…"

He steps away suddenly. The absence of his touch almost painful. "You're not a virgin, are you? Oh god, I'm so sorry, Olive. I never would have come on so strongly. I should have read the room."

"No." She shakes her head. "I'm not. I've never fooled around here on the boat. It rocks if I get up too fast, I can't imagine what kind of waves we would make. And…I don't know. It's like my parents are everywhere in here. It doesn't feel right. I know it's silly." She leans against the counter and rubs her eyes, wishing she is back in his arms.

"It's not silly," he assures.

***

She's trembling. Vic watches Olive as she reaches for the tea basket again. *Say something.* She turns around with a wide smile.

"How about some green tea?" she asks softly.

"Yeah, that sounds good," he responds, settling back against the table. "You know, I can take off if you want me to."

"I don't." She shakes her head, pulling two tea bags from the basket. He watches as she reaches for two mugs from the cabinet. She moves with fluid grace, as if the air itself longs to embrace her.

"You want to watch a movie or something?" he asks.

"I don't have a television."

"Of course, you don't," he replies, looking around the walls of bookshelves filled with books.

"Don't get me wrong. I watch plenty of stuff. I stream it on my phone though. I've got years to make up for. So many terrible sitcoms and movies I never knew existed. Sometimes, when it rains, or when it's cold, I'll watch an entire series in one weekend. I'll barely leave my bed. It's decadent." She chuckles at herself, pouring the steaming water over the teabags.

"We all do that."

"Glad I'm not the only one. I'm sure my folks roll in their graves every time I do it. They believed humans should be outdoors. When it was too cold to be outdoors, it was time for the smaller creative endeavors. I wrote a novel by the time I was twelve. It was garbage. But I wrote it."

"I'd love to read it someday."

"No, you wouldn't." She shakes her head vigorously and laughs. "It was about a fairy princess in a bunny kingdom I believe. There were a lot of illustrations. Lots of flowers."

"I've never written a novel. Or spent a winter without a TV for that matter. I bet it was brilliant."

"Sure thing." She hands him a steaming mug. "I don't have much for seating in here. You'll have to behave yourself," she says over her shoulder as she crosses through the doorway and sits cross-legged on the bed piled high with a rainbow of pillows and blankets.

He feels oversized as he follows her through the doorway. The lights and the ceiling seem lower. To one side is a chair with some clothes piled on it. Beside it is an alcove with a sink, a mirror, and a small closet door. The walls are full of shelves and cubbies with clothes and books tucked neatly away. The boat rocks beneath him; he stands still steadying the teacup.

"Here, let me get that." Olive springs up and moves the clothes pile to the floor space at the foot of the bed.

"Thanks." He sits slowly as the boat continues to rock under their movement.

"Sorry, I'm not used to company," she says, settling herself back on the foot of the bed.

"Don't be. This place is great. So bohemian. I bet Amanda would love it."

"Why don't you call her Bunny like everyone else?" Olive asks, sipping her tea.

"I don't know." He shrugs. "Mike doesn't call her Bunny, and we spend a lot of time together, the three of us. She's Amanda to me."

"It must be weird to have two names like that."

"I guess I never thought about it before, but you're right. It must be. How do you like yours?"

"I don't think it's going to become a second name any time soon. But I like it. It sounds magical."

"It's fitting then," Vic says, watching her sip her tea surrounded by glowing lights and a rainbow of colors. The thought of climbing into the mountain of pillows with her and covering her with kisses is almost more than he can handle. Instead, he brings the warm mug to his lips and sips the mild, earthy tea.

"Stop." She laughs, looking away.

"Stop what? It is a fitting name. You're like a dream up there." He sips his tea again. The air smells like incense though there isn't any burning. He watches over his mug as she glances his way, blush rising to her cheeks.

"Thank you." She blinks slowly and holds her mug with both hands, hiding a bashful smile. They watch each other for what feels like an eternity. The distance between them insurmountable.

"Are you excited about tomorrow?" he asks in an attempt at polite conversation.

"I am. I can't believe it's happening already. Or that I'm actually going to do it." She lowers her mug to rest it on her knee and leans back into the pillows with a smile.

"You're going to be amazing. The show is going to be amazing. You're all setting the bar pretty high for the next show."

"When do you think the next show will be? I'm already sad this one is over and it's not even opening night."

"You guys keep selling out shows, and we'll keep producing them. I never would've thought this would be where our club was going to end up, but I'll be damned if I'm not beyond pleased."

"I understand what you're saying. I wouldn't have imagined even six months ago I would be performing with a burlesque troupe in front of four sold-out crowds."

"Funny how life does that, isn't it? Even this morning my life looked completely different. I was thinking about gutting my workout room to build a nursery."

"Were you?"

"Yeah." He nods. "I was."

"Now what are you thinking about?" she asks casually, bringing her mug to her lips.

"You," he answers without hesitation.

Olive lowers her mug, her bright mossy eyes sparkling despite the low light. She tilts her head slightly, opens her mouth to speak, then looks down at her hands. "I think about you too. Like all the time." She lets out a little nervous chuckle without looking up. "But," she looks up again, "if I'm being honest, I don't know what the hell I'm doing. I have never been with a man. I've never had a relationship."

"I thought you said…"

"I did. And I'm not. But the last time I had sex was when I was sixteen and he told me he was gay shortly after. So, you know, that didn't last. Then I lost my family, and sex never seemed like a priority. So, here I am in this new world that's fifty percent glitter and fifty percent sex and I have no clue what I'm doing. Then there's you. And you keep showing up with your beautiful fucking smile." Her voice softens as she looks away again. "I feel like a foolish little girl."

"There is nothing foolish about you," Vic says, his heart swelling with admiration. *She has no idea how stunning she is.*

She huffs, "Thanks."

"Olive, I mean it. You are an amazing person. You've been through more than most and you haven't lost your kindness. You shine despite it. Maybe because of it. I don't know." He watches as she swirls her tea in her cup, then raises her gaze to meet him.

"If you stay tonight, can we take things very slow?"

He wasn't prepared for her question. His mouth goes dry. Suddenly he's a foolish kid without a clue. "I would rather die than make you feel the slightest bit of discomfort."

She nods and unfolds her long legs, then stands and takes his mug without a word. She whisks through the doorway. He hears the latch turning on the lock, then the light goes out in the kitchen. She reappears in the doorway with a shy smile. "Come sit with me." She crosses to the bed and settles in her pile of pillows and blankets.

Vic's transported back to a time when a girl's bedroom was the holiest place a boy could be. When the thought of kissing alone in a room was enough to stiffen his eager cock to a painful degree. He barely remembers the faces of the girls or what their rooms were like. But the feeling is as real as if he were thirteen again. He steps slowly as the boat rocks and sits at the opposite end of the bed. His heart is beating wildly at the prospect of taking it slow.

Chapter 17

Vic sits as far away as he can while sharing the bed with her. Olive shifts to face him. "I feel like I made this more awkward than it needs to be." She chuckles, pulling a blanket over her lap.

"You didn't." He offers an encouraging smile.

"Okay." Olive laughs, her heart racing. "It's weird. I can't count the nights I've slept alone in this boat. But now that you're here, I know it's going to feel oddly empty without you." He smiles and says nothing. "Oh, for shit's sake. I need to stop talking. I keep making it worse."

"You aren't. I can't think of a place I would rather be, or a person I would rather be with." She thinks his affection is genuine. Her bedside lamp casts a golden light across his face, highlighting his deep smile lines. She looks at the several small scars on his cheeks, eyebrows, and chin and remembers Simone recounting their childhood.

"You're sweet," she says.

"That's not how most would describe me. But I'll take it." His grin shines brighter than the lamp beside him.

"Oh, come on." She laughs and watches as he relaxes into the pillows behind him. He lifts his legs onto the bed and rests his foot on his ankle.

"It's true. I can't recall the last time someone, other than my mom, called me sweet."

"Well, I think you're sweet." She shakes her head and wonders how to close the distance between them. She wants to be in his arms, wants to kiss him and be kissed by him. She shifts again, sinking deeper into her pillows. They stare at one another with a tension that fills the small room. Olive wonders how to make the next move. She thinks of Emily, of her bold, sexy confidence. Surely, she wouldn't sit awkwardly on the foot of a bed, while the object of her desire sits at the other end, waiting for a move to be made.

"Are you okay?" he asks softly, his brows coming together.

"Yeah. Feeling silly, I guess. Pretty sure I'm failing the whole art of seduction thing." A snort escapes her as she attempts to laugh. A genuine smile spreads across Vic's face.

"What do you want right now?" he asks, sitting up away from the pillows and scooting himself against the wall.

Olive's taken off guard by his question. She takes a deep breath and gives her head a subtle shake. "I'm not sure. No, that's not right. I'm sure of what I want. What I'm not sure of is how to get it."

"Let's start with what you want." His voice is smooth and calm, with a hint of playfulness. His eyes twinkle.

The fire burning behind her cheeks must be shining like the sun. Her heart buzzes where it once beat. Her skin hums with expectation. "I want to be closer to you," she says breathlessly.

His wide grin shows both dimples. "That's easy enough." He shrugs and moves swiftly, sliding up beside her on the pillows. "Done." He's so close she can feel the vibration of his voice. "You're in the driver's seat here," he says gently. "If you want me to stop, say the word. If you don't like something I'm doing, tell me."

"You don't have to be so careful." Olive chuckles at the absurdity of it all.

"I do, though. I have to know that you're comfortable."

"I'm a big girl, Vic. I'll be okay. It's new to me, that's all. I don't know the etiquette for most moments, let alone this one."

"I don't know that there are any. It's up to you and me. What I need is to know you'll tell me if I'm doing something you don't like."

"Now *you're* making it awkward." Olive laughs again, doing her best to ignore the nerves coiling in her stomach.

"Better now than later." He offers a half smile and seems to search her face for something. Then, his hand is on her cheek, his fingertips in her hair. Her scalp tingles as he combs them through to the ends, lifting the strands from her shoulder. A trembling sigh escapes her lips. Their shoulders touch against the pillows. He's solid and warm. His hand rests on the crook of her elbow; the rest of her body aches to know his touch. As his knuckles skim her upper arm to her shoulder and back down to her hand, she relaxes into the moment. No longer worried about etiquette, she closes her eyes and lets her head fall to the pillows closer to his.

He's kissing her, barely grazing her top and bottom lip. Then he pulls away slightly, his mouth lingering near enough she can feel his breath. He kisses again with more force. She shifts to him, their bodies nestling together, her breasts against his chest. His fingertips trail the length of her arm, over her shoulder, along her neck, into her hair, spiraling around the locks. Her skin comes alive, all her tiny hairs standing up. Her nipples tingle against him, begging for the same attention. She whimpers in response to this new and aching need.

"Is this okay?" he breathes, his mouth still on hers.

"Yeah," she barely whispers, bringing her hand to his cheek, pulling him into a deeper kiss. As his tongue flicks along her parted lips, she loses herself in the desire. She slips into a world where only their bodies and lips exist. Pure joy radiates from wherever their bodies meet. She's hungry for more, longing to be closer still. It seems the fabric of their clothes are a mile wide, separating their skin. She stretches her legs out beside him. The blanket she'd covered herself with is bunched between them. He moves his hand from her hair and yanks the blanket free, tossing it away. The empty space is filled with their bodies coming together.

The anticipation would be almost painful if it weren't so beautiful. As they grow more comfortable, their hands roam. She's amazed by his shoulders, his pecs, his back. Every rolling, solid inch of his body. She presses her pulsing mound against his bulging zipper. A low groan escapes his lips, setting her ablaze. She rolls her hips against him, pleasure coursing through her. His hands grip the back of her t-shirt, stretching the fabric tight against her breasts.

"I don't know if I want to take this slow anymore," she whispers into their kiss. The sound that emits from Vic's chest is foreign, animal.

"Olive, we have to."

"Why?" She's vibrating with desire, the idea of stopping the most terrible thing she can imagine.

"I don't have protection."

She whimpers, burying her face in his chest, the heat of his body offering little comfort, his scent making things worse. She wants to know every inch of him, to be as close as physically possible, to consume him and be consumed by him. The wild wanting is like nothing she's ever known. She kisses his chest then moves to his neck, begging without words for more. His fingers are in her hair again, the muscles in his neck twitch as she finds his most sensitive spots. "I don't want to stop," she breathes between kisses.

"We don't have to." He shifts his weight, rising over her as she settles into the pillows. "There's plenty I can do for you."

"What about you?" she asks, gazing at him.

"Don't worry about me," he says, lowering his lips to hers.

He moves excruciatingly slow with tender kisses on her mouth and face. He follows her jawline to her ear, where he nibbles delicately. She squirms in joyful discomfort. His hand rests on her stomach, fingers playing at the hem of her shirt, inching it up slowly. Then slipping under the fabric, he explores the length of her torso under her shirt, continuing with his deep, soul-crushing kisses. Gently, he cups her breast, kneading, tracing one finger around her nipple. Her head falls back. His lips move to her throat. He pushes her shirt completely above her breasts, his hand moving from one to the other. The cool air becomes part of the ecstatic torture. Then his lips are gone, and he's easing her shirt over her head. She opens her eyes to see him watching her. "You're the most beautiful thing I've ever seen," he says with a dreamy smile.

"So are you," she replies.

His smile stretches across his face as he strips off his shirt and lowers himself back into her arms. Slipping into his silken embrace is like slipping into a warm pool. She runs her hand over the patch of golden hair on his chest. He pulls her close, squeezing tightly, his lips finding hers again. They're tangled together in exquisite delight.

His hands travel her body, their masculine presence setting a match to the primal flame she's long ignored burning in her belly. He moves to unbutton her jeans, pausing with his fingers in place. She answers his silent request with a subtle roll of her hip.

Strip me bare, do what you will. Just don't stop.

He slips his hand between her open zipper and cotton panties, cupping her completely. The weight of the base of his hand rests against her pulsing clit while his fingers undulate against her swollen lips. His smallest movement sends vibrations of pleasure up and down her spine through to her fingertips and toes. Then, he drags his fingers over her clit, rubbing small circles with gentle pressure. His kisses trail over her chest to her bare nipples; he flicks each one with his tongue before pulling them into his warm, soft mouth. She pushes hard against his fingers until he hooks one around her panties, finding her wet and swollen parts. She gasps at the intense sensation. He stops his exploration and lifts his head from her breast.

"Don't stop," she sighs. A small, gruff sound comes from his throat as he takes her nipple back in his mouth and slides his finger along the length of her labia. As she moves her hips, he slides one finger inside, then a second. The base of his thumb presses against her aching clit skillfully. She arches her back as the crescendo of pleasure builds. She pants as his lips travel the length of her neck again, then move to her mouth. The rolling pulsing begins, then wild quivering. She gulps for air and finds kisses instead. Tingling warmth envelops her entirely as she explodes and contracts from one breath to the next. He slows, slipping his hand from her panties, then cups her as he had before while the writhing bliss slows to a gentle hum.

His kisses are light on her cheek, forehead, and lips.

***

Olive's eyes flutter open and are dazzling. A shy smile plays at her lips. "All these years, I've been doing it myself. It never felt like that." She chuckles and buries her face in his neck. He slides his hand from the warm confines of her pants and pulls a blanket over her bare shoulders. His cock throbs behind his zipper. Her words bring to mind images that are sexier than what he's seen already. Her smooth skin burns against him as she snuggles closer to his bare chest. He pulls the blanket over himself and wraps her in his arms. "It's your turn," she purrs into his neck. His straining cock twitches at the playful sound in her voice.

"I'm okay," he lies, kissing the top of her head.

"No, you aren't." She laughs.

"Yes, I am," he insists.

"But what about this?" she asks, boldly stroking the bulge in his pants. He hears her breath catch in her throat and clenches his teeth at the sensation as she explores his length and girth over his pants. "Oh my," she breathes. "Is there a beginner's model somewhere?" she jokes, adding a nervous chuckle.

Vic joins her with his own laughter; it rumbles from deep in his belly. Her honest reaction endearing her even more. Having spent so many years with jaded women, or those who were pleasantly aloof, Olive's perspective is refreshing. "Very funny." He gives her a gentle squeeze, trying to keep his mind on her voice, her words, not her hand stroking his cock through his jeans. She's more curious than clumsy.

"Can I take it out?" she asks, almost giddy, unaware of the effect her blatant interest is having on him. He's unaccustomed to her directness, no games, no toying with him. It delights and terrifies him.

"Olive, I don't know." He cringes at the thought of what he's about to do. Deep down he knows he's not worthy. "You said you wanted to take it slow."

"I did…" She holds her hand over his jeans, cupping his shaft and balls, mimicking the way he held her only moments before. "…and we are."

"Olive." He feels his resolve failing. She unbuttons his jeans and slides her warm hand into his boxers. It's like the first time all over again.

He's a thirteen-year-old boy sneaking through a girl's bedroom window. A tiny sound escapes his lips at the shock of the pleasure of it. She wraps her hand around the shaft, sliding it up and down, exploring every inch. Her finger tracing the ridge around the head, then the tip. She's unapologetic with her exploration, sighs and giggles all the while. His heart races uncharacteristically as her hand dips lower to cup and explore his balls. She handles them gently, but thoroughly before she goes back to stroking. Her lips find his throat again. She kisses and nuzzles as she strokes.

Her muffled words reach his ears as pleasure builds. "I'm both terrified and enthralled by this," she barely whispers as she gives his shaft a light squeeze. Her words are more than he can bear, her normally light voice, low and husky. Her breath, warm on his neck with her trail of kisses. The moment takes control of him. He's climaxing before he knows what's happening. His cheeks burn with embarrassment as he is once again a teenage boy wondering how to clean up the mess of warm semen on his stomach.

"Jesus, Olive," he chokes the words out. "What did you do to me?" She giggles. The sheer joy in the sound is enough to make him forget his shame at popping off like an adolescent.

"Let me get you something," she says as she hops off the bed, retrieving a towel from a shelf. It wafts patchouli through the air as she tosses it to him. "I don't know if you'll even fit in my bathroom," she says, sliding the folding closet door open and flipping the light on.

"No worries," he calls through the door, wiping himself clean, laughing at the situation. "That hasn't happened to me since I was a kid," he calls, his shame rising.

"What hasn't happened?" she asks with innocence or grace as she pushes through the small door. He couldn't tell which, maybe both.

"Thanks," he says flatly, looking up at her smiling face.

"Really. What?"

"Don't make me say it. It's bad enough it happened."

"I thought it was fun." She shrugs, standing in her pale blue panties and nothing else. Modest cotton briefs have never looked so amazing. Her high full breasts stand proud and tan from what he imagines are hours of sunning herself on the deck of her boat somewhere in the middle of the Mississippi. She climbs back onto the small bed and pulls the blanket over her bare skin and snuggles her back into his chest. His arms fall comfortably around her.

"I should go," he says after a long silence.

"I figured." There's disappointment in her voice.

"I don't want to. Believe me, Olive, it's the last thing in this world that I want to do. But tomorrow is a big day and you've got to rest. If I stay here, I'm afraid we'll be up all night."

"You're right," she sighs, snuggling closer still.

He kisses the top of her head, caresses her shoulder, and holds her tight. "Will you stay with me tomorrow, after the show?"

"Yes." She turns to him, still wrapped in his arms, and kisses his mouth, matching the need and urgency he feels to be so close to her.

***

"Olive, if you don't give me the details, I'm going to scream," Chris demands from his place in front of the mirror. She's sitting next to him, laying out her makeup and brushes.

"There aren't many to give," she says with a sly smile, knowing her refusal to share anything about her evening with Vic is driving Chris mad.

"I never knew you were such a heartless bitch," he says, leveling his gaze on hers in their reflections.

She laughs at his displeasure. "From you, I take that as a compliment," she replies pertly, pulling her hair into a messy bun on the top of her head.

"Damn it, woman."

They are alone in the dressing room. Everyone's not there yet or upstairs sharing the space with the out-of-town folks. Olive looks around to be sure. "Okay fine. We biked back to my place and I made him tea."

"You made him tea?"

"I didn't have anything else, and he didn't want the grilled cheese I offered."

"He didn't want the tea either." Chris rolls his eyes. "I swear." He shakes his head.

"Do you want to know what happened or not?"

"I'll stop. You talk." He pushes his makeup aside and turns to face her directly, resting one elbow on the table.

"You're right. He didn't want tea." Olive's cheeks warm with the memory of him taking the tea basket from her hands.

"Duh."

"You know I don't have a lot of space. There weren't too many options for places for us to sit. We ended up in bed." Chris's eyes grow wide, his jaw drops. "Not like that. I mean, we did fool around some. But he was a perfect gentleman."

"That's all you're going to give me, isn't it?"

"There's not much more to give." Olive shrugs, looking back at her reflection. "I promised to stay with him tonight after the show."

"You didn't."

"I did."

"You little minx." Chris shakes his head with a sly grin and returns his attention to his reflection.

"I'm not sure which I'm more nervous about. The show or afterward."

"What's there to be nervous about?"

"I don't know, everything. Aren't you?"

"Not really. But I've been on stage a time or two in my life. I'm thrilled really. Though, I might be a bit nervous about spending the night with Vic. From what I saw in his gym shorts, you might have reason for concern."

Fire burns from her deepest places, spreading to her face at the mention of Vic's gym shorts. "He's very..." She sighs and looks down at her makeup and brushes. "Skilled."

"Oh my god. You are terrible. You'll eventually drop this innocent girl façade and give me all the goods. Until then, just know I know, you are every bit as dirty a dog as the rest of us."

"You may be right." She gives him a side-eye half grin and lifts a makeup brush to begin the process of transformation. Over the months she's studied makeup tutorials on the internet and taken all of the advice she could get from their online support network. Cin has been especially helpful, sending her specific videos for her face and style.

As the evening progresses, more people fill the small backstage space. Olive watches as each one is transformed from their regular daily appearance to the splendor that is their burlesque persona. Bunny, Bridgette, Cin, and Calvin appear to be gods of another time and place, sparkling perfection in brilliant costumes, makeup, and hair.

Each one's individual style shines through in their costumes. Cin is pure elegance with her last-minute pride routine. Long, smooth black wig, long glittering black gown. Calvin's wrath is all leather and post-apocalyptic flare. His golden dreads are shaped into a wild mohawk while only his eyes are visible from above the leather face mask. Bridgette channels the most beautiful of mid-century cinema starlets in her pink chiffon peignoir. Though Bunny wears a little devil costume for the opening group routine, her genuine chef's uniform complete with the tall white hat hangs on the garment rack. It, along with a crisp white bra and panty set, will soon be covered in frosting and sprinkles as she makes love to several layer cakes on stage. "The audience knows it's going to be good once we bring a tarp out," she's said several times over the weeks.

Olive's plans to spend the night with Vic are never far from her mind, but she's so immersed in the thrill of the moment, the promises of what's to come are a mere whisper. She, Chris, Susan, and Julie have made their own transformations, each one more glamorous than they thought they would ever be. Susan and Chris, though their faces are made up for their individual routines, wear costumes to match Olive and Bunny. Julie looks like another person altogether. The body she normally hides behind sweats and baggy t-shirts is stunning. She's larger than life, six feet tall with perfect proportions. Olive does a double take upon seeing her in the deep red corset and shiny pleather leggings paired with knee-high boots. She walks in the high heels as if she were born in them.

As Olive admires her friends coming and going, she catches her own reflection in the mirror. Her hair falls in loose curls over her shoulders, a subtle change from her thick, straight locks. Her eyes are painted with more green and gold glitter than she's ever seen. Her lips are a soft glossy pink. Her red little devil costume squeezes her around the middle. She hardly recognizes herself.

Marty and James pop through the curtain in their matching ties and suspenders. "Starting to fill up out there," James says with a sweet grin. He's a man of few words with a kind heart. On stage he takes a verbal beating from Marty. By the end of the show, he'll be the audience's favorite.

"You all look amazing," Marty says to the room, his eyes falling on Olive's cleavage. She turns away to look back at her reflection, her heart quickly rising to her throat, beating rapidly. The noise from the other side of the curtains grows with every minute. She fiddles with her hair, applies another layer of lip gloss, and looks around the room for a sign that anyone else is as nervous as her.

"Hey." Bridgette approaches from behind. "You're going to kill it out there." "Thanks." Olive laughs nervously.

"I mean it. You're incredible. Don't let the nerves get you."

"Easier said than done."

"We all had that feeling. The sick stomach, swirling mind, racing heart. You've got to channel it. Instead of nerves, think of it as energy. The energy you're going to use to make them all love you. And they will. They will love you."

"Thanks. I feel like I'm going to fuck something up."

"You won't. And if you do, run with it. These folks are here for one thing and it's to be entertained. You've got a few short minutes that are yours completely. Don't forget you own those minutes. For the time you're up there it's you, your music, and the stage. You're allowing them to watch."

Bridgette's words settle over her like a protective blanket. *You're allowing them to watch,* she tells herself over and over. The words are like a mantra as she breathes through the nerves. Music plays from the sound system, setting the mood and masking the noise from the growing audience. Then Marty and James are welcoming the crowd. Cheers and applause greet them, louder than Olive could have imagined. After what feels like an all-too-brief exchange of humor, laughter, and more applause, Olive follows Bunny, Chris, and Susan onto the stage right on cue. The minutes go by, distorted. At first music and lights are all there is, and time feels slower. Olive moves through the steps of their dance easily. She sees Chris smiling and taking her hand. They spin and step and kick and bend. The song ends to the sound of thunderous applause.

She rushes backstage, her heart still racing. Cin is waiting behind the curtain for her cue. "You guys did great," she says with a genuine smile.

"Thanks," Olive pants, helping Susan out of her first costume into the many layers of pale pink and blue. Cin exits on her cue and time is moving too quickly. Julie is there, ready to help Susan. Olive rushes for her costume change. Time and space are irrelevant, the moments backstage are surreal, full of music, banter, and applause. She combs through her hair and adjusts her costume one last time before Susan appears beside her panting and full of joy.

"You'll do amazing."

Olive nods, her heart in her throat again. The black curtain hangs still, inches from her face. More banter, more laughter, more applause. Then her cue. "Give it up for this magical creature, *La Fae Verte*." Her music begins low at first. Julie is beside her, holding out her feather fans.

She follows the music as she has many times before. The crowd is silent beyond the glare of golden stage lights. She steadies herself and thinks of Vic, knowing he's out there watching. She forgets the crowd, the lights, and everyone backstage. She dances for him. Every word of the song is for him, every movement of her body his. As she unsnaps her gown and it falls away, the silent crowd erupts with applause. The only thing separating her from them are the fluttering feathers, and sparkling thong and pasties. Twirling, stepping, reaching, she allows a glimpse of a thigh, an arm, her belly. The fans hide most of her until the end of the song, when she raises them above her head. The gentle music is lost behind wild applause. Olive basks in it. It rushes over her, through her, down to her bones. The whistles and cheers cascade like rain. She covers herself with her fans and bows before running off stage. "Let's hear it for *La Fae Verte*." James shouts as he takes the stage. The applause thunders in her chest. As the emcees announce intermission, she slips a light cotton robe over her shoulders and ties it in place.

Walking to the bar through the audience, she's stopped by more people than she can count. They all tell her how wonderful she was. How much they are enjoying the show. She smiles and thanks each one, all the while scanning the room for Vic. She spots him standing with Mike and a handsome, dark-haired man she's never met. *Where are all these beautiful people coming from?* she asks herself as she's surrounded by her burlesque family. Bunny begins the group hug, then there are more arms than she can count around her. The group is congratulating her and each other. They're ecstatic over the success of the show so far. "You were amazing," Bunny says.

"So beautiful," Bridgette agrees.

"Everything has been perfect," Calvin says through his leather mask.

Olive's heart is full to bursting in the arms of her friends. Through their embrace she meets Vic's gaze. He's shining with joy as he moves easily through the sea of people. She steps away from the group's embrace directly into his.

Chapter 18

Vic stands with Mike and Henri, who arrived only that afternoon from New Orleans. The two men provide a welcome distraction from the anxious joy that's been spiraling in his gut since he left Olive's place the night before. Henri, as is his custom, grills them about club ownership. Vic finds it laughable a man of Henri's means would ask for advice on anything. With money like his, he can hire dozens of lawyers and business professionals to do all the work. It seems, however, he wants to roll up his custom-tailored sleeves and do the dirty work himself. The dirty work, from the sound of things, is being neck deep in beautiful, creative women and men in two major metropolitan areas.

"I don't know how you do it," Mike says to Henri over the music signaling intermission. They stand at the end of the bar, making way for patrons to order their drinks. "This place keeps us busy enough. I can't imagine having two."

"It's surprisingly easy. The theater in Chicago runs itself. All I do is visit from time to time with Bridgette. Back home, Lilian does it all." He continues talking about traveling with Bridgette and watching the two theaters grow. Vic stops listening as Olive appears on the darkened stage, a worn and pale floral kimono cinched tightly at her waist. She moves down the steps slowly, as if unsure of her steps. People speak to her from their seats. She pauses for each one, listening and nodding, offering them her lovely smile. As she approaches the group of performers in the center of the room, she's enveloped by them. He breaks away from Mike and Henri, his only intention to have her in his arms again. The hours without her beside him have been torture.

Her face appears to stand out from the others. She meets his gaze and moves out of their collective arms into his. It's like he's breathing again for the first time since he left her sleeping in her bed. Her sweet patchouli scent wraps around him. He kisses the top of her head and inhales deeply. She squeezes him around the waist, pressing her forehead against his chest. "That was incredible." She sighs.

"Should have seen it from down here," he says, stepping back to take her in. As glorious as she looks in her glittering stage makeup, he longs to see her face pure and clean, wearing only the blush he causes with his touch.

"Thank you." She bites her bottom lip and looks away like an awkward child receiving a compliment.

Bridgette approaches from the broken group hug and wraps an arm around Olive's waist, whisking her away. "Come on, I want you to meet Henri." Olive glances over her shoulder. Vic's left alone, feeling the chill of her absence. Amanda follows close behind them, giving him a side-eyed glance and a knowing half-smile.

"Much better choice," Cin says from his side, nudging him with her hip.

"You think so?"

"I don't like to say I told you so."

"Don't lie."

"You're right. I do like to say it. But I'll spare you this one time."

"I don't know you've spared me anything," he says through gritted teeth. Their banter had been cat and mouse since the day they met, though he never knew if he was the cat or the mouse. He'd always admired Cin, despite never understanding her.

"I was worried about you, but I can see I had nothing to worry about."

"Aw, Cin, I never knew you cared."

"I can't help but care. You became part of our family the moment our Bunny transplanted herself here."

"Well, thanks for caring." As they chat, he watches Olive with Henri, Bridgette, Mike, and Amanda. She fits seamlessly into his world, like she's always been there. She glances his way, and her face lights up.

"Go get her, tiger," Cin purrs and wanders away into a crowd of admiring fans.

Vic crosses the room back to Olive's side. Amanda and Bridgette leave to head backstage for the second half.

"You don't want to miss curtain call," Amanda says over her shoulder to Olive, though her gaze is firmly on Vic.

"I won't," Olive calls back, stepping nearer to Vic. "I'm so excited for the second half," she says against his ear. A tingle runs down his spine. The houselights go down, the emcees take the stage. Their banter is lost on him as they announce Dave the magician. His performance is incredible, leaving the audience spellbound.

Vic is under another spell, however. Olive's every move catches his eye. She wanders to the bar to chat with Simone, who eyes him suspiciously as she fills a glass of water. Olive's kimono does little to cover her long legs, barely grazing the bottom of her ass. The bottoms of her bare feet are dirty from the Speakeasy floor. He remembers the moment on his roof when he caught her dancing in the setting sun. If only he'd realized what she would mean to him then. He could've avoided so much heartache.

She returns with her water and he wraps his arm around her waist. As she leans into his embrace, he hooks his thumb under the belt at her waist, wishing more than anything that they were alone so he could pull the bow free and watch the kimono fall open. He longs to feast on her breasts, to taste her skin, to be tangled in her hair, lips, and limbs.

The show goes on with one amazing routine after another. Chris follows the magician with a darkly humorous greed routine. Amanda strips to barely anything and sits in a layer cake, smashing another one into her breasts. She rolls on a tarp and covers herself with sprinkles, eating clumps of cake off her chest. The crowd loses it.

Vic steals a glance at Mike, who's hooting and whistling louder than anyone. Olive bounces up and down in front of him, cheering wildly. Calvin is almost frightening as he performs his version of wrath.

Bridgette closes the show with her sultry lust routine, all pink and sex. Vic notices the intensity on Henri's face as he watches her dance. He understands completely, realizing how he must have looked watching Olive on stage.

As Bridgette exits the stage to the rumbling of applause, Marty and James enter, calling for the performers to join them. Olive turns and smiles at Vic before heading to the stage. The show is coming to a close.

She'll be in his apartment before he knows it.

***

Standing ovation. This is a standing ovation, Olive thinks to herself as the shadows of the audience rise on the other side of the blinding stage lights. Their applause rises to a near riotous level as they stand, clapping and shouting wildly. Olive's heart is full to bursting. Her face hurts from the grin she's worn since she joined her troupe on stage. Music blares over the crowd and the entire room begins dancing. Chris squeezes her and spins her into Bunny's arms, then Bridgette is there and Susan. Cin spins her again and hugs her closely. Then they form a line and exit the stage together to form a receiving line near the door.

Smiling faces and laughter fill the room. The energy is electric. Vic is behind the bar, helping Simone close out tabs. The rest of the bar staff clears tables. Olive poses for picture after picture as the happy audience members file their way out the door. It's not long before only the performers and staff are left.

Vic calls from behind the bar for a round of celebratory shots. Olive declines and he leaves his own untouched as well. Discussions of where to go and what to do next fill the room. Olive looks for Vic's reaction; he's watching her silently.

"I don't know about you all, but I'm beat," she says to no one in particular.

"Yeah right," Chris says with a conspiratorial wink.

"I am. It's been a long day," she answers as innocently as she can, despite her stomach doing flips.

"Sure thing." He laughs. "I'm not ready to turn in yet. Who wants another drink?" he shouts to the room at large. "Let's get out of here." Everyone cheers in agreement as they filter their way out of the Speakeasy.

***

"Here we are," Vic says in a low voice. They're standing at his back door. He's carrying her bag of clothes. The October air chills her bare legs. She's regretting wearing nothing but her robe up the stairs.

"Here we are," she agrees, shifting her weight from one foot to the other.

He pushes the door open and holds it for her to pass through. The muscles in her shoulder are tight, and her anxious heart is pounding. His heat radiates as she brushes past him. His apartment is dark, quiet, and cool, a stark contrast to the post-show Speakeasy.

"You okay?" he asks, following closely.

"Yeah." She nods, and turns back to him, the light through the door shining on his face.

"You sure?" he asks, his brow coming together.

"I don't know." She shrugs, blinking back tears forming in her eyes. Her chest constricts. She's suddenly fighting a wrenching sobbing sensation.

"Olive." His hands are on her cheeks. "It's okay," he says softly, stroking her cheeks with his thumbs.

"I don't know what I'm doing. I don't know why I'm crying," she squeaks with a trembling voice.

"Hey." He gathers her to his chest, shushing into the top of her head, warming her hair with his breath. She crumbles in his arms, quiet tears soaking his shirt.

"I'm sorry," she whispers, her tightly coiled muscles relaxing with each soft sob.

"You have nothing to apologize for," he says softly, kissing her head. "Do you want me to take you home?"

She shakes her head. "No," she sighs. "It's overwhelming. All of it." Another sigh. "I don't want to be alone. I don't want to be away from you. I don't know if I'm ready. I mean last night was wonderful. And you're so patient with me…" She wiggles out of his embrace and steps into the kitchen, also lit by the outside lights.

He follows her, flipping the light on. As her eyes adjust to the stark white kitchen, he fills a glass with tea and sets it on the counter. "I said it last night and I'll say it again. You are in the driver's seat. Nothing will happen if you don't want it to. You want to borrow a pair of sweats and play Scrabble all night, I'm game."

Olive sips her tea and chuckles at the thought of playing board games with Vic all night. "Thanks. I think I'll feel better after I wash my face."

"I'll show you the bathroom."

Vic's bathroom is insanely luxurious with more mirrors and jets than Olive knows what to do with. His shower is larger than her entire bedroom. The water pressure seems to strip away the top layer of her skin. She lathers and scrubs away the makeup and pasty glue, letting the warm water run over her tense muscles. Then she towels herself dry and dresses in her own sweats.

Vic is in his, sitting in the living room, a bottle of wine, two glasses, and true to his word, a Scrabble board set up on his coffee table. Olive laughs at the situation, sure that this is not how he planned his evening with her. "So, this is what burlesque dancers do after their shows," she says as she settles herself next to him on the couch.

"Looks like it's what this burlesque dancer does," he says with a playful grin.

"I don't want to play Scrabble," she tells him.

"Good, because I'm terrible at it. Not sure how I even got the game to be honest. You want some wine?"

"Thanks." She takes the glass he offers.

"It's not Moscato, but I think you'll like it."

"No, thanks for this." She gestures at the board game. "I don't know why I was so worked up. I think it was the whole night and being here, finally alone with you…"

"Hey, it's no problem."

"I know. But I want this to be perfect. I've been dreaming about it for weeks, and I don't want to mess it up."

"You've been dreaming about this for weeks?" he asks with genuine surprise.

"Maybe longer," she admits. "I mean, I know I ran off pretty quickly after the accident back in Marquette, but I'd be lying if I said I didn't think of you and that face more than once afterward. Especially the way you stared Kyle down that night."

"Well damn, Olive. I've been a fool longer than I thought."

"You aren't a fool."

"Pretty sure I am. When I think of all the time we've lost. All the time I missed with you."

"It's past. Let's try thinking about now."

"Okay. What do you want, right now?"

"I want you."

He slides to her on the couch, taking the wineglass from her hand and placing it on the table beside his own. "I'm yours," he says, gathering her into his arms. She reaches one hand to his face, running it over his cheek, slightly rough with stubble.

“Kiss me.” His lips are on hers in an instant, bold yet gentle. He’s searching her mouth with longing kisses, his hands stroking her lower back. She shifts and leans in. He pulls her onto his lap. She places her arms around his neck. His hands roam her body over her shirt. She pulls at his, remembering how delicious his skin felt against hers. “Show me your bedroom,” she says between kisses. He pulls away quickly, his initial surprise clearing the way for lust.

“You sure?” he asks.

She nods quickly and slides off his lap. He stands and takes her hand, leading her down the hall. His room is decadent, completely opposite of the rest of the apartment with its airy and light neutral tones and comfy modern furniture. The bedroom walls are painted a deep leather brown with a four-poster bed in the middle. The pillows and blankets of gold and fawn have a sheen of luxury. A large mirror on one wall reflects the whole thing. Olive’s heart is in her throat as she remembers his experience in comparison to her own.

“Be gentle.” She giggles with nerves as they approach the bed. He tilts his head and opens his mouth to speak. She steps close and presses her lips to his, stealing his words with her kiss.

***

The amount of restraint it takes to not devour her is a feat any man would be proud of. Vic stands beside his bed, holding Olive in his arms. She’s kissing him as deeply and surely as any more experienced woman would. Though the purity in her longing is more than he can bear. She pulls something from him he thought long dead. Excitement and joy he’s never truly known. She wiggles and pulls away from their embrace, peeling off her shirt over her head. Vic stares at her full, lovely breasts, scrubbed clean and red from the pasty glue around her dainty nipples. He strips away his shirt, and she wraps her arms around him, kissing his neck and chest hungrily. His sweatpants do little to hide his growing excitement.

He looks over her shoulder at their reflection, the length of her tan and beautiful back, her long, dark hair hanging damp and wavy over it. Her baggy gray sweatpants sit on the swell of her hips. She inches them down as she continues to kiss him. The sight of her ass like a ripe peach appearing slowly in the mirror is too much. He lifts her gently and places her on the bed. She smiles up at him. Keeping his pants on, he slides beside her, still watching their reflection. She turns to see where his attention is and laughs. "Oh my," she breathes. "You can see everything we do." The blush rises to her cheeks.

"I can turn out the light," he offers.

"Leave it on," she says and pulls him close for more kisses. His hands roam her body, and he explores every rising, falling inch of her. In turn, her hands travel his torso, running over his chest, back and forth over his pecs. She glances at the mirror between kisses. He moves his lips to her breasts, from one tender nipple to the next. She clutches his head, little moans escaping her throat. He tastes the skin of her stomach, clean and fresh from the shower. A sprinkling of glitter still remains. Her hip bones rise to meet his kisses as he breathes her in.

***

What have I been so afraid of? Olive asks herself. The utter bliss she feels in Vic's arms, in his bed, watching in the mirror as he floats around her body, leaving kisses wherever he may, is beyond surreal. She feels like a goddess being worshipped as she leans into a pile of cloud-like pillows. His attention to every inch of her brings out feelings she didn't know existed. She relaxes fully as his head dips lower and lower, his tongue darting around her belly button, then tracing her hip bones. As his breath whispers over her most sensitive places, she moans softly. His tongue follows to those sensitive places, and her breath catches in her throat. She cries out. The feeling of his hot, soft, wet tongue tickling her clit is a shock. A million tiny fires set to blaze at once. She clutches a fist full of his golden curls and pants while he laps at her moist and swollen parts.

In the mirror she watches the tiny movements of his hips while he feasts on her. His pants are completely out of place in the picture. "Take off your pants," she says, barely able to form the words. He looks up at her face then into their reflections. She smiles and says, "Please." A sound not quite human comes from his chest as he slips out of his pants, kicking them on the floor.

She's shocked at the sight of him completely nude. Visions of Greek gods float through her mind as she takes in every inch of his beautiful body. He appears to have been cut from marble. She rises to her knees and moves next to him, watching their bodies in the mirror as they come together. His cock, like heated stone, brushes her hip. He watches her in their reflection, with a look of absolute hunger. Words are lost as they sway and move together, both watching the mirror. The golden haze swirling around them is magic. The moment beyond a dream. They're moving as one, lips, hands, arms, and legs have no boundaries. She aches deep inside to have all of him.

Lying back against the pillows again, she opens her legs and looks away from their reflections into his face. She blinks and arches her back slightly, begging him without words to take her. He pauses for a moment for protection then moves over her, lowering his body over hers. Slowly, the head of his cock slides into her beckoning sex. The initial shock of his girth is softened by the absolute pleasure that follows. Tingling delight travels the length of her spine, starting in her core. She cries out again, moving with him as he inches deeper still. She's filled completely, panting with joy as he pulls out only to enter her again. One slow and driving thrust after another until her rapturous cries ring from the ceiling. Her heart races, her vision blurs. She clings to his shoulders. His body tenses above her as he rocks himself to his release.

He falls beside her, resting his head on her chest, kissing her breast, stroking her belly absently.

"I love you, Olive," he says as quiet as breath. Her heart bursts with joy. Love hadn't been what she was looking for when she decided to audition for the troupe. But it's what she needs.

"I love you too," she says, a joy she thought long lost rising in her chest.

TURN THE PAGE TO SEE HOW IT ALL BEGAN…
BURLESQUE RIVER

BURLESQUE RIVER

"Ladies and gentlemen, Bunny Demure."

The music starts. As she saunters across the stage, and makes love to every person in the room. Peeling off one smooth satin glove with the beat, one finger at a time, the other. Then, she drops her gown strap off one shoulder and slides it back into place. Batting her lashes, she plays with them. Her hands find the zipper of her gown. She pulls it slowly, seductively. The crowd erupts with applause and whistles as the dress falls to the floor. She steps out in stockings, heels, and a hand-beaded corset that catches the light with every sequin.

"Damn, I'd like to keep that little hula hoop girl on the dashboard of my truck. You know like those little hula girls?" Mike says, leaning toward Vic. The drinks are going to his head. He's taken to talking over the MC in between dancers.

Vic laughs and motions for another round.

"I'm glad you came and dragged me out tonight. Glad I didn't miss this."

"Drink up, buddy." The bartender hands them both a shot of something. Mike knows he'll regret drinking it.

"What the hell. Bottoms up," he says, the shot glass to his lips. "What the…" he lowers the glass and steps away from the bar. "You gotta be kidding me."

"What's up, man?" Vic stands up straight and follows Mike's gaze.

"I thought you'd like her. She seems like you're—" Mike raises his hand, speechless for the moment.

Twelve years. It'd been twelve years since he last saw her. Twelve years since she placed his ring back in his hand and said *sorry* with tears in her eyes. Twelve years since she left him and never looked back. And those years had been kind to her. Back in the day, she'd been all legs and bones. Now she was curves and hips, shimmering in the stage lights like a dream.

Mike rubs his neck. *It can't be.* He steps closer, shaking the buzz from his head. That face, though. It's her. He would know that face anywhere: those eyes, those lips, that smile. How many nights had he dreamt about that face?

His shock fades as cheers and whistles remind him of what's about to happen. He has to fight every muscle in his body not to charge the stage and throw her over his shoulder kicking and screaming. "Bunny Demure, my ass," he says under his breath. Teeth grinding, his fists clenched.

Vic steps behind him. "What the fuck, man? What's going on?"

Mike glowers. "I gotta go." Then he mumbles, "The last shot was poison," and heads for the door.

The heat hits Mike as he pushes outside. Nothing could've prepared him for that. He blows all the air out of his chest, shoves his hands into his pockets, and with his head down heads toward his apartment.

Where has she been? This is what she's done with herself? This is what she left me for? "God dammit." *I'd come so close to forgetting. Should've stayed home.* He shakes his head and walks on.

ABOUT THE AUTHOR

Kitty Bardot juggles a life full of excitement and love. By day, she's a chef with her own catering company, by night she puts ten years of burlesque experience to use in various venues in the Quad Cities. She writes from her country home not far from the Mississippi River, enjoying every moment with her husband and their three children. Currently, she is working on her next Burlesque River story.

Connect with Kitty:
website: kittybardot.net
instagram: @ktbardot
twitter: @KittyBardot
facebook: facebook.com/Kitty-Bardot-312641412082507

Boroughs
Publishing Group

www.BOROUGHSPUBLISHINGGROUP.com

If you enjoyed this book, please write a review. Our authors appreciate the feedback, and it helps future readers find books they love. We welcome your comments and invite you to send them to info@boroughspublishinggroup.com. Follow us on Facebook, Twitter and Instagram, and be sure to sign up for our newsletter for surprises and new releases from your favorite authors.

Are you an aspiring writer? Check out www.boroughspublishinggroup.com/submit and see if we can help you make your dreams come true.

Made in the USA
Monee, IL
14 October 2021

79574586R00105